DIGITAL SAMURAI

LIQUID COOL: THE CYBERPUNK DETECTIVE SERIES

From the Crazy Maniac Files
BOOK TWO

AUSTIN DRAGON

WELL-TAILORED BOOKS

Published by Well-Tailored Books, California

Digital Samurai
Liquid Cool: The Cyberpunk Detective Series
From the Crazy Maniac Files (Book Two)

978-1-946590-64-0 (paperback)
978-1-946590-62-6 (ebook)

http://www.austindragon.com

Book cover design by Leslie K.

Printed in the United States of America

CONTENTS

Introduction

Classic Cyborg may have been the first of my "Crazy Maniac Files," but it wasn't the only "File." When you're a busy street detective working the low-life, high-tech mean streets of Metropolis, it's easy to get into the routine of solving a case, then moving on. In the world of private investigation, even the dangerous cases with the potential to shoot you between the eyes with a laser blast, you close out and take on the next one. I hadn't forgotten one particular case; I'd filed it away in a spare office of my mind. What made me recall it was watching "Shark Week" with the wife on TV.

After my second major case, the Blade Gunner Case, my eyes were quickly opened to how frightfully hazardous corporate cases were to the average detective. Major detective firms handled them, often on retainer to specific megacorporations. I dipped my toe into those very lucrative waters and not only did I almost get my toe bitten off multiple times, but I almost got figuratively swallowed whole—including getting shot for real. But that's not what made my Blade Gunner Case so deadly dangerous. I saw for the first time the world of black megacorps. I saw sharks that could swallow the shark that swallowed me whole, and sharks that could swallow the supercity of Metropolis whole! Super cyborg cults and sinister, secret megacorps that not even the other megacorps knew about. It was because of this case that I decided to be very picky when it came to what corporate cases I took on. It wasn't a big concern because most never hired sole proprietor detective agencies like mine. They had their own in-house intelligence divisions, complete with corporate soldiers and assault teams.

However, that didn't mean that these megacorporations weren't part of those "mean streets" that I needed to know everything about. Even if I never did another significant corporate case in Metropolis in my life, I needed to know about this world. Earth had the über-governments on one side and the megacorps on the other—locked in an eternal stalemate. My hobby used to be restoring and building hovercars. Now, it was studying criminals. There were a lot of criminals lurking around the streets of Metropolis below, and in plenty of corporate megatowers above. I had to familiarize myself with them all.

Megacorps employed corporate soldiers and more elite samurai soldiers. Digital samurai was a term I'd first heard from cyberpunks, gamers, and V-Lers (virtual life)—people who spent most of their life on the Net, and in the Net. I learned more about this world than I'd ever care to from my Electric Sheep Massacre Case. Digital samurai were hit men—the street name for enforcers, who used laser swords patterned after Up-Top technology. Their unique sword weapons were giant switch-on laser blades. Then, I learned about a specific assassin within the black megacorp underworld. Not from any of these geeks, gamers, and hackers. In a supercity of over fifty million people, they would never know of such a person, any more than I would.

How, then?

One rainy afternoon, a real live samurai master, a suave Asian gentleman wearing an expensive silk suit and slippers, walked into my Liquid Cool office to retain my services. But he didn't come for himself, or his megacorp boss. I'd learn he was sent by *The Digital Samurai*—a mysterious assassin rumored to be able to travel via the Net to find and kill her victims. Why couldn't I have normal clients like every other detective agency and firm in Metropolis? She was the crazy maniac who wanted to hire me. And a galaxy of trouble and mayhem followed two steps behind her.

I'M CRUZ, PRIVATE DETECTIVE

A s I lay there on the bio-bed, staring at a white glossy ceiling, I thought about how much I hated hospitals. I viewed them as giant petri dishes—nasty people with their nasty germs, despite the facade of cleanliness. All I could think about was how long I'd be in my super-shower at home the moment I left the place.

I'm Cruz. The president, CEO, COO, and detective-on-the-go of the Liquid Cool Detective Agency. Besides my own detective firm, I have a wife, a kid, a classic hovervehicle, and a cool hat. But this morning I wasn't at my office or working a case on the "mean streets" of Metropolis. I was stuck at Metro General.

My big, high-profile cases in my relatively short career as a licensed Metropolis private detective got all the attention from the media and public. However, it was the smaller cases that filled up most of a working street detective's calendar. They were every bit as dangerous as any of the big ones. I'd met many I'd call crazy maniacs—criminals and clients alike—from all walks of life, in all kinds of neighborhoods. Slimy, low-life gangster wannabes; shifty working-class Average Joes and Janes; and off-world, filthy rich tycoons. Most were ultimately forgettable. I solved the case and moved on, storing the data file away in the archives of my computer. But every so often one of those "smaller" cases couldn't be forgotten.

I was born and raised in the supercity of Metropolis. Like every other resident, I complained constantly about the city but wouldn't work anywhere else on the planet. Not even those booshy Up-Top colonies in space, the Moon or Mars could ever coax me away. I loved my city, crime aside. As a private detective, crime was what paid the bills and put food on the table for the family. I was very good at catching bad guys and solving cases. So good that more than a few people said it was like I had been born for it. Laborer to hovercar restorer to private investigator. Not the normal career path for a detective.

My beat—Metropolis—was the largest and most powerful supercity on Earth. Fifty million people stacked on top of one another in flashing superskyscrapers that reached high into the dark rainy skies, some as tall as three hundred stories. The ground was overflowing with life in constant motion. Flashing neon and video signs of a concrete jungle. In the "good" districts there were lots of lights—street lampposts over every corner, doorway, and building surface. The "bad" districts were places Average Joes stayed far away from; they were the stomping grounds of gangs, thugs, and the underworld. Good or bad, the gray masses bustled about with their glowing eye-wear under the ever-present rain.

Above it all, hovercars, hovervans, hovercycles, and hovertaxis filled the sky—twenty to fifty feet up.

Metropolis was my home. My actual office was my Liquid Cool Detective Agency. But instead of being there, I was here—at Metro General—for a follow-up checkup. My last paying client, tried to kill me, but it's okay because I sent her straight to the morgue with my omega-gun. A short detective career and I'd already dealt with killer cyborgs, killer robots, and killer clients.

The doctor finally returned to the hospital room. He wasn't the first expert I'd visited, more like the third. I still didn't know how my late client, NeuroDancer, had mind-controlled me and so many others. We had lots of theories but nothing more. I'd had brain scans, eye scans, bio-scans, brain wave analysis, bloodwork, the works.

The doctor sat down in a single chair in the room. He had a chestnut complexion, with slicked-back silver hair with a full beard. He had my digital chart in his hand.

"What's the word, Doc?"

"Mr. Cruz, it's all negative."

"Nothing?"

"You are in perfect health."

"But that isn't the problem. The problem is that I don't know how I was mind-controlled by this person."

"Mr. Cruz, I do take issue with the term mind-controlled."

"What would you call it?"

"I wouldn't call it anything. We simply do not know. My theory is she used some type of external hardware, technology we've never seen. Something only she knew of."

"I'm sure she wouldn't want anyone to use it against her. But that's not a concern of hers anymore."

"Don't trouble yourself about it, Mr. Cruz. You don't need to see any more experts either. You have a clean bill of health."

"Can you give me that in writing for the wife?"

He chuckled. "I'm sure I can manage a note."

"It's just that I don't like loose ends, Doc."

"I know how you feel. No one does, really. But it is the way of the world. Not everything has a clear resolution. A lesson that I'm sure you'll impart to your son."

"Cruz Jr.? That's an intellectual conversation far in the future for his mother and me. He's more interested in practicing to be a teleporting ninja."

"Sounds like my son."

The doc stood from his chair and reached into his pocket. He showed me a digital card with rotating photos of a boy my son's age. I jumped off the bio-bed to show him pictures of Cruz Jr.

"My little ninja."

Metro General wasn't the best hospital in Metropolis, but it was the largest and in the center of downtown. I didn't need best; I needed good enough. Why get charged five times more and go out of my way in busy sky traffic to have a booshy doctor tell me the exact same thing?

The hospital's megatower was always extremely busy. I got to the elevators and then to parking as quickly as I could. Another thing I hated about the hospital was its chaotic parking bay. It was the type of place where defensive driving training paid off. Always the most dangerous drivers were teenagers and the elderly. They would've been banned from all forms of hovervehicles if I were dictator of the Earth.

I drove a classic Ford Pony and I didn't want any non-drivers near it. Bright red, sleek, high-performance, supercharged, advanced nitro-acceleration hydrogen engine, muscle-hovervehicle coupe. The sight of it made the average person gawk and the mouths of the genuine hovercar enthusiasts and collectors hang open. I'd found the shell in a junkyard when I was in middle school and in high school, I built and restored it, spare part by spare part, and had been upgrading it ever since. No one believed that I found and built such an expensive muscle hovercar from scratch, but it was true, and I drove it every day. My Pony was considered a true classic and always got me genuine offers to part with it, but one doesn't sell a classic Ford Pony; it's a purchase for life—like a legacy residence. My Pony had been featured (without my permission) in so many hovercar magazines that I'd lost count.

I slowly coasted out of the parking bay without revving the engine. I'd parked in valet but didn't let the college-kid valets touch it. But they knew me and were happy to let me park myself as long as they could snap photos of it.

Before heading to my office, I decided to stop at Good Kosher in the district of Woodstock Falls. Woodstock Falls was a working-class, multi-ethnic, mostly Jewish neighborhood. Like similar working-class neighborhoods, residents and business owners fiercely kept the trash—human and otherwise—away. The reason why was simple—the residents didn't just work here; they lived here. The bottom half of the monolith skyscrapers were the businesses and all above to the top was residential.

Good Kosher sat on Graffiti Alley, but despite the name there wasn't a speck of graffiti anywhere ever. It was secluded and dark, and though it was a main street, had the feel of an out-of-the-way back alley where bad things were supposed to happen. But Good Kosher had a rabidly loyal client base that included all of Metropolis.

Good Kosher Market took up the entire length of the street, and that's saying a lot, since streets were ginormous in Metropolis. Food came in three categories—processed (practically everything sold on the market), organic (supposedly the "healthier" alternative"), and natural—or, as I'd say, "straight from the dirt." I never shopped anywhere else. I didn't eat processed and felt the whole "organic" thing was nothing but a scam (by the unholy coupling of government and megacorps) to overcharge people for food. I only ate natural food, and Mr. Watts and his five sons had been serving nothing else for more than a century. It was like many generational businesses. I was a devoted customer and member of its select clientele for almost fifteen years.

As a fixture of a neighborhood for so long, popular among the local residents, employing the same workers and catering to the same clientele, it didn't take long for everyone to feel as if they were all part of the same family. Every family had a sage—the wise, ol' uncle or grandmother. Mr. Watts was our sage. You did your shopping first, one of his five sons rung up the order at the register, and then you spent however long chatting it up with the Good Kosher Man himself.

I didn't know how old Mr. Watts was—he had to be in his late fifties at least—but there was nothing old about him. He had a full beard and mustache with the hair graying at the temples and the edges of his beard. Like his sons, his uniform was a khaki jumpsuit with a fully equipped utility belt, beaded strings around the neck, and a pointed Chinese bamboo hat to protect from the constant exposure of the artificial daylight ceiling lamps, which all its indoor natural plant life depended upon. The skin techs at Eye Candy, where my wife Dot worked, would be proud. He probably had the rare hats shipped directly from the Southeast Asia territories, back when they were affordable.

Good Kosher was also a secret flower shop with its own interior gardens in the back and off-limits to customers, growing a wide variety of roses, tulips, and other flowers. Watts and sons would go back into that room, with its steady rain mist falling, and handpick bouquets for customers. No one had better, if you wanted real ones and not the synthetic ones everyone else sold.

"Mr. Cruz, how's the family?" Mr. Watts asked me at the register as his sons rung up my groceries.

"Cruz Jr. will be as tall as your sons in no time."

They grinned.

"I'm sure. How's the detective business?"

"Busy and good."

"And dangerous."

"And fun."

7

"And dangerous."

"Don't you know I'm famous now? You have a long-time client who's famous."

"Never was one to think much of being famous. Often it brings more problems than benefits."

"It's bringing in a lot of clients at the moment, so I'll ride that wave to the bank."

"Hopefully, you'll be more selective in the cases you choose going forward."

"Mr. Watts, it wasn't my fault. How was I to know my client was a crazy maniac? She mind-controlled me."

"Mind control?"

"Yes."

"Sounds like an excuse to me."

"It's the facts. But I still solved the case, and dealt with the bad guys—multiple bad guys."

"When I cook a meal, I never cook multiple dishes. Multitasking tends to lead to multi-problems and multi-sloppiness. One excellent meal, then move to the next."

"I agree, Mr. Watts. But I didn't know it was so many criminals at the beginning. Doesn't matter. I solved my NeuroDancer Case, like I solved my Blade Gunner Case."

"At least, you're giving these cases better names."

"I still don't know why everyone doesn't like my The Guy Who Scratched My Vehicle Case."

They chuckled.

Two of his sons helped me to my vehicle with my ton of groceries. Half of it was diapers. We loaded up the trunk and back seat of the Pony. We exchanged our goodbyes as they pushed my hovercart back into the store while I got behind the wheel of my vehicle, and closed the door.

In Metropolis, the weather was mostly always the same: "rain with a chance of rain." It started to drizzle a bit, but looking up I could see darker clouds moving in. I was glad it was an "in the office" day for me instead of an "out on the streets" soliciting new business one.

My eyes stopped on my rearview mirror. I turned my head to look out the rear window. I saw someone—a shadow, but now it was gone. I didn't like it. I powered up and rose into the air. In moments, I was merging into the sky traffic. I did a quick glance down to the ground out the passenger window, and for a moment I thought I saw a shadowy figure again, but couldn't be sure.

I'd been seeing shadows and silhouettes for the last week or so. Each time I couldn't be positive whether there was actually someone there or if my mind was playing tricks on me. The doc had said I had a clean bill of health. Maybe I needed to visit a few more doctors.

PUNCH JUDY, MY CYBORG SECRETARY

My Liquid Cool office was in Buzz Town. As far as districts went, it wasn't the best of areas, but it wasn't the worst either, like a Free City or Mad Heights. I told everyone that the presence of Liquid Cool classed up the entire neighborhood. Though I wished all the tenants of my megatower on Circuit Circle—simply known as the Circle—shared that opinion.

Liquid Cool was on the hundredth floor. Since beginning my new career as a detective, I'd made the office into my own personal fortress, complete with additional surveillance of the parking lot, elevator, and hallway to and from the office. The cases I'd already worked on and the clients and criminals I'd already encountered told me not to do so would be suicidal. I liked a clean office; I liked a safe office. We weren't one of those big, fancy, thousand-person detective firms taking up multiple floors. I was a one-man show with one employee.

I started the Liquid Cool Detective Agency not even three years ago, leaving my previous line as a classic hovervehicle restorer and sometime illegal hovercar racer behind. It started out as simple favor for a friend. Already I had solved some of the biggest and most dangerous cases that not even the big, fancy detective firms with their thousand agents could boast.

My one employee had the street name of Punch Judy. When you knew she was a cyborg with two very impressive bionic arms that made sense. But she was Punch Judy even before her "accident." My ex-felon, cyborg secretary was a soldier in the punk-posh gang *Les Enfantes Terribles* in Neo-Paris, France. She got her street name because she liked to punch people and was quite good at it. Now, she could even punch a three-hundred-pound cyborg through a steel and concrete wall—and had. She only wore sleeveless tops to show off her buff, bionic arms.

Today, PJ had short, crimson hair and a simulated mole—a dot above her lips, matching her crimson lipstick-covered lips. Hip, female business suits were what she wore nowadays—sleeveless tops, knee-high skirts, heeled leather boots. We started out as frenemies, but she was my respectable second in command these days.

I walked through the front door and was met by her French ska music playing.

"Ah, you've decided to come to work after all," she said from behind her reception desk.

She'd turned the main office area into a shrine to all my high-profile cases. There were framed pictures covering practically every inch of the reception area. Pictures of me at press conferences, at police scenes, with megacorporation senior executives, with the Council of Corporations president, me shaking hands with the mayor, but my favorites were those with just the Average Joes and Janes of the supercity, including the client from my very first major case, Carol Num, after I successfully rescued her kidnapped daughter. These were the cases that made it all worthwhile, despite all the crazy maniacs I had to deal with and those who shot at me. I didn't like getting shot.

"Did the doctors say you're cuckoo?"

"No, I am in perfect health, top to bottom, in and out, mind and body."

"So they don't know what made you cuckoo?"

"I'm fine. Since she's dead and she's the only one who knew how to do her mind-control trick, I'm not too concerned."

"If you say so. You have many messages on your desk. You need to review them first."

"I can't drink a cup of coffee?"

"No, you were late to work so straight to working. No coffee."

I laughed.

PJ's reception desk was a workstation behind a metal barrier, but it didn't look like a barrier with all her decorations. Psychedelic posters filled the wall behind her, her fancy glass desk had see-through glass drawers, and her boombox sat on top along with her own mobile computer.

About eight feet from her was the door to my private office. On the wall outside of it was her neon light sign in big letters: LIQUID COOL. Underneath, in smaller neon letters, DETECTIVE AGENCY.

Her vid-phone rang. "Hello, this is Liquid Cool. Why are you calling?"

I stopped next to her desk. "Please tell me that's not how you're answering our phones."

"Why are you calling me?" PJ asked whoever she was talking to. "I'm not your secretary. Call him directly."

Whoever it was couldn't even get a word out.

"Bye!"

She hung up on whoever it was.

"PJ, who did you hang up on?"

"It was stupid man."

"Stop calling Phishy stupid man. What did he want?"

"He'll tell you when he calls you."

"Then why isn't my phone ringing?"

"That's Phishy for you."

Phishy was my associate, slider, and gun dealer.

PJ's phone rang again. It wasn't Phishy, but I walked to the office's waiting area with its geometric, purple couches around a glass table on a shimmering, neon powder-blue rug. The reception table held many more French fashion magazines than I was comfortable with. Where were my hovercar racing mags? Where was the reading material for my male clients who waited?

PJ was on her headset and brushed past me and dumped a stack of my hovercar racing magazines on the table. She returned to her desk. I made a disapproving sound as I bent down and arrayed all the magazines to be visually pleasing. I stood, admired my work, and nodded to myself. What was PJ doing with my hovercar racing magazines?

PJ was busy on the phone so I walked back to my private office. I eavesdropped as I passed by, but the conversation didn't sound like a legitimate client. The man sounded like a "window shopper." They came across the name of an agency on the Yellow Pages site. My agency sounded cool, so then they called to ask endless, inane questions about hiring a detective. But ultimately, they'd schedule no appointment at all. They'd call someone else.

The Good Kosher Man was right about that. Fame attracted all types. We had people who'd call to talk to me just because they saw me on TV or read about me on the newsfeed. PJ would, of course, tell them "no!" in that rude, French way she was so good at. Who said gatekeepers were bad? I had the best. They could waste her time, not mine.

I walked to my desk. She loved prioritizing my messages. I had the "hot" pile, the "hold" pile, the "hell no" pile, and a few other miscellaneous ones. I had her print them out because I didn't like to deal with messages on my phone. I was old-fashioned that way; I wanted the paper. I could mark it up, take notes, and throw away when done. Probably was an OCD thing, but it worked for me and made me more efficient than constantly looking at my mobile to read them.

"Cruz," PJ called out.

She didn't yell, but her tone was a bit off.

"What is it?" I walked back out into the main office area.

Near the main door stood a middle-aged Asian man, in an expensive silk suit, staring at us.

ECHO, SAMURAI MASTER

"How did you get in here?" I asked.

"You speak like children. Westerners banter much but say little," he said, not looking at me but gazing around the office.

"I think I read that in a fortune cookie once," I said.

He locked his eyes on mine. "I will walk from where I stand into your office. In your office I will slice your desk and every piece of furniture to pieces. I will leave and you will not see me again."

"Why would you come to my office to cut it into pieces?"

"I come to see if you can stop me, Cruz-san."

"If I do?"

"Then we can talk further. We must see if you are worthy to be hired by the Hiero Corporation. Worthy to be in the company of neo-samurai."

We never saw the sheath. He pulled his samurai sword from his right sleeve. It was a real sword, and it could do more than slice a wooden desk to pieces. Depending on the material, it might be able to slice PJ's bionic arms to pieces too.

"This is a mistake," I said.

"For you?" he asked as he took a side stance, sword held with both hands and angled pointed to the ground. The man was wearing slippers, which meant he was a real samurai soldier.

"I'm not going to let you come into my office and slice up my furniture."

"Cruz, don't joke with him," PJ said.

"Then stop me," he said to me. "Maybe your woman can, after I cut off her arms."

He shouldn't have said that.

"Only one man ever cut off my arms," PJ yelled.

"You found him and killed him?" the samurai asked.

"No," PJ said. "He's standing right next to me."

I could draw a gun faster than most people but a real samurai, even a mediocre one, could move faster than I ever could. But that wasn't my aim. I fired my omega-gun at him as soon as I could pull it from my shoulder holster. He swatted both laser blasts with his samurai sword like they were nothing. That told PJ that the material of the sword might very well be able to slice off her bionic arms. She wasn't having any of that.

She punched the metal barrier that made up her receptionist desk at him. He jumped up, knees up to about his eye level, nearly touching the ceiling as the barrier smashed into the wall behind him. I fired three more shots at him as he was jumping. Again, he swatted all my blasts away.

PJ grabbed and flicked her chair at him with maximum bionic force. It flew at him at sonic speed but he sliced it in half; both pieces went around him. I switched my omega-gun to machine-fire. He seemed to know I'd done so and threw something at me. I never saw it because it moved too fast. I heard the shuriken hit the wall behind me with a tremendous thud. My reflexes couldn't have moved me out of the way in time. He intentionally missed me but likely cut off a piece of my ear or something just to show me who was master. I realized my hat was gone.

PJ was doing her own throwing. Anything her hand grabbed, she threw at him faster than my eyes could follow. Vases, scissors, cups, pens—all turned into deadly projectiles.

I pretended to stumble dropping my omega-gun. I could see the surprise in his face. I grabbed a handful of beans from my jacket and desperately threw them at him. He laughed, catching one in his hand, looking at it and tossing it—while he was swatting PJ's projectiles.

He thought they were peanuts, I'm sure. My Mexican jumping beans began to explode, making sounds like loud firecrackers. He was startled but before he could stop his own reaction, I shot him point-blank with my pop-gun, hidden under my left sleeve. He crashed into the wall.

PJ had already grabbed her electric shotgun and shot him again. I aimed my omega-gun and fired an explosive round. There was an explosion, but also an explosion of black smoke. I dove at PJ, pushing to the ground. Shurikens embedded themselves into the wall around us.

We couldn't see him and that was bad news. I fired, machine-gun style, around PJ's desk. She fired her shotgun, then she opened the bottom drawer of her desk. I had no idea, until then, that she kept grenades—a lot of them.

As I heard my office being blown up the phone rang. I grabbed PJ's hand to keep her from throwing another grenade. She looked at me.

"It's okay," I said.

She was surprised to see me stand. She jumped up from the floor too to look around. The office was black and blown up. The door was closed, but the samurai soldier was nowhere to be seen.

I leaned over and answered the vid-phone. His face appeared on the display screen. He wasn't in the hallway. He stared at us from our parking lot surveillance cameras. PJ and I were so angry we could explode. We looked around the office again. The walls in front of us were riddled with bullet and laser blasts, the waiting area furniture and the magazines were blown to pieces, the paint was all black and burnt. The office looked like it had been hit by artillery fire. We turned around and the wall was covered with deeply embedded shurikens, including my Liquid Cool neon sign.

We looked back at the monitor. He watched us. We were shaking with anger. He showed no emotion.

"Your skills are poor," he said, "but you did demonstrate misdirection, though rudimentary, and an element of surprise. It is only because of that last action we are talking. We can talk. You may be suitable."

He moved away from the camera and disappeared, hanging up. We looked up at what had been my beautiful office. We wanted to kill that samurai soldier real bad. And he was on his way back up.

We had enough firepower in the office to fend off an army, but PJ and I were nervous. Our eyes were glued to the monitor of our surveillance cameras. I had a completely illegal laser machine gun in my hands; PJ had a heavy pulse rifle.

I glanced to the side. My tan fedora rested on the floor. One of those throwing stars knocked my hat right off my head. That hat could stay on my head in a gale force wind, but there it sat. It looked undamaged, but my nerves weren't.

We heard the elevator beep.

A petite Asian woman in a black suit and white blouse underneath exited. She was followed by a young Asian man, then another. They filed out of the elevator in a column. The door opened and they entered. She saw us and smiled, then did a Japanese bow and continued inside. All those who followed stepped in, smiled, bowed and entered. PJ and I didn't know what to make of them. They didn't look like corporate soldiers.

The elevator beeped again and we watched a paint crew, then laborers in overalls arrive. Another group arrived and set up a hover-platform. They arranged three chairs and a table on it. The young Asian woman gestured for us to have a seat, sitting across from each other. The samurai master entered with three large men, definitely corporate samurai soldiers. I'd seen their type before. Our attacker sat at the head of the table on the hover-platform as it rose about six feet in the air. He handed me his business card: ECHO. There were Japanese letters underneath, then a phone number. More people arrived, male and female.

Sometimes in life, you have no idea what the hell is going on. That's how PJ and I felt sitting on the hover-platform with Japanese waitresses serving us tea and crackers. The man blew up my office and now his people were serving me tea. All around us his crews were restoring the office—buffing then repainting the walls, repairing the bullet holes and laser blasts. They replaced the carpets, swept then buffed the floor. My Liquid Cool neon sign was replaced. They repaired PJ's workstation. They replaced our waiting area for clients. One of the men gave my fedora a professional spray wash and brush in front of me and placed it back on my head perfectly. As each crew finished, they faced us, bowed, and left the office. Moments later, all the crews were gone. The first Asian woman stepped out of the office, followed by the three large men, who closed the door. It was now just the samurai man, PJ and me.

"How do I address you?" I asked the man.

"EE-KO," he said.

I looked at the card: Echo. Good thing I asked him. I didn't want to make him mad and have him blow up my office again.

I said his name, heavily stressing the "E" as he did. "Well, Mr. Echo. You have my attention. Though, you could have accomplished that in a less dramatic way."

"It was a test."

"Yes, you weren't trying to kill me. However, we were trying to kill you."

He smiled. "I was never in any danger."

"My little son is practicing to be a ninja himself. But to meet one in real life. I really liked the throwing stars. I didn't know they were still used."

"I am a samurai master. No ninja. We have many tools, many weapons, many you do not know of."

"How did you sneak into my office without being seen? PJ and I were right here."

"Your eyes were open but you were not seeing."

"Tell me, did you really hear me switch settings on the gun? You couldn't have."

"I did. Your weapon is from off-world. I know of it."

"You withstood our weapons-fire. Skintight body armor? Did you get that from off-world?"

"Our body armor is made here on Earth. It's better than any off-world."

"So Mr. Echo, what may I be suitable for?"

"To assist me in my task."

"You don't look like a man who needs assistance from anyone, let alone me."

"I will not be successful unless I change the game. In any battle with an enemy, we know who shall win and who shall die. We know before we touch a weapon, or draw a sword. I am a samurai master. I command an impressive army of samurai solders. Do you know of digital samurai?"

"Yes," I answered. "Enforcers who used laser swords with switch-on laser blades."

"My enemies are samurai masters. They have digital samurai too. My master wishes to hire your services."

"You are here on your master's behalf."

"I am."

"Will I meet your boss?"

"No. You do not understand. The boss pays my salary. My master is the one who I cannot defeat in battle. They are two different people."

"Do I meet either one?"

"You will meet my boss, not my master."

"What services do you wish to hire me for?" I asked.

"I require you to accompany me on my investigation."

"Accompany you?"

"I conduct an internal corporate investigation. My company is the Hiero Corporation. We are set to acquire the Macro Corporation. I have been tasked to review the efficiency of Macro. Hiero is a Japanese-owned megacorp, three centuries old. Macro is not. An infant company. Barely a century old."

"Mr. Echo, I've done corporate cases before, but this sounds to be out of my realm of expertise."

"Macro is a devious company. We believe their goal is to allow themselves to be acquired. Once within, they will seek to take over Hiero. That is the true purpose of my investigation. I do not know the Western mind. I am of the Eastern way of things. I need a Westerner to accompany me on my investigation. My master chose you."

"As flattered as I am, Mr. Echo, I'm not sure I will be much help."

Echo clapped his hand. The main office door opened and the young Asian female entered. She closed the door then walked to PJ. The woman handed her a large certified check. I could see PJ's eyes almost pop out of her head.

"Our retainer is paid, Ms. PJ," she said.

"We will begin tomorrow," PJ said.

"My office will call you," Echo said.

Echo stood and stepped down from the hover-platform. He turned to face us, bowed, then left through the door.

"I will return later to collect the platform," the woman said.

She also bowed and left.

I leaned over to look at the check. PJ had the biggest smile on her face.

"PJ, haven't we gotten in trouble doing this before?"

"Cruz, look at this money."

"PJ, to do what?"

"Never mind that. I'm putting it in the bank today. It's simply a retainer."

"They know your name, probably all about me," I said.

"So?"

"Look at this. They knew our exact furniture."

"Cruz, stop complaining. They fixed up the entire office as good as new. You'd never know anything happened in here."

"You mean an entire gun and laser battle, along with multiple explosions? I didn't know you kept live grenades in the bottom of your file drawer."

"Cruz, you have no cause to complain. No one was killed. Office was fixed. And big money. I call that a good day."

"And he's not the ultimate client. You know I don't work with go-betweens. I need the meet the real client."

The front door opened and a few tenant neighbors peeked in. We didn't know their names, but we recognized them as fellow tenants from surrounding offices. They gave us dirty looks as they looked around.

"We'd ask what the racket was about, but we know you'll lie," one said.

"We're reporting you to the landlord—again!" another said.

They closed the door, disappearing.

"PJ, under no circumstances are you to tell Dot what happened here today."

My wife was still very overprotective of me after my NeuroDancer Case. She was the one having me visit multiple doctors in the city.

"Tell her? What am I going to tell her? We got big money, but other than that I have no idea what happened here today or why, and I was here. Oh, what about those stupid Mexican jumping beans? You promised never to use them again after your first case. Cruz, you're a big-time private detective. If people were to find out about them, everyone in Metropolis would be laughing at you."

"They saved us, didn't they?"

"Saved us? He was trying not to laugh at you. A grown man throwing children's toys at him when he can block lasers with his sword."

"He said he wanted a detective who could bring an element of surprise to the table."

"Don't use them again. Liquid Cool is a high-quality detective firm, and you will not be allowed to damage its reputation."

"But I'm the boss."

"No excuses!"

THE MICK, LET IT RIDE'S VP OF COVERT ACTIVITIES

Peacock Hills was one of Metropolis's upper-class business districts. Every time I went there, its monolith buildings reminded me of gargantuan fingers extending into space through the city's rain-cloud cover. Megatowers were illuminated in the conservative colors of white, light yellow, and blue. The roof lighting made the structures look like they had angelic halos.

My best friend, Run-Time, President, CEO, and COO of the megacorp *Let It Ride Enterprises* was out of town with his wife, Crystalline, on a weeklong business trip. I always consulted with him if one of my cases had to deal with politics, high finance, or the corporate world. His megacorp owned all the top car washes, hovercar body shops, hovercar rental shops, hovercycle rental shops, hovertaxicab and hoverlimousine services in the city. Anything that had to do with private transportation, Run-Time had his hands in it. Hovercars remained the top luxury item in the city, despite ubiquitous public transportation and commercial hovertaxicab services. He was a certified member of Metropolis's business elite.

I left my Pony with the valet. It was one of the few places I felt comfortable allowing others to park my hovervehicle. The elevator from the parking level to the executive offices was silent and fast; the floors counted up in large digital numbers on the door.

Three women sat at executive reception, evenly spaced apart from each other. "Good morning, Mr. Cruz," the receptionists greeted me in unison. I knew them all on a first name basis. This visit, the Caucasian woman with the British accent was dressed in metallic blue, the Asian woman with the Southern accent was dressed in shimmering yellow, and the Black woman with the West Indian accent was in deep indigo.

I greeted them and chatted for a bit to catch up with their lives. Run-Time had three vice presidents. Mrs. Phoenicia was a tall Lebanese woman, and Mrs. Role was a West Indian woman. Both were also out of town at business conferences. However, neither of them was who I came to see.

I came to see The Mick, the stout blue-eyed Irishman and Run-Time's third vice president. I never knew his first name. He just told me to call him Mr. Mick if I wanted to be formal. He came out of the elevator in a black suit and tie, white shirt. He was very Japanese in his demeanor and mannerisms. Exactly what I needed.

He led me to his office—or an office he said was his. It was one level down. The upper level was all Run-Time's office. He offered me refreshments but I declined. The office was Spartan and very Japanese. The only Irish motif was a carved green leprechaun on his desk wielding a samurai sword. I saw no pictures of family, or of anything on his glass desk. Other than the desk and our chairs, there was no other furniture.

"You have one of those pop-away offices. All your file drawers and cabinets disappear into the walls and floor when you have visitors."

"Of course."

"You mean I guessed right?"

"You did."

We sat in our chairs.

"You need help with a Japanese megacorp. Is that what you said?" he asked.

"I may have a Japanese client. I wanted to brush up on Japanese protocol. I know I'll never master it. I just want to be able to conduct myself so I don't offend or annoy anyone."

The Mick nodded. "Good. I'm glad you came to see me. Japanese company."

"Yes."

"Can you tell me the name, or is that confidential?"

"Hiero."

Immediately, I saw the change in his face. He was surprised. His eyes looked down at his desk.

"Hiero? Why would they hire you?"

"Not sure, but I'll know soon enough."

"Who hired you?"

I hesitated. I decided not to tell him the name, but I told him about PJ and my encounter with him. The Mick listened closely.

"Hiero has acquired the Macro Company—a Euro-Russian megacorp."

I nodded. "Yes, but it didn't say much about them on the Net. Actually, the Net has very little on either company."

"Most of the major megacorps list very little on their public Net presence. They deal with other megacorps and governments, not the public."

"Is there something more I should know about this merger?"

"No," he replied.

"No, meaning you won't tell me."

"No, meaning the less you know about their inner world, the better for you. You're an outsider so they'll keep you at arm's length in that regard. Maybe that's why they want you. You're an outsider and you have a public profile they can scrutinize. Your background checks out. You have a family. Very important to such companies that a man has a family. You have business and political connections, off-world connections. All those things will elevate your standing in their eyes. You're an outsider but not a lowly outsider. They can do some business with you. Your interaction with the Orochi Corporation was probably what put you on their radar to begin with. Orochi's CEO quietly stepped down."

"I didn't know that."

"You wouldn't. The funeral was last month."

"Funeral?"

"Funerals usually follow resignations or ousters at those high levels in a megacorp."

I shook my head. "Hazardous life being a senior exec these days."

"At these companies, yes."

I remained quiet, slightly amused. How many questions was he going to ask me?

"I'm here for Japanese business etiquette lessons," I reminded him.

"Cruz, I strongly recommend you withdraw from working with them."

"Why?"

"Have you forgotten the last time you dealt with a Japanese megacorp involved in illicit activities?"

"I'll never forget Gidrah. I'll never forget the Asimovians either. Are you saying Hiero is like Gidrah?"

"Yes."

"I'm taking the case. How many megacorp members of the Council of Corporations are involved in illicit activities? Probably all of them."

"True."

"They all have corporate samurai soldiers."

"As do we, but we don't have any samurai masters on payroll. Families work exclusively for companies, going back many generations. They are in service to their company from the time of birth to their death."

"I'm only talking to them at this point. That's all. Find out what the full job is. I've turned down cases before, retainer or not."

"Don't cash the retainer. Doing so is acceptance of the job."

"I know that. Samurai masters have bosses?"

"Yes, the company's president."

"Do samurai masters ever have their own masters, separate from their bosses?"

"Why did you ask that question? How would you know to ask such a question? Did he tell you that?"

"We were talking."

"Cruz, you should walk away. I'm very serious. These are not the common street thugs you're used to."

"I know that. I was the one fighting him."

"You weren't fighting him. There is no fighting them. There's killing you in less than five seconds."

"I know that too. PJ was with me. We were fighting him. He was taking a nap while standing up."

"Why then—"

"I'm curious, Mr. Mick. And don't tell me about curiosity killing the cat. I'm curious to know why this serious samurai master came into my little detective agency office to hire me, of all people."

"Why indeed."

"I'll indulge that curiosity. My prerogative."

"Don't trust him, or anyone at either one of these companies. Whatever reason they give you for hiring you, you can be certain it's not the true reason. They may never tell you the true reason. You're the outsider. It's customary to first test an outsider before bringing them more into their business. An initial case to see how you perform, then, if they are satisfied, the real case. But again, the truth of things will not be shared."

"I never trust anyone." I smiled. "Except at Let It Ride Enterprises. Oh, and the wife. Not sure about Cruz Jr. yet."

He grinned.

The Mick gave me nearly two hours of Japanese business etiquette training. Mostly it was when it doubt: shut up and observe. When we were done, rather than shake my hand, he held his arms at his sides and gave me a slight bow, Japanese-style, to say goodbye. I didn't even bother to try doing the same; I waved.

JUDO, ECHO'S LIEUTENANT

When police went into a situation that was likely dangerous, they called backup. As a street detective, I had none. I'd need to remedy that in the future. I already put together my own network of street informants, who I felt were as good as Metro PD's—my Sidewalk Johnny Brigade. I needed the equivalent of my own street backup because sidewalk johnnies didn't do gun battles.

However, I was going to be in the care of the Hiero Corporation, so I felt safe enough. Any fighting that needed to be done, they'd do it and I'd step back, keep my hands at my side, and keep quiet.

I'd asked The Mick what the Hiero Corporation did. He told me "import-export." That was like a gangster telling me they were a "businessman." The Mick gave me a non-answer answer. A gazillionaire megacorp around for nearly three hundred years, and no one could tell me what they did.

The Hiero hoverlimo picked me up from the parking bay of my Liquid Cool office. The vehicle was made of a reflective dark silver material that I hadn't seen before, but based on my hovercar restoring experience, I assumed it was a dense metal alloy armored exterior. The hoverlimo was as long as a hoverbus. The rear door facing the street opened and a young Japanese man exited. Black suit and tie, white shirt. He held a sheathed katana in his hand. He stood before me.

"Judo," he said and bowed.

"Cruz," I said and bowed my head, not the full body bow of Japanese tradition. The Mick told me, as an outsider, I would immediately be perceived as giving respect. Since I didn't want anyone else blowing up my office, I was going to remain on their good side. My fancy, Up-Top omega-gun meant nothing if they riddled my body with twenty throwing stars before I could reach it.

I was directed to the back seat facing the front. Judo sat across from me. Next to him was another corporate samurai soldier, a much larger man holding his sheathed katana, and wearing dark glasses.

The hoverlimo rose in the air and quickly merged into sky traffic.

"Will I be visiting with Mr. Echo again today?" I asked.

"No. Mr. Echo will join us when we meet Hiero's CEO. I will attend to you until then."

"May I know the name of Hiero's CEO?"

"Mr. Ming."

"Thank you. May you advise me on proper behavior for today?"

Judo grinned. "Do not be so eager to please. Mr. Echo has hired you to be yourself, not to try to be us."

"I could never be that."

"No, you could not. I am confident you have done the necessary preparation not to embarrass the name and honor of Mr. Echo, who has retained your services."

"I will be on my best behavior."

"At Hiero headquarters that is required. When we visit Macro, we expect your behavior to be the opposite of your best. There we expect you to be the wild man that is your reputation."

"Wild man?" I smiled to myself. "I have never been called that before."

"Translation is always an imprecise thing, but I am confident you know what I mean."

"I do. Do that thing I do to make people want to punch me."

Judo smiled.

"But what if they really try to punch me?" I asked.

"I will be with you at all times. No one will do so—who wishes to keep their arm."

The Hiero Corporation building was nestled in between several other megatowers in the ultra-wealthy district of Silicon Dunes. The wealthiest of humanity lived Up-Top, but if they had to live on Earth, Silicon Dunes would be on their top ten list. The hoverlimo glided over the roof and we were bathed in light; the roof folded open as we descended.

The parking bay had more security than I'd ever seen in my life. Corporate soldiers were standing guard everywhere with laser machine guns or handguns. We exited the hoverlimo and I followed Judo. The other man followed behind us several paces back. I must have stuck out like the sun in a black void. Every last one of them was in a black suit and tie with white shirt, no hats. I strolled along in my tan fedora and slicker. I did wear a white shirt, but no tie, and did wear black pants to be as conformist as I'd ever be.

We walked to the elevator bay. A dozen doors in an oval waiting area, but it was the entire floor than began to descend. It stopped one level down at the top of some stairs. Judo led me down the steps as the floor went back up. As far as I could see were people at their cubicle work areas on computers and wearing headsets. Most were talking. At a glance, I guessed that the workforce was half male, half female.

"Are all your employees Japanese?" I asked.

"We are Japanese owned. Hiring only Japanese would be employment discrimination."

Judo could see my grin. I wasn't seeing anyone else other than Asians.

"Japanese, Chinese, Vietnamese, Mongolian, Singaporean, Thai, Korean. Hiero Corporation is a very diverse, multicultural company."

I couldn't help myself. I laughed. He wanted to laugh too. We walked from the steps through the main aisle between the many cubicles on either side. I scanned the employees, but not one of them looked at us. They kept working as if we were invisible.

Our destination was a conference room. Smaller than I expected. A simple table with three chairs. Judo gestured to me to sit. He sat in the other. The glass door closed and the larger man stood outside.

Judo sat with his right hand on his sheathed sword and his left hand flat on the top of the table. His eyes were closed. I looked around, then I clasped my hands together. Not too chatty, these Hiero people.

I had no idea how long we'd been waiting. They didn't know I was the stakeout master. I could stay quiet and calm for days without being bothered a bit. Only I didn't need to close my eyes. I picked out a spot on the wall, fixed my gaze, then went into stakeout mode, like switching from single-shot to machine-gunfire on my omega-gun.

In stakeout mode, I was oblivious to the passage of time. Judo never moved a muscle; neither did I. At some point, I became aware that Judo had opened his eyes. He was staring at me. I didn't move my gaze from the wall in front of me, but his expression looked worried. Was this a test?

It was so slight at first, but I could see he was shaking. He moved his mouth; a switch. His eyes closed then opened. In an explosion, he yelled out and slammed his left palm against the table. He jumped up from his chair, cursing. It wasn't in English, but I knew it was cursing. He stood there, his head downcast.

"Mr. Cruz." Someone called my name.

I turned my head to see Mr. Echo standing at the open door. Through the glass wall I could see many people watching me, men and women.

"Mr. Echo." I stood and bowed my head.

"My second has embarrassed me."

"Mr. Judo is young," I said, not knowing what the junior man had done wrong. "He can learn from any mistake. I know I have."

"How many hours do you believe you've been in this room?" Echo asked me.

"I was once on stakeout after a criminal. I watched his apartment for four days straight. I caught him at gunpoint. He asked me, 'How many hours were you waiting in that hovercar to catch me?' I said to him, 'That is the wrong question. The right question is, do I care?'"

"We can see my boss, Mr. Ming, now. I will be authorized to continue with your services."

"Will Mr. Judo be allowed to continue as my guide? I've been enjoying our deep conversations and his guidance."

Echo chuckled, then nodded. "Yes, he can remain."

Judo yelled and burst out of the room.

Echo frowned, then returned his gaze to me. "Maybe he can benefit from your guidance."

It wouldn't be until I had a chance to speak to Mr. Mick again that I'd learn I'd saved Mr. Judo his job, and saved myself from being fired. It was a test. I'd been waiting in that conference room for five hours. Mr. Echo led me from the conference room. We waited with his people outside the male restroom until Mr. Judo emerged with his head hung low.

MING, CEO, HIERO CORPORATION

The Mick told me that in Eastern cultures the greater the age, the greater the status. However, the actions of junior members of the family could shame the senior leaders of the family. In megacorps like Hiero, the company was more family than one's blood family.

Echo led me into the single office at the other end of the floor. Since I wasn't in "stakeout" mode anymore, I did very much feel the passage of time. It took us a hell of a long time to get to the other end of that office. Judo and the rest of the men were left outside the door. I was almost blinded by the whiteness of the room. At first, my eyes couldn't perceive the edges of the room. It was like a vast white void with a single Asian man standing in the center, wearing all black—suit, tie, and shirt. He had a white Fu Manchu mustache past his chin. Echo led me to him and stopped. The boss glared at me as if he wanted to slap me.

The boss yelled something in Japanese at the top of his lungs. I heard the door open behind me and there was Judo standing beside Echo, his head tilted down, his gaze to the floor. I didn't like the look of this situation.

"It wasn't his fault," I said.

I was not supposed to have talked. The boss and Echo shot glances at me.

"You have my profile," I said. "You know about my previous OCD tendencies. I cured myself by learning how to channel those energies into other activities. I could remain still for days on end. It's quite abnormal. I don't even know my limits, but I'd guess they're far greater than your best samurai soldier. I take no credit for the ability. I was simply born with it. Mr. Judo was not at fault."

Echo looked away. Mr. Ming turned around and raised his hand with a grunt. Judo disappeared and I heard the door open and close.

"You, Mr. Cruz, are an oddity to me. Mr. Echo was not authorized to contact you. Hiero does not need an outsider to conduct its affairs."

"I can leave at once," I said.

"However, in light of your behavior today, I have been moved to Mr. Echo's way of thinking. You may aid us after all."

Ming turned around and walked back to us, with his hands clasped behind his back.

"What do you know of the Macro Corporation?"

"Imports and exports, Mr. Ming."

"Legal business and illegal business, like all others. I have resisted such mergers in the past. Generational companies such as Hiero must grow from within. Growing by acquiring others risks corrupting the spirit and culture of the company. However, for the first time in my tenure the board has overruled me. They are too eager to expand into other markets."

Ming walked to Echo.

"You may proceed as you wish," he said to Echo.

The samurai master nodded.

"Mr. Cruz, Mr. Echo told me of your encounter."

"Yes."

"Did you learn from it?"

"Mr. Echo is a formidable adversary that I'd prefer to keep as an associate."

"Yes, but did you learn from the encounter?"

I heard the door open again. I had learned from it. I wore my own skintight body armor under my clothes. In my hand, between my thumb and index finger, I kept the pressure at all times. I didn't need to reach for anything—simply release.

A round hit the ground and the volley of throwing stars that came at me were magnetically yanked out of the air. All of them smacked against the round at the base of my feet. I'd modified my pop-gun and with the flick of my left arm blasted the men away with a plasma pulse.

Echo stood beside me, emotionless. Ming nodded.

"Good," Ming said. He looked at Echo. "Good. I am satisfied."

"Thank you, Mr. Ming," I said.

Any other detective in Metropolis would have quit the case right there. Two major cases ago, I would have too, but I wanted "in." I wanted to know I could hold my own in this murky, frightful megacorp world with its corporate soldiers and retained samurai-for-life.

Ming looked at Echo. "Conduct your investigation of Macro. Have the detective review your findings. We know Macro is a Trojan Horse that must be exposed. We must do to them what they plan to do to us."

Echo nodded.

Ming extended his hand to shake mine. "Pleasure, Mr. Cruz. On behalf of the Hiero Corporation, we are honored to retain your services."

MR. ABLE, MACRO'S MAN

Despite my skill with weapons and my calm composure, I was actually very risk adverse when it came to private investigation. I was more than content running away from a gunfight rather than running in guns blazing. Gunfighters survived by not having gunfights, not seeking them out every day. I had entered the megacorporate world of high violence. Mr. Mick didn't have to warn me about the Hiero Corporation. I already knew how extremely dangerous and likely criminal they were. Yes, they had plenty of legitimate businesses on paper, on the surface. But who knows how many illegal ones they had off-books? My intent was to stay quiet and off to the side, accompany Echo as he did his audit of the company they acquired, advise him of anything that looked shady to me, leave, and collect my fees. Did I think it would turn out so easy? Hell no, but I had a mountain of expenses after my last two major cases, and I had no intention of returning that Hiero retainer.

We were back in the Hiero hoverlimo. Echo had joined us. He sat in the middle across from me, with Judo and the larger man of either side of him. Judo had not made eye contact with me once.

His gaze was to the ground. The larger man had his dark shades on again. Echo alternated between watching me and glancing out the dark tinted windows.

"At Macro, there are many Caucasians," he said. "They always smile and laugh. They became the megacorp they are by smiling and laughing before killing and burying people. They surround themselves with ...is the word bullies?"

"Thugs," I said.

"Yes."

"I was almost killed in my last case by a smiling, laughing person. A whole building full of them will only make me more on guard."

"Yes, be on guard. You will stay with me. Judo will follow. If anything happens, return to this limo."

"Excuse me, Mr. Echo, but doesn't Hiero already own Macro?"

"Hiero owns fifty-one percent of the new company."

My poker face was always good, but Echo realized that he'd said too much, which he never would have intentionally done. If Hiero only had a bare majority of the new company, were they really in charge? Was Ming the boss? Or were we going to see the real boss of the new company?

I'd been driving in Metropolis sky traffic for over fifteen years and illegally before then. I'd never seen it slow virtually to a halt. Judo yelled to the driver who I hadn't seen behind a dark partition. Echo's number two obviously wanted a traffic status.

"How far away is Macro?" I asked Judo.

"We should have arrived already," he replied.

"Curious there would be this much traffic at this time of day, going in this direction," I said.

"The driver says a dignitary has arrived at Metro International Airport and there is increased police activity."

"Or Macro has orchestrated all this to make us arrive late," I said. I was answering Judo but looking at Echo.

Echo said something to Judo in Japanese. The junior man looked at the watch patch on his left wrist.

"I'd recommend hovercycles," I said. "Use back alleys only."

Echo muttered something to Judo, and the junior man yelled to the driver.

We didn't wait long. I heard a knock on the passenger side. Judo got up and opened the door. We were at least twenty feet in the air. He jumped and disappeared. Echo gestured for me to follow. Can't say I ever jumped out of a hoverlimo without knowing where I was landing, but I wasn't concerned.

As soon I jumped, I saw about six hovercycles below. Suddenly, one of them was under me. They were two-seater models with a driver and tandem passenger pod. The helmeted driver handed me a helmet. I didn't see Echo and the larger man jump out, but when I turned they were on their hovercycles and putting on their helmets.

I was grateful I was a former amateur (meaning illegal) hovercar racer. These hovercycle drivers weren't playing. We'd dove and were moving at well past two hundred miles an hour through the back alleys as I'd suggested. They were true professional racers themselves making all the high-speed turns and dips with precision. Many times we came inches from hitting the side of a building, a hard sign, an antenna array, communication or electric wires. But never were we in any danger.

We soon arrived at the Macro Corporation building, pulling into their parking bay. I glanced back and the hovertraffic was as heavy as I'd ever seen in my life. Dignitaries visited Metropolis all the time. Never was sky traffic so congested.

The Macro Corporation building was nestled in the center of the several megatowers. We were still in Silicon Dunes, but at the other end. The entrance to their parking bay was the same as most—in the middle of the building. Often megatowers had the executive levels at the top, the parking in the middle, then the general levels.

Since we were on hovercycles we were able to bypass the normal valet and land directly in the small vehicle area. The drivers remained on the cycles with their helmets on. Echo, Judo, the larger man, and I gave them our helmets. Echo's men also left their sheathed swords behind.

Echo and his men checked their clothing and grooming. I did the same.

"Judo will lead. We will follow," Echo said to me.

The Macro parking bay had as much heavy security as Hiero. Actually, it looked identical to Hiero's—corporate soldiers with laser machine guns or handguns. All dressed in black suits and ties with white shirts, no hats. That would be the last similarity as we walked to the elevator bays.

Was this a real company? Even the stoic Mr. Echo couldn't believe what we were seeing. Out of the elevator capsule we stepped onto the first of the executive levels. We were treated to a floor that was a cross between a coffeehouse and a dance club. The reception area of the lobby wasn't a modest area for waiting. They'd created a monstrosity of beanbag lounge chairs in every color, equipped with full entertainment audio and screens. Every chair was occupied by someone listening to music or watching a movie on the screen. Moving through them were young women dressed for clubbing on hoverskates and serving refreshments.

At executive reception were a cluster of receptionists, tall Caucasian blondes who looked like they were poured into their clothes. Their business attire consisted of female business suits over their bras—interesting dress code. All of them had headsets and were busy talking, answering phones.

One spotted us and held up a finger as she finished her call.

"Mr. Echo," she said.

He nodded.

She handed him an access card. He immediately gave it to Judo.

"You can proceed to the penthouse level, sir. Mr. Able will greet you. Executive elevators are behind me."

Echo nodded.

The elevator opened and a perfectly tanned man in a dark green suit and turtleneck stood, waiting. He was Caucasian, tall, muscular, wavy brown shoulder-length hair. He wore glasses that had a slight bluish tint.

"Mr. Echo," he greeted. "I am Able. I report directly to Macro's CEO, Mr. Glyph. I'll take you to our conference room."

Hiero's had an open floor with workers in cubicles. Macro had one office after another packed with people at workstations.

"I see you made it here, despite the traffic," Able said as he led us down the hallways.

"Traffic was no bother," Judo answered.

"I know your security aide, sir. Who is the civilian?"

"He is nobody," Echo answered instead of Judo.

"Will 'nobody' be attending the meeting with Mr. Glyph?" Able asked.

"My aides will accompany me," Echo said.

We reached an open conference room. Nothing fancy or gigantic. It was a modest room with simple tables and chairs.

"I'll get service staff to attend to you while you wait," Able said and left us.

We sat quietly as the large man took his post standing outside the door. None of us talked, as we all knew the room was certainly being monitored.

GLYPH, CEO, MACRO CORPORATION

The game was as old as humanity. Heads of state would build the biggest, gaudiest, receiving rooms imaginable to intimidate visiting diplomats and dignitaries. Law enforcement and district attorneys would have suspects wait for hours in rooms too hot or too cold. Board members would vie for the biggest and plushest chairs, and be seated as close to the head of the table as possible. Grown people acting like kindergarten kids. I'd seen it all before. We should've been brought straight to Macro's CEO; instead we were sitting in a little conference room. We hadn't even been offered refreshments. I spoke too soon.

Not one, but two buxom women entered wearing what I was guessing was the Macro dress code for females—business suits but fancy bras instead of a blouse or shirt. One had a tray of ice-filled cups. The other had an assorted tray of canned drinks labeled in Japanese. They smiled as they set the trays on our table, nodded and left.

I could see Judo glance at Echo, but his boss focused on opening one of the canned beverages. Judo followed suit, but not me. Echo poured his can into one of the glasses with ice, set it in front of him but didn't take a sip. In fact, he never touched it again. Of course, Judo did the same thing.

We waited and waited, then we heard a commotion from outside the door. Judo stood from his chair and left the room. I heard loud yelling in Japanese.

"What now?" I said and stood from my chair.

I opened the door. Three Hiero men from the parking bay were with them. "Can you both step in here and tell me what's happening?" I said to Judo and the large man.

They stopped yelling, looked at me, and I could see them both look past me—obviously to Echo.

They stepped in and Judo closed the door.

"What's happening?" I asked again.

"Our drivers called. They must move the hovercycles. Hovertrucks arrived and are taking up the space."

"Mr. Judo, stay here. What is your name?" I asked the large man.

"Pro."

"Mr. Pro, you and I will deal with this. Mr. Judo shouldn't have to lower himself to deal with this nonsense. Let's go."

I opened the door and stepped into the hallway. I could hear the three men speaking Japanese in whispers. Pro stepped out and closed the door behind him. I'd memorized the path Able had taken, so I led Pro to the elevators.

When we stepped out of the elevator we were greeted with a cloud of dust. It was more than the arrival of hovertrucks. The vehicles that were trying to pull into the bay were the largest hovertrucks I'd ever seen. We saw our three cycle drivers, without their helmets, yelling at Macro security.

One of the guards ran to us. "Gentlemen, you have to go back to your floor. We—"

"Shut up!" I startled not only the guard but Mr. Pro. "Who's in charge?" I yelled. "Right now! Take us to him."

Another guard approached us, but not alone. Several guards walked with him.

"Are you the one in charge?" I yelled.

"I am. Who are you?"

"Nobody. You are not allowed to fly galaxy-class hovertransports into a parking bay for standard commercial hovervehicles. They need to enter your industrial receiving bays. Are you going to move them on, or do we need to talk to Mr. Able? Does Mr. Glyph, the CEO, know the two of you are doing this?"

I got the man's attention now. He led his men away and started barking orders at security. I looked at Mr. Pro.

"Mr. Pro, get your sword and Mr. Judo's. I don't think we're dealing with honorable people here. We may need them."

Pro didn't hesitate. He marched to the hovercycles with the drivers. As he did that, I watched security direct the mega-hovertransports back out. They were massive machines. If their hoverengines ever failed, they were heavy enough to possibly punch through one or more levels of the building.

Pro returned with a sheathed katana in each hand. He gave me a nod. When we both were satisfied, seeing one hovertransport reverse out of the parking bay and the three behind it already gone, I waved goodbye to the three cycle drivers. They gave me a thumbs-up.

We walked back to the elevator. Before it closed I pushed my hand out to stop them.

"On second thought," I said.

I hadn't flown a hovercycle in a while, but I'd tried my hand at the hovercycle racing scene. The Hiero hovercycles were so high-end and high-tech they could fly themselves. The drivers let me drive and take the lead. Into the elevator, we went and I flew the lead cycle out with the driver, another driver with Pro, and a final driver following. We sped down the hallways to our conference room. Hoverbrakes on these models were so precise and silent, you literally could stop on a coin. Your only enemy was knowing basic physics, or you'd easily flip the vehicle and crush yourself. We parked the cycles against the wall, the drivers removed their helmets with big smiles, and we all noticed that everyone in the offices we passed was in the halls gawking at us, chattering away, laughing and smiling.

Pro and I stepped back into the conference room. Both men saw the cycle drivers. Judo stood from his chair and took his sword. Pro returned to his post outside the conference room.

Echo said softly, "We hired well."

"If Able doesn't return in five minutes, we'll show ourselves to Mr. Glyph's office!" I yelled out, talking to the office workers.

Able did walk back into the conference room three minutes later. I immediately rose from my seat and stopped right in front of him.

"Stop it," I said to his face. "Stop your games. This is the behavior of children and two-bit criminal punks on the street. You're supposed to be a nearly one-hundred-year old megacorp of some prestige. Should I inform your boss, though I'm sure he's the one behind it all? If not, you'll be fired for acting like a child. If so, you'll be fired for me figuring it out. I don't want to tell you again. Are you taking Mr. Echo to your CEO this instant or not?"

"I am," Able replied, with a slight smirk.

"Then I have nothing more to say."

I returned to my seat.

"Mr. Echo," Able said. "Mr. Glyph is ready to receive you."

Echo stood, then Judo and I did.

Able said nothing as he led us past our hovercycles in the hallway. Pro followed us, leaving the drivers behind. We returned to the elevators but Able waved his hand over a part of the wall in the corner, and a new elevator door appeared.

The Macro elevators were already plenty large. The new elevator was twice the size. We went up one level. Now, we were on the real penthouse level with the exclusive offices of Macro's CEO.

I hadn't been in the detective biz long, but from the corporate clients I had it seemed the unwritten law was that presidents and CEOs had to have the most outrageously large offices compared to anyone else. Mr. Glyph's office was the entire penthouse floor.

There were no partitions at all, only an executive desk with chairs that we figuratively had to walk a mile to.

The space reminded me of photos of Mars because it all had a slight red brownish tone. There were huge paintings on the wall, and between each were busts of historical figures I didn't know on column stands. The office also had its own long rectangular reflecting pool in the center, with a fountain shooting up tens of feet in the air.

But the megacorp CEO wasn't at his main executive desk. He sat stuffing his face with food at another black table to the side. Another buxom female was pouring him a drink. He already had two empty glasses in front of him. The man was eating one of the messiest, though tasty, meals with his fingers—barbecue ribs lathered in sauce. His silver-gray hair had a military vet style, full beard and mustache. Impeccable striped suit. Shirt with diamond buttons and diamond cuff links.

We all waited quietly for him to acknowledge us.

"Have a seat, gentlemen. I do apologize. I've been in back-to-back meetings due to the merge and have literally not eaten in two days."

Able offered us seats at the main desk. Echo sat first, Judo on his right, and I sat on the other side. Judo stood behind us with Pro. Able joined them.

Mr. Glyph finished his meal and stood. The female quickly cleared it, picking up the entire clear tray that I hadn't noticed. The top of his meal table slid away, converting to a sink. He washed his hands, the water drained away, then we heard air blowing as he heat-dried his hands. He stepped to his desk and sat in his high-back faux-leather chair.

"Gentlemen," he said.

"Mr. Glyph," Echo said back.

Glyph looked at me. "Mr. Cruz of the Liquid Cool Detective Agency."

"Nobody," I said.

"Why are you in my building, Mr. Cruz, in my office?"

"The Hiero Corporation has hired me as a records consultant, nothing more. No need, sir, to read anything more into my presence, Mr. Glyph."

"How can I not? A famous private detective before me."

"I work for Mr. Echo. I'm nobody."

"Mr. Echo, my man, Mr. Able, will also work for you for the duration of your review. How long will Hiero's review take?"

"Mr. Glyph, my intent is to complete the review in no more than three weeks. Is that acceptable?"

"More than acceptable, Mr. Echo. Whatever you need, Mr. Able will see to it."

"Thank you, sir."

"After your review, I look forward to spending time with Mr. Ming."

"He also looks forward to many productive meetings with you."

"When would you like to begin your work?" Glyph asked.

"Whenever is convenient for you, sir," Echo replied.

"Then you can start tomorrow at noon," Glyph said.

I slowly raised my hand. Glyph's icy blue eyes locked on me. "Yes, Mr. Cruz."

"I'm sorry, Mr. Glyph. Since the traffic was so bad, maybe, if it's convenient, we can start the work right now. That terrible hovertraffic. Galaxy-class hovertransports. Limited parking in your bay. I'd forgotten to tell Mr. Echo that this part of Silicon Dunes is more like Silver City with the traffic. In fact, I'd be willing to work through the entire night to get back on schedule for Mr. Ming."

Glyph said nothing. He examined his perfectly manicured hands. Finally, he looked up and smiled.

"Mr. Able, what do you think?"

"We're ready to accommodate Mr. Echo and his team," Able replied.

"I will leave you to Mr. Able," Glyph said.

"Thank you, sir," Echo said.

Echo stood. Judo and I also rose from our chairs.

"Tell me, Mr. Echo," Glyph began, "is Mr. Ming angered by something Macro has done? I wish for the union of our two companies to be mutually beneficial to all."

"Mr. Ming regards the Macro Corporation in the highest esteem."

"Then why is an outsider involved in our private business?" the CEO asked.

"He is simply a consultant—"

"Mr. Echo, is Mr. Ming available for a call?"

"I am not directly knowledgeable of his schedule, but the office will connect you if at all possible. Is it a matter than I am unable to assist you with?"

"I want you to fire the outsider."

The two men stared at each other.

"Mr. Ming authorized him."

"I do not authorize him."

"Hiero retains the authority to hire whoever it wishes, for whatever purposes, and for however longer it decides."

I slowly raised my hand again.

Glyph flashed a bit of anger at me. "It's not necessary to raise your hand. Speak!"

"Is there some reason why you're delaying Mr. Echo's records review, sir?"

"Excuse me?" Glyph asked.

"Mr. Glyph, I have observed that the Macro Corporation has attempted to delay Mr. Echo's review of company records from the time this day began. Mr. Ming personally asked me to report back to him, separate from Mr. Echo, on an hour-by-hour accounting of any problems or resistance to Mr. Echo's work. Sadly, sir, I will have much to report today, and Mr. Ming will not be happy."

Glyph stood from his seat. "Did you threaten me, Mr. Cruz?"

"I told you already, sir. I'm nobody. Mr. Ming, the CEO of the Hiero Corporation, is directing me. I don't see why you'd view that as threatening you. I'm doing my job. Mr. Echo will begin his work right now. And he will bring me along, if he so chooses. Mr. Able can take us where he needs to so you can get back to your post-merger meetings and ribs eating."

At that moment, Glyph's desk flew across the massive office and crashed to the ground. The CEO stepped to me. I saw his muscles bulging and heard what sounded like crunching rock. He was either a cyborg or wearing a bionic suit underneath his clothes.

"You have no idea how dangerous I am," he said to me.

"Mr. Glyph, I'm not worried in the least. I know how this works and know a lot more than you think. I work for Mr. Echo. I work for Mr. Ming. You touch me or any of your people, including your bouncy, half-dressed females, they'll kill you."

"Are you certain, Mr. Cruz?"

I stepped closer to him. "Yes, Mr. Glyph, I'm certain."

AGENT DELPHI, METRO PD CYBERCRIMES UNIT

I knew that Glyph could have accidentally ripped off my ear lobe or kicked my gonads up into my skull, so I had to give him an out to de-escalate his rage.

"Take a look at this," I said. It was a photo from a year ago of Macro executives and staff. I showed it to Echo. Echo's eyes narrowed. Glyph looked like a teenager caught doing something inappropriate. "I notice that none of your female staff were dressed as they are today. Why the one-day change to the dress code? I was so impressed by your little show you put on for us in the executive reception area, I took a picture and sent it to Mr. Ming."

"The women here at Macro are not your type, Mr. Cruz?" Glyph asked me.

"I'm married, Mr. Glyph, and I've never been interested in the bimbo type regardless of nationality. My wife is high-class all the way. I married up. So let's stop the games, Mr. Glyph, because I am the master of games. Ask all the criminal types sitting in Metro

Prison, or you can try the morgue too. Lot more of them there. Mr. Echo came here to work. We thought we were dealing with a professional company. Seems like its run by college frat boys."

Glyph burst out laughing. "We love our practical jokes at Macro, Mr. Cruz. Mr. Echo knows. All initiates have to put up with it. I do know how the Japanese executives love the European ladies."

"I'm Cambodian," Echo said.

"I'm Korean," Judo said.

"I'm Hong Kongese," Pro said.

"I'm Puerto Rican," I said.

Glyph belly-laughed. Echo laughed with him. I laughed in my pretend way.

"You have to loosen up, Mr. Cruz. When you work at a company most of your waking hours, you have to find fun where you can. Mr. Ming is well aware of my elevated sense of humor. Able, get these men what they need, and practical joke time is officially over. Return the executive lobby to normal, and please do have the women change so that Employee Resources will let me alone."

"Yes, Mr. Glyph," Able said.

Glyph, still laughing, patted me on the shoulder and walked back to his desk.

"And call maintenance," he said to Able.

Everyone was laughing and having a good time. I was glad Judo and Pro had their swords back, though, and I was standing right next to Mr. Echo, just in case.

I made up a story at the spur of the moment so I had to stick with it. We did work through the night. There was no way I'd use my own mobile. Macro would hack in and turn my own mobile into a listening device or maybe make it blow up in my face at their discretion. Maybe an urban myth about megacorps, but I wasn't taking any chances. I used Judo's mobile to call my wife and tell her I wouldn't be home. Then I learned that PJ had already called her to blab about our new megacorp client.

Echo had Judo and me reviewing financial records. I had no idea what I was looking at—numbers, numbers and more numbers. The only written text was in Japanese. At least Judo seemed like he knew what he was doing. I simply looked on.

Echo soon left us to review Macro's confidential files. He took Pro with him. We didn't see either man until the early morning, when Echo announced the review was over.

The Hiero hoverlimo was waiting for us in the parking bay. The hovercycle drivers had already been released earlier in the night, so we loaded into the vehicle. As I sat there, I wondered if I was in the middle of another corporate war. It wasn't uncommon, especially in this supercity, for a client to hire a detective for ulterior motives other than their stated case, just as Mr. Mick had said. I'd caught more than a few clients wanting to use me, whether to establish an alibi while involved in criminal activity or as a decoy. This smelled like a power struggle and ordinarily I'd pass on the case, but they paid me a lot of money. However, the only thing worse than a gang war was a corporate war. I'd been in one already in my Blade Gunner Case. I was not about to be dragged into another.

"Mr. Cruz, our review of the Macro records is complete," Echo said.

"Do we need to return for additional days?" I asked.

"All is complete tonight," he answered.

"The contract is complete then?"

"It is, Mr. Cruz. Our courier will arrive in your office tomorrow with final payment of all your fees."

"Thank you. I hope I was able to provide the services you needed, Mr. Echo."

"You did, Mr. Cruz. Mr. Ming was given a full report and was extremely impressed by your assistance. That appreciation will also be reflected in your final payment."

"Thank you, Mr. Echo. Though brief, I'm glad to have had the chance to work with you, Mr. Judo, and Mr. Pro. Feel free to visit me and my secretary again, but remember, you don't have to throw any shurikens at us to get our attention. You can simply say, 'Hello.'"

Echo chuckled. Judo and Pro joined him.

"Yes, Mr. Cruz. I will remember that."

They took me home to Rabbit City, dropping me in front of my residential building the Concrete Mama. I waved as their hoverlimo rose into the air and at about three a.m. I walked into the lobby. At 3:10 a.m., not wanting to wake up Dot, I threw myself onto the bed in our guest room and fell fast asleep. My Hiero case was over, and I'd be getting a bonus!

Who was touching my toes?

My eyes opened to glance at the wall clock. I'd been asleep for only four hours. I knew I had to move fast. I reached down and snatched a giggling Cruz Jr. from the bottom of the bed.

"Leave my feet alone," I said and laid him down next to me. "Go to sleep because I have to sleep."

I knew he'd behave for only a few moments. He pretended to sleep, then sat up, laughed, and was gone. I heard feet running. He did that to try to trick me. Cruz Jr. loved his new found ability to move on two legs, but reverting to baby-crawling remained a part of his bag of tricks. His plan was to sneak back into the room. I sat up and watched the door, waiting. He appeared crawling on all fours, saw me, and fell to the floor, laughing hysterically.

"I was your age too, you know."

I had to accept the fact that I wasn't going to get any more sleep unless Cruz Jr. was asleep. And that wasn't until thirteen hours later. I heard noise in the kitchen so Dot was up too.

Almost noon. The sky was slightly overcast but we hadn't had rain in a few days. I couldn't remember the last time I was on my way to the office so late. Even though I drove a bright red hovervehicle, I tried to vary my routes to the office. Once I hit the Circle there was only one way to go, but there were endless ways to get to the Circle.

My dashboard vid-phone rang. I answered it and PJ's face appeared on the screen.

"I'm on my way," I said.

"Not yet, you have a pickup."

"Pickup?"

"We have a check waiting at the Metro Courts."

"I got all our payments."

"Cruz, when the government says it wants to give you a check for money, don't argue. Metro Municipal. Check. Bank. In that order."

I laughed. "I'm on my way to Metro Courts then."

At least I wasn't going back to Metro General. Downtown Metropolis was the center of Metropolis. The monolith towers were no bigger or taller than any others in the city, but they always looked different when I flew by in my vehicle. Some said it was its historic architecture of lighter-colored paint for its exterior, in contrast to the dark hues of the surrounding towers. I agreed with whoever said it was a state of mind, a projection of swagger. You knew it was the center of power, so you intuitively saw that in its buildings when, in reality, it was the same as everywhere else.

I worked hard to be a generalist detective. I had my Average Joe cases, megacorporation cases, and government cases. I didn't want to be pigeonholed because I liked the variety. Lately, most of my government cases were skiptracing verification, process serving, and witness statements for the municipal courts. There was so much work to be done, far beyond what their full-time staff could accomplish, that they had to bring in licensed contractors like me. You had to stay on them to get paid on a timely basis but once they tagged you as reliable and getting results, they made sure to keep you happy, especially as a contract investigator.

The Metropolis Municipal Court Building wasn't a building; it was an endless maze. The Criminal Courts were bad; the civil court system was worse. But I adapted and always knew where to go and who to see to bypass the lines and any waiting. I gave my name to a regular I knew at the lobby desk, and they told me where to go.

This time I was going to the seventieth floor. When I came out of the elevator I went to Room 32. I'd never been on the floor before and there was very little hall traffic, unlike all the other floors I'd been to. I gave my name to reception.

"Cruz," the female counter attendant said as she scanned her computer screen. "Yes, Mr. Cruz. Go straight to Room 80 at the far end of the hall."

The other thing about government buildings was the numbering. It made no sense at all. There were signs that clearly marked where to go, but there was no logic to it. I did as directed and walked to the other end of the winding hallway to the far end. There it was.

I opened the door and it was a small office. A man sat at a desk in front of me, behind a big terminal. He looked up at me.

"My name's Cruz. I was told to come by and pick up a check."

"You can wait in the conference room."

I walked to the open door. It was not a conference room.

"What's this about?" I asked. "This is an interrogation room."

"It's an interview room."

"To-may-to. (Tomato) To-mat-to. What's this about? Do you have a check for me?"

"My boss is on his way over."

"What agency is your boss with?"

"It's best if he speaks with you."

"Is there a check?"

"No, Mr. Cruz, there isn't. He'll explain. I can assure you it's important and my boss is with law enforcement."

"Just not Metro PD."

"Part of Metro PD."

I didn't like it, but I sat in the interrogation-interview room. I sat with my back against the wall and watched out the door. I heard the main door open, a brief conversation, then a tall man appeared with a leather-bound notepad in his hand. Asian, long slicked back hair to his shoulders, nice suit jacket but with ratty jeans and sneakers. He saw me checking out his attire and smiled. He closed the door and sat down at the table.

"Good afternoon, Mr. Cruz."

"Good afternoon."

"I'm sorry for the deception, but we didn't want you coming down to Police One."

"Why not?" I asked. "They have interrogation-interview rooms too."

"They do, but you'll soon understand the reason for the precautions."

"My ears are open."

"My name's Agent Delphi with the Cybercrimes Division."

"Who can verify your identity for me?"

He grinned. "You are welcome to visit Metro PD, discretely, to verify my identity. Please speak to Chief Hub only. We were speaking about you yesterday."

"Were you?"

"We were."

Chief Hub was Metropolis's top cop and head of its five-hundred-thousand plus police force—the largest on Earth.

"About what?"

"Background."

"Satisfied?"

"Yes, I've spoken to others too. You have lots of fans and lots of enemies in law enforcement, but it's the fans that matter most to me."

"Wilford G. is a good friend."

"Yes, Mr. Cruz. We know you're good friends with the head of the Police Union."

Delphi opened up his pad and took a pen from his jacket. "Are you still working for the Hiero Corporation?"

"Hiero? Is that what this is about? I wrapped up my work with them early this morning."

"Yes, they dropped you off at your residence at three this morning."

"Do you have me under surveillance or them?"

"Both."

"Why is that, Mr. Delphi?"

"What work did you do for them?"

"Are you kidding?"

"Did they have you sign a confidentiality statement?"

"Why would they? I didn't do anything."

"They paid you a lot of money for not doing anything."

"I have mouths to feed. Delphi, I'm not telling you about my clients, unless it's something criminal. It wasn't. Besides, it's done."

"I don't think so."

"What do you mean by that?"

"We believe they'll contact you again."

"Why?"

"Mr. Cruz, what do you know about the Hiero Corporation, really?"

"Really? Nothing. Import, export. That means nothing."

"They have many legitimate import-export businesses, but Cybercrimes is not interested in that. We are interested in their criminal 'import-export' activities on the Net."

"Delphi, I worked for them for one day. Whatever you think I can do, I can't."

"The reason we believe they will contact you again is because there has been an explosion of background checks and life searches on you from individuals from the Hiero Corporation, the Macro Corporation, and others."

"Others? What others?"

"Criminals, Mr. Cruz. If they were done with you, the interest would have dropped off immediately, not continued and expanded. It's not unusual for megacorps to hire someone and test them out first. See if they're capable and can be trusted with the real job."

"What's the real job then, Mr. Delphi?"

"When you find out, we want you to tell us."

I sat back in my chair with a big smile. "You know, Mr. Delphi. This could be part of their test too."

"If you're suggesting that I'm a mole for the Hiero Corporation, your suspicions are misplaced. Their criminal activities thrive not because they have moles in law enforcement. It's because they're good at their criminal activities."

"Better than you?"

"As you know, the Net is a vast universe, Mr. Cruz. Most of it is hidden from the public eye."

"Mr. Delphi, what are you looking for? Fishing expeditions don't work on these people."

"I can't tell you that for obvious reasons."

"You're not being very persuasive, Mr. Delphi. You have me under surveillance. You're tracking my movements. You want me to spy for you on clients I no longer have."

"I understand, Mr. Cruz. Trust is something that's earned. I'll ask you this: what is your assessment of Hiero's acquisition of the Macro Corporation?"

"I have suspicions, but that's where they'll remain after interacting with them for only a day."

"Mr. Cruz, I can't tell you much other than to say your dealings with Hiero and Macro are not over. I believe you know that. I can share with you that Hiero began its checks on you six months ago. That's how you came to our attention."

"Interesting."

"Macro's interest began this week, and especially as of yesterday."

"I'm sure. I bet I can pinpoint the hour the checks began."

"After a cordial meeting with Macro's CEO?"

"Cordial would be one word for it."

"Mr. Cruz, all I can say is, I'm here. Your life may become quite complicated shortly."

"The life of a Metro street detective is always complicated."

"True, but yours is far more than most. Hiero and Macro are very dangerous companies. Do you know why they merged?"

"I thought Hiero acquired Macro?"

"A merger to avoid a full-scale corporate war, but all that means is that the war will be behind closed doors."

"And you're telling me I'm in the middle of it?"

"Hiero is using you to tip the scales in their favor, and Macro knows that."

"Mr. Delphi, I agree with you that these companies are 'nice' criminals, but these megacorporations are not reckless, low-end street punks. They merge to end fighting, not to bring it behind closed doors. Fighting kills and hurts business for everyone. None of them want the Council of Corporations breathing down their necks."

Delphi nodded. "I see that you do understand."

"I do. What's this about then? If you say I'm going to get a call from them or they're going to show up at my office again to hire me for the 'real' job, then I'd appreciate you telling me what you know. It's my neck on the line, not yours."

"Mr. Cruz, I'm here, and so are the full resources of Metro PD's Cybercrimes Division. We're here."

"We're here." That was it. He sounded like a life insurance or accident attorney commercial. As soon as my meeting with Mr. Delphi was over, I marched from the Metro Court Building straight to Metro PD and Chief Hub's office.

DIGITAL SAMURAI

Chief Hub was waiting for me. He'd told the front desk to just send me through. After I verified Delphi was Delphi, I asked Hub the same question: "What's going on?"

Hub was as forthcoming as Delphi, meaning he said nothing.

"Cyber-crimes deals with cyber-warfare, cyber-espionage, cyber-terrorism, cyber-extortion. Any crime there is, put 'cyber' in front of it and they deal with it. I'd do as he says, Cruz. When you find out what they're up to, I'd make him your first visit, not me. I have my hands full enough with crimes in the real world. I'll leave the cyber ones to them."

In my "bible" *How to Be a Great Detective with 100 Rules*, written by my posthumous mentor, Mr. Wilford G., a ninety-five-year-old private eye who had worked the streets of Metropolis for seventy years, said: "Always trust your instincts, especially when they say you're about to walk into a laser blast."

Everything Delphi told me I already knew. Both PJ and I were expecting a return visit from Mr. Echo. Maybe he'd send Judo in his place to fetch me back to Hiero.

As I drove back to Liquid Cool, I now had possible answers to my recent heightened paranoia. I'd felt I was being watched, because I was. I'd seen the shadowy figures. If Hiero had been checking me out for six months, that explained it. However, "others" had taken an interest in me too. There was also Cybercrimes. I didn't like it at all.

This time I called PJ at the office. She answered right away.

"Did you get the check?"

"There was no check."

"No money? What then?"

"Warning from pseudo-friends?"

"Pseudo-friends? Is that fake friends?"

"Fake friends are not friends."

"But pseudo-friends are?"

"Yes."

"Cruz, that makes no sense."

"It makes sense to me, and you too, if you think about it. But that's not why I'm calling. Weapons, PJ. However many weapons we have, it may not be enough."

"Why? We have plenty."

"I'm not feeling very secure. Look at the trouble we had against Echo. That was one man. And he wasn't trying to harm us."

"He's coming back?"

"I'm not worried about him. He walks through the door and that means more money."

"Money is good. Is he coming back?"

"Money buys weapons. He's coming back."

"That's not what I'll use my money for. Who's coming that I should worry about?"

"I don't know."

"We need to be ready though."

"Ready for anyone or anything. PJ, I got to go!"

I immediately disconnected the vid-phone.

A big, black, fully-tinted hovercar had been following me close. It picked me up as soon as I turned onto the Circle. They made no attempt to hide they were following because they didn't care that I knew. I'd had my office blown up. I was not about to have my prized Pony damaged or destroyed. I dove.

The modern hovercar had so many safeguard sensors and features to avoid crashes and to alert the driver. But crashes still happened. I was possibly going to cause a lot of them by illegally diving my vehicle. I was practically a professional driver. I was about to see how good the driver on my tail was. As I descended toward the ground fast, I saw hovercars swerve and one honk. Metropolitans never used their horns. I'd almost forgotten what one sounded like. I heard a small crash; a hovercar hit him on the way down. I expertly avoided any collision and when I was on the ground, hit my nitro-accelerator and shot around a corner.

Pedestrians ran for their lives, but they were in no danger. I was too good to hit a person. There was no sign of the other hovercar in my rearview window as I shot around another corner. I combat parked, hopped out, and ran across the street. The door closed itself and I left the engine running.

The black hovercar appeared the second I reached the other side of the street and screeched on their brakes. They saw me, so I stopped to face whoever they were. Out came three men with laser rapiers—Japanese sword-like weapons with switch-on laser blades. Their faces were covered with red neon tattoos with their dark shades. Digital samurai. But the street enforcers were far from their turf.

"What d'you want?" I yelled.

All three ignored me as they approached. I couldn't see the driver behind the black tint, hovering in the vehicle. I wanted answers but I wanted to live more. I fired laser rounds at the driver side of the black hovercar, shattering glass, and inside caught fire. The digital samurai yelled out and charged with their switched-on weapons. There was nothing to do but finish it. Unlike Echo, they couldn't swat lasers out of the air. The volley of my omega-gun cut them down with ease, but that's when I immediately ran for cover. People had already scattered at the sight of the gangsters. I threw myself through the door of one of the street establishments—it was some takeout restaurant. I didn't care about the food—people were on the ground, cowering—I cared about their own tinted window.

It was as I thought. The first hovercar was to keep me busy while the rest of the crew arrived. Two black hovervans landed. I kicked myself for leaving my own vehicle. I needed to be in the Pony, not hiding in a takeout place. Out came more digital samurai, but these had a laser sword in one hand and a gun in the other. Again, they showed me they weren't professionals. I watched them but they couldn't see me.

I burst out of the restaurant and sprayed them with laser-fire before most had a chance to even move. Half I hit; the others scattered for cover behind parked hovervans. My goal was to get to my vehicle and go. I kept spraying laser-fire as I ran past and to my vehicle. I launched into the sky before they could get even one shot off.

In my Pony, I could do some serious damage. I modified it with all kinds of "extras" but it was still a classic, and I didn't want any bullet holes or laser blasts in the Miami Vice red paint. Before I hopped back into the Pony, I'd memorized the license tag of the main hovercar. I was in sky traffic and was gone.

The landlord of my Liquid Cool building hated me. He loathed me. He'd hire contract killers to get me if he thought he could get away with it. Most of the tenants on my floor were equally contemptuous of me and my business. They claimed I brought the low-life streets to their office doors. I told them that it had only happened a couple of times, and it wasn't my fault. Crazy maniacs are...crazy.

I parked in the building next door to mine and ran over. PJ had already called me. She told me that digital samurai had arrived in force in our parking level and she went down to deal with them—carrying a bag of weapons. (No, we weren't going to call the police! We'd already reached our call complaint quota for the month.)

The elevator opened one level above. I could already hear the gunfire. The police must have been called a million times already with all the noise, but sadly that didn't necessarily mean they'd arrive soon. We were in Metropolis. There were lots of gun battles in this supercity. I'd walk down one flight of stairs.

When I opened the door, a digital samurai jumped out at me. He swung and I fired, hitting him in the chest. I blew off his sword hand to make sure he didn't try to slice me. He didn't scream at all, but reached into his jacket with his other hand. I stomped on his chest. He screamed.

"Why are you after me?" I yelled.

He glared at me.

"I never did anything to you, or your gang. Why are you after me?"

"Voodoo Child will find her."

"Who or what is a voodoo child? And who is 'her'?"

"No lies! We know you work for her. We know."

"Know what? I don't know what you're talking about, but you can tell the police all about it when they get here."

"I tell nothing."

The man slowly stuck out his long tongue, then chomped down hard enough to draw blood. I almost gagged in disgust.

His mouth began to foam up with a white substance. His head tilted to the side and his eyes drifted off. The man was dead.

If there was one digital samurai in the stairway, there might be more. I picked up the man and threw him through the doorway to the level below. I saw flashes of light in the darkness. The bulbs had been blown out. I shot multiple times at every laser sword I saw. Grunts. Falling bodies.

The sound of gunfire had subsided. I slowly moved down the steps and opened the door on my parking level. When I stepped out into the light I saw more bodies. Two hovervans were illegally parked with doors open. So that I didn't get shot by own employee, I took cover behind vehicles and called her on my mobile.

"I'm here. Near their hovervans. Don't shoot me."

I hung up and stood up. I cautiously surveyed the area. PJ came out from around the corner at one end. She carried an extremely large laser rifle.

"What is that? I thought you liked your laser shotguns."

She made her way to, kicking bodies to make sure they were dead. "I wanted to try something new."

"Did they say anything to you?"

"Cruz, say what exactly? They're gangsters."

"Digital samurai on our parking level. Why are they here?"

"They're dead gangsters now. They picked the wrong detective agency to mess with," PJ said.

"This is the police!"

The audio announcement rumbled from outside the building and sent a shockwave of fear through our bodies. It was an arriving police hover-cruiser. PJ and I ran so fast to the elevators that I'm sure we broke records. We had to get to the office, stash our illegal weapons, switch the video recording of our private parking level cameras back on, and put on a show that we were working all along and didn't know anything about the shootout.

The police had arrived! They'd visit Liquid Cool for sure. They always did. At least this shootout wasn't on our office floor, so neither our grumpy landlord nor unfriendly fellow tenants could complain about us. But they'd find another reason or two.

BUBBLE BAHA, GHOST MARKET GREMLIN

PJ had locked up the office but opened back up in a second. She ran to her workstation with her rifle and bag of weapons. I ran into my private office. I heard PJ's music playing again and lots of noise. We had all kinds of secret safes built into the office.

For my part, I took off my jacket and planted myself behind my desk. Many people didn't know it, but the police could see elevated heart rates with their enhanced glasses. My heart was racing. So I calmed myself as I walked to my pop-open mini-kitchen and casually made myself a cup of silk coffee. I'd be calm and relaxed in no time.

As I sipped from my cup, I stepped back out into the main office area. PJ was working, typing a million miles a minute with her bionic fingers. She looked calm and relaxed too.

"The mission of the day is to find out the meaning of this name: Voodoo Child," I said.

She gave me a quizzical look. "Who's that? Did those digital samurai tell you that's who sent them?"

"Yes."

She smiled. "Good work. You got to interrogate them before you shot them."

"I'll search through the database and look at neon gang tattoos. That should give us clues too."

The door opened. We both looked up. Two large Metro PD officers stepped into the office. In standard silver-and-black body armor, visored half-helmets, full weapons assault vest. PEACE in big bold white letters on their chests, though, like all police, they could kill you in an instant, if you did the wrong thing.

I smiled. "Good afternoon, Officers."

They moved to us; one of them scanned the office.

"Hello, Cruz," one said. I didn't recognize either of them, but all beat cops knew me by sight.

"Have you two been here all day?" he asked.

"I got in around thirty minutes ago," I said.

"I opened up the office at nine a.m., Officer," PJ said.

"Actually, I met with Chief Hub before I got in," I said with a big smile.

"What happened, Officer?" PJ asked.

"You two don't know?" the second officer asked.

"No, Officers. Know what?" I asked.

"There's a pile of bodies down in one of the parking levels," the second officer replied.

PJ and I feigned shock.

"Bodies?" I said. "Who was it? What happened?"

"See boss, I told you. The criminal element here is getting bolder," PJ said, glancing at me.

"What happened, Officer?" I asked again.

"Yes, what happened?" PJ said. "Now I don't feel safe with all the violence around us these days. What's the world coming to?"

The officers started to chuckle.

"Officers Break and Caps say hello," the first officer said.

"Oh, the officers are good friends of mine."

"They'd be here instead of us, but they're on a major call. But they did tell us one thing: if it's a shootout, you and your felon secretary were involved."

"Now wait a minute," I protested. "We've been in here, and I was with Chief Hub."

"Officers, I paid my debt to society and I'm an honest, law-abiding citizen."

"We're not even going to bother playing your games," an officer said. "The parking level will be yellow-taped for investigation, we'll go through the motions, but we know who the principle suspects are."

"It wasn't us, Officers," I said.

"Sure it wasn't, Cruz."

"The police cruiser on scene spotted two unidentified figures running away on infrared," the second officer said.

"I hope you and your felon employee got all of them, because these types tend to keep coming," the first officer continued.

"Do you have video surveillance of the parking levels?" the second officer asked PJ.

She looked at me with disapproval. "The boss here is too cheap to pay for it. We only have surveillance of the elevator and the hallway outside the office. See boss, even the police say we should have surveillance of the parking level."

The police officers watched us. If it were someone else, we both would have been arrested and taken downtown, but I was a "friend of the police.

"Lucky day, Cruz. The gangsters had so many arrests and outstanding warrants on them that you're getting a pass," one of them said.

"Gangsters?" I said. "Do you know which gang?"

"Why? And have us do your work for you? You saw their tattoos when you shot them. Figure it out yourselves." He tapped the top of the reception station. "You two have a fine day."

The police officers turned and left the office.

Unfortunately, this was a "client call" day. PJ had three clients scheduled, each appointment about an hour apart. I was tempted to reschedule them, but PJ wouldn't let me.

"Having satisfied clients isn't good enough anymore, Cruz. We don't want to be a good company. We need to give great client service because we need to be great. People never forget how great companies make them feel."

"Reading those business books still."

"I'll have you know that I'm the VP of Great Client Services at Liquid Cool."

"Thanks for informing me. I'm only the boss."

PJ had already rescheduled these clients because of my all-night work with Hiero the day before.

"You speak to your clients. I'll do the research," she told me.

"Anything yet?" I asked her from the doorway of my private office.

"Cruz, let me do my work. What about the tattoos?"

"Nothing yet."

"Then you have work to do too."

"Keep an eye on the surveillance because—"

"Cruz! I know how to watch out for gunmen."

I thought for a moment.

"What?" she asked me.

"You're right."

"What do you mean?"

"You always watch the surveillance cameras. How did Mr. Echo sneak into the office that day? He was just standing there."

"Maybe he was wearing one of those illegal Up-Top cloaking suits."

"But he wasn't wearing any mask."

"Maybe he is a real ninja."

"Maybe. Well, we have a lot of work to do, and I'll be out of commission with these three clients."

"Don't blow off good-paying clients."

"I won't." I saw from the clock in the office that my first client would be arriving in less than thirty minutes. "PJ, that thug who said what he said. I lucked out big time. He gave us a clue that we shouldn't have, and I didn't kill him."

"No?"

"He committed suicide."

"Suicide?"

"I thought it was because I got the drop on him, but I think it's because he realized that he slipped when he said what he said to me. He was worse than an informant to the police. His bosses would have brutally killed him in ways neither of us could imagine when they found out. He couldn't reach his sword. He wasn't going to try to kill me. He killed himself."

"Seppuku," PJ said. "Japanese ritual suicide. Gangsters still do it."

"Suicide by poison. PJ, I need to know what Voodoo Child means. Every reference you can find, no matter how remote or seemingly silly."

"You got it, boss."

There was an even bigger question for us: why did the digital samurai come after me? Honestly, despite their flashy weapons, these digital samurai were not very good, which raised more questions in my mind. But I had my client calls.

My first client was a middle-aged woman with a pale complexion and short dark hair.

"Mr. Cruz, I want to hire you. My husband's cheating on me and I want you to prove it," she said, seated across from me in my private office.

In a supercity where it always rains, only the droplets are more plentiful than all the cheating spouse surveillance cases. However, I never wanted them to be more than a quarter of my overall cases. They were easy and paid quickly, but took no real skill and sometimes could be dangerous. Usually, the wealthier the spouse, the more chance of violence. My potential client's husband was very wealthy.

"I'll take your case," I said.

As soon as I was done with the new client, I was back onto my computer scrolling through thousands of neon tattoo designs of Metropolis gangs. I'd sketched an image of the tattoo and had the computer auto-searching for me between client appointments, but it was not an exact process. The problem was that it was a neon tattoo, which meant that not necessarily the whole tattoo had lit up, only a piece of it did. So I still had a lot of images to review.

The second potential client was the kind of case that I liked. A young woman who'd turned eighteen wanted me to find her birth mother.

"If she put you up for adoption, there could've been legitimate reasons for it," I said.

"I know."

"Did you not get along well with your adoptive parents?"

"My adoptive parents are my real parents. They raised me," she said. "I'm simply curious, Mr. Cruz. I'm not trying to show up in their lives out of nowhere. I want to say hello. I want them to know I turned out okay."

I gladly took the case. I told her if I found her birth mother, it'd be up to the birth mother if contact was ultimately made. The young woman agreed.

Since my second appointment was shorter than usual, I had more time to view my computer search results. PJ was speaking to the second client and getting her retainer—I gave her a reduced rate. I found a few designs that seemed to match with my digital samurai attackers. My search continued.

PJ popped into my office. "I'll start the search for her birth mother."

For my second client, PJ would probably end up "solving" the case from her computer.

"Great. How's your search?"

"I may have something, but I'm not done."

"Good. Oh, how many people am I seeing for the third appointment?"

"Maybe twelve people."

"Twelve people?"

"It's an easy case. Easy money."

"Okay."

"ABC. Always be closing cases!"

The third client call was a neighborhood watch group. I'd worked for a few of them in the past. Usually, it had to do with some type of surveillance. The group of residents and business owners wanted me to help them catch a gang of graffiti bandits plaguing their neighborhood.

"Do you know the name of their leader?" I asked the group clustered around me. We were meeting in my private office's waiting area for more room.

"Some punk named Halley," one of the men in the group answered.

"They call themselves the Pixel Posse," a woman said.

"What did the police say?" I asked.

"Nothing. They took our statement but told us to our faces they wouldn't do anything unless it escalated."

"The police do have to prioritize," I said. "I think we all can agree that we'd prefer them to be going after murderers and rapists."

"What about quality of life?" another man said. "This is where we live and work. It's quality of life."

"Thankfully for you there's the private investigation industry. You gave me what I need. I'll take the case."

"Don't you need to interview us more? Ask questions?"

"The Pixel Posse run by a punk named Halley, and I know your neighborhood boundaries. What else do I need to know?"

They all looked at each other.

"Nothing, I guess," a man said.

"You've filed police reports, so I'll get copies of all of them and I'll take care of it."

The group was visibly relieved. As I stood, a few of them offered to help me move chairs back to their original places in the office.

My mind was already in high gear. PJ would wrap up the case of our second client by day's end. I had an idea to use my third clients' misfortune to help me with my digital samurai mystery. I walked them all out of the office to the elevators as we chatted about life. Our small talk in the hallway outside the elevator was longer than the actual client visit.

"PJ," I said when I got back to the office, "I may have a task for you."

"What task? I'm busy."

"Remember that demonstration you once did for those gang kids messing around the Concrete Mama?"

She smiled from her desk. "Punch Judy punch power."

Gangs were about their turf. This new graffiti crew, the Pixel Posse, had picked the district of Rainlight as their turf. Finding them was easy. From police reports, they weren't dangerous at all. All they wanted to do was "share" their art with the world by defacing apartment tower walls, storefront windows, pavements, sidewalks, and even hovercars.

A group of them stood outside in the rain near an out-of-the-way eatery, smoking. They spotted me the second I came around the corner. I was told they weren't violent, but I kept my hand on my weapon anyway. Tall, lanky, skinny kids in black slickers, collars up, neon tattoos covering their faces and hands.

"The Pixel Posse," I said.

"You the guy?" one asked.

"I'm the guy," I said.

"Your sidewalk johnny friends said you wanted to hire us," another one said.

"I did, but first thing first."

"What's that?"

"Rainlight will be off-limits for anymore of your tagging."

"Why?"

"Because PJ said so."

"What's a PJ?"

"That's a PJ. PJ stands for Punch Judy."

The ground parking lot was across the eatery. I watched in amusement; they watched in horror as they saw a figure punch one of their hovercars to pieces.

"What's she doing?" one of them yelled, his cigarette dropping from his mouth.

The kids ran to the parking lot. PJ stood there, with her arms folded.

"Why did you smash my car?" one of them yelled at the top of his lungs.

PJ said nothing. The five of them noticed me casually walking to the parking lot myself.

"Why did she do that?" one of them asked me.

My attention focused on a bystander with long hair, who wore glasses and looked like he never heard of shaving, watching. He had no face tattoos but he did have neon tattoos on his hands. I walked on over to him.

"You must be Halley," I said.

He was not happy that I knew who he was. "What do you want?"

"Rainlight is off-limits to your gangs' tagging from this day to the end of time."

"Did the neighborhood goodie-two-shoes hire you?"

"They did."

"I didn't know private detectives did that kind of work."

"Neighborhood watch group support. Yeah, we do that."

"Tell your woman cyborg to stop destroying our vehicles."

"I am not his woman!" PJ yelled.

His eyes widened.

"I'd apologize if I were you. She punches you and your boys will find the upper half of your body in the eatery, but your lower half will still be standing here."

"I'm sorry!" he yelled at her.

"Don't worry. Your insurance will take care of it. That's what hovercar insurance is for," I said.

"Okay Detective, you made your point. We'll move on. We always do."

I put a picture in front of his face. He squinted a bit and then took the photo from my hand.

"Know it?" I asked.

He was thinking. His fellow taggers joined him, each of them looking at the photo too. I wasn't sure about Halley yet, but one of the kids definitely recognized it.

He handed me the photo. "No."

"No, what?" I asked.

"No, I'm not getting involved. Tell your goodie-two-shoes they won't see the Pixel Posse on their streets again. And you, Mr. Cruz, we don't want to see you again either."

"Why so unfriendly?" I asked.

"I know about you."

"Then why won't you help me?"

"No way. We're urban artists. We not involved in violence and we're not involved with violent people. We're pacifists."

"A pacifist gang?"

"Why not?"

"Good luck with that. The picture."

Halley shook his head as he pointed to the photo. "They're violent."

"They who?"

He shook his head again and started walking away. His gang followed.

"Give me a name and I'll pay you for it. Simple transaction."

Halley and his posse stopped. He walked back to me.

"How much? Because of you I have to buy a new ride."

"The real question is, how do I know the name you're going to give me is legit?"

"He's legit all right."

"How would I know? I pay you. You give me a made-up name and disappear."

"Disappear where? You know who I am and my gang. You and your sidekick—"

"I am not a sidekick!" PJ yelled.

"Maybe you should not refer to my employee at all. You're going to get punched."

Halley was nervous and got more so as PJ joined us.

"Why's a grown man hanging around boys?" she asked.

"We're not boys!" the gang members yelled at her.

"I'm nineteen," one added.

"That's a boy," PJ said.

"To a senior citizen like you."

I grabbed PJ's arm before she could raise it.

"Lady and gentlemen, please," I said.

"I'm their teacher," Halley said to her.

"Teacher?" PJ said.

"I teach graffiti art classes. They're my students."

"You are crazy," PJ said.

"Halley, I want a name," I said.

"I'm giving you a name. Bubble Baha."

PJ and I started to chuckle.

"But you won't find him until you pay me."

He turned and headed back toward the eatery with his gang-students. PJ and I looked at each other. We watched them disappear in the shadows between streetlights and reappear entering the eatery.

"Are we going back to the office?" PJ asked.

"No. You have your mobile computer in your hovercar?"

"Of course."

"Do a criminal search on that name. If it's legit then I might as well pay him now and get it over with."

"What kind of stupid name is Bubble Baha?"

"Let's find out."

Halley got his money. More than I wanted to pay, but far less than a real criminal would have extorted from me. Bubble Baha wasn't a joke after all. I was sure Metro Cybercrimes had a fat file on him—or her. Someone like that would never meet me in person with all my connections to law enforcement, but I'd lucked out. Halley told me that Bubble Baha was a fan and had even purchased a Liquid Cool T-shirt from my agency's virtual storefront after my highly publicized Blade Gunner Case.

In the criminal world there was the Shadow Market—the ultimate shopping center for the criminal class. However, there was also its Net counterpart called the Ghost Market. There, criminals mostly trafficked in the stolen information of gang cartels, governments and megacorps. Bubble Baha had been an operator within the Ghost Market for decades. I still couldn't believe he'd meet with me in person as I waited in a dark bar I'd never been to before in a seedy outskirt of Tokyo Town.

Dark bars were where criminals met to discuss their criminal business over drinks and a meal, maybe catch a live show too. The saying was if that's what legitimate businesses did, why not the criminal world. The bar was dimly lit like similar establishments, the music was bad, and the clientele was what I'd expect from the criminal class—loud and crass.

Bubble Baha could have been a man, woman, or even a whole group of people. Whoever I was going to meet might not even be the real Bubble Baha.

"Mr. Cruz."

I'd been sitting in a secluded booth near the back. I gave my name at the front. A female waitress checked my ID and had a male thug-in-a-suit take me to the table. The entire establishment was filled with enclosed booths on three levels. They reminded me of giant hollowed-out acorns, each equipped with privacy and security screens.

The man who arrived was wearing a tight-fitting hoodie; his hands were gloved, but most intriguing was his white mask covering his face from his forehead to his nose.

"Always wanted to meet the man in person," he said, shaking my hand and sitting. He touched a button and a tinted glass came down on the open side of the booth.

"What should I call you?" I asked.

"B.B. is fine."

"I never thought I'd meet you, B.B."

"Yes, but are you meeting me."

"My thoughts exactly."

"We are actually a large conglomeration of activists who live, breathe, work, and play in the Net. I call myself a Ghost Market gremlin, stealing chunks of data for profit from whoever I choose to cause a little chaos here and there."

"Halley told you what I'm looking for?"

"Mr. Cruz, I do own quite a few of your T-shirts, but that's not why I'm meeting you. I thought it best to tell you in person that I may have inadvertently jeopardized your life."

"How did you do that?"

"I knew of the digital samurai who belong to the neon tattoos you're inquiring about."

"Do they have a name?"

"Japanese-named gang. Translates to 'Silver Snake.'"

"Great," I said. "Another secret gang named after snakes. Don't they know there are other animals in the universe? Who do they work for?"

"They work for a handful of megacorps on a regular basis. The problem is that I checked to see if anyone else was inquiring about them. I shouldn't have done that."

"Why?"

"They know that someone is looking into them."

"B.B., these digital samurai were not what I'd call professionals."

"Why do you say that?"

"I had a little confrontation with them."

B.B. laughed out loud. "I envy your life, Mr. Cruz. I travel the universe from the confines of a single room, but it's still a single room. No matter the dangers I face, I can never be killed. You face real death on the streets. Maybe I'll be brave one day and venture out from my single room onto the streets."

"Just don't get yourself killed."

"Yes, I promise I won't."

"What do you think about what I just said? Why would a megacorp hire street amateurs?"

B.B. began typing on one of his palms then turned over his forearm. A screen turned on and I saw a list of names.

"Any of these names look familiar?" he asked.

The list was of megacorporations, and Hiero and Macro were two of the names.

"Yes," I replied.

"What does that mean to you?"

"Low-rent gangsters trying to kill me pretending to be a specific gang of digital samurai. A specific gang of digital samurai who in fact work for the very megacorps who hired me to do a simple job."

"Hired you? One of the megacorps on the list?"

"Yes."

"I'd say you have some problems, Mr. Cruz. I can disappear with ease. You, however, can't."

"Can you tell me more about those megacorps?"

"Mr. Cruz, I trade in data between interested parties. I know only what I can see. I hear the same rumors as everyone else. But the reality is only the megacorps know what vast criminal activities they're involved in. They have a public board of directors and executives, and then the true one. A single megacorp could exist forever without those two sides ever coming into contact with each other. They're better at secrecy than I'm at breaching that secrecy. When that secrecy is breached, people die."

"Interesting structure."

"That's how it's done."

"Megacorps know how to keep their secrets. They don't want me to know, then no amount of my poking around will reveal those secrets. They know that."

"I know that the Hiero Corporation hired you."

"You do?"

"Yes, and so do others. Only a thought, but maybe someone wants you to know some secrets."

"Why would that be?"

"I don't know. There could be a million reasons why. People within Hiero, people within Macro."

"You know all about my activities."

"That's what I do. Maybe people within any one of their many rivals here on Earth, the Lunar Colonies, Mars, maybe not even a megacorp, maybe the government of Metropolis or a foreign government, maybe a criminal cartel wanting to be a megacorp."

"That's a lot of suspects."

"Too many for you to ever get to the bottom of."

"Sounds like all I can do is wait."

"It is all you can do. Maybe the players will get tired of playing and move on to something else. It's a hope. The digital samurai were a one-off, a mistake. It'll all blow over and you'll move on to other exciting cases."

"I'm glad to hear you say that, B.B., but it occurs to me that maybe you wanted to meet me in person because you didn't think I'd be around for you to meet in the future, just maybe."

Bubble Baha said nothing.

THE DIGITAL SAMURAI

Whenever I was about to do some serious driving I wore my open-knuckled leather driving gloves. I now knew that the crew PJ and I tangled with were not the real digital samurai gang whose neon tattoos they appropriated. The real one was still out there. I also didn't know who sent the fake one and why. Or who or what a Voodoo Child was. Then there was the question of when Mr. Echo and company would be revisiting me, and their involvement in all this. I had too many questions and unfortunately no way to get answers. Bubble Baha was absolutely right. I wouldn't know unless someone on the inside wanted me to know—no police, cybercrime unit, or intelligence service could help me. Though, B.B. did give me a way to contact him again.

I'd already closed two of my three cases from yesterday. Halley and the Pixel Posse moved onto another turf for their in-the-field schoolwork. And I put Ms. Page in touch with her birth mother, who said she'd been thinking about the daughter she gave up for adoption every day lately. Some said twins had psychic links; maybe some mothers and children did too.

My other case would have to wait, as I was wondering if I should make the first move and call Mr. Echo. But what would I say?

I saw a flash in the corner of my eye from the other side of oncoming sky traffic. Instinctively, I moved a lane below but still heard a thud outside my hovercar.

Panic set in. I exited out of the sky traffic and descended my Pony toward the ground as fast as possible. I air-braked ten feet off the ground, opened my driver's side door, hung out, and shot the metal tracker fixed on the side of my vehicle with my omega-gun. It could have only been a tracker; it could have been a bomb. I was back inside and gunned the hoverengine. I jerked the steering wheel to do a sharp one-eighty a split-second before a laser blast barely missed me. I was officially under attack.

I knew every street and alleyway in Metropolis proper. They picked the perfect spot to ambush me because there were no secret ways for me to escape. If they knew that, then they knew the terrain as well as I did. Wherever I went, they'd already be there, or would arrive right after me.

Normally, I'd feel safe racing down the alleyway I was flying, but at the moment I kept my eyes on my rearview mirror and above. I saw two, then three dots appear, moving fast. I turned and crashed through a bay window into a warehouse. The Nil Point district had plenty of warehouses, but this one wasn't empty. The crates were huge and I had no idea what was in them, likely machine parts. As I raced the Pony to the other end, I saw the crates were arranged in rows. The three dots appeared on my rearview mirror; I turned again. I slammed the brakes!

I would have smashed right into a metal wall. Quickly, I reversed and sped away. I did another one-eighty and saw a space, one of the large support columns of the warehouse, and that's where I drove.

When I reached the mega-column, I went straight up using the column as a shield. My driver's side window went down; I fired at the massive skylights above. I drove through the open skylight as glass rained down. I did another one-eighty, up and over, and landed the Pony on the roof. Once parked, I got out and ran to one of the large roof vents for cover. Three black hovercars made the same maneuver and landed near the end of the roof.

The men wore black suits with laser sword weapons, faces and hands covered with the same neon tattoos. I knew I was looking at the real Silver Snake digital samurai gang.

I watched from behind the vent. They saw me and marched to me, all thirty of them. For a brief second, I wondered how ten of them could fit in a hovercar. Were they sitting on each other's laps?

"Why are you chasing me?" I yelled at them.

No answer as they continued to me. I came out from behind my cover.

"I'll ask you again. Why are you chasing me?"

One said something in Japanese. The other men laughed.

"Why don't you say that in English?" I taunted.

"I said: thank you for bringing me my new hovercar."

"A Ford Pony is a classic vehicle, not a hovercar, Neanderthal."

The explosion near my Pony startled them, but I was only able to shoot one of the digital samurai dead, before the rest scattered in every direction.

I ducked back behind the giant roof vent as multiple throwing stars missed me. As I added an attachment to my omega-gun, I looked up and couldn't believe what I was seeing. From behind me, Echo approached wearing his slippers with Judo, Pro, and three other samurai soldiers.

"Mr. Echo," I said. "I was expecting you at the office, not on a roof."

"We can meet here after this is done," Echo said as he walked past me with his men.

All I heard was a nasty exchange of yelling in Japanese between Echo and the digital samurai. Judo and Echo's men stood quietly, never taking the sheaths off their swords. The digital samurai were yelling loudly, wildly waving their arms all around, but never moving to Echo. They were scared of Echo. I could see it in their faces, behind the neon tattoos and enhanced dark glasses. Soon the yelling was over and the digital samurai grudgingly backed off and returned to their hovercars.

The hovercars rose into the sky and blasted away.

Echo and his men walked back to me. He looked at the attachment I added to my omega-gun and smiled.

"You might have actually defeated them," he said.

"Mr. Echo, are you going to tell me what this is about? This is the second time I've encountered these digital samurai."

"These were digital samurai. The ones you encountered at your office were not."

"Is this a new case?"

"My master will explain it all to you."

"Where is he?"

"She is below."

She?

Echo was no joke. Thirty of those digital samurai, real or pretend, would be nothing to him. I might have defeated them with my sneaky attachments I added to my Up-Top omega-gun. He probably had been a samurai master before I was born. If he had a master, then the person would have to be older and far more powerful. But then he said "she." He was part of a highly patriarchal, machismo, alpha-male clan structure that dated back centuries, no, millennia. Not only were women not part of it, they were never leaders. Echo already told me that his master was the only person he couldn't defeat. Now he revealed that person was a woman. Women could be every bit as vile and dangerous as men, but it was done differently—male-canine versus female-feline. A wild dog knocked you down with strength and mauled you to death. A wild cat snuck up on you with cunning and ripped you to shreds.

"What is your master's name?" I asked as Echo led us down the roof stairs.

"The Digital Samurai."

We reached the ground floor and came back out of the stairway into the open warehouse. More samurai soldiers waited at the base of the gigantic metal crates. While Judo and the men stood still, Echo led me to the open area at the base of the same mega-column that I'd flown past not too long ago. I saw a flicker. As I stared, a figure came into view.

Echo led me to the woman.

"Mr. Cruz, The Digital Samurai."

I couldn't tell her ethnicity because her skin had a greenish-yellow hue. She wore a hooded slicker, and her hair dangled down to cover the right side of her face. Her eyes had a green glow. This woman with dark lipstick was Echo's master?

"You must forgive me for my directness, but I'm having trouble believing that you could defeat Mr. Echo even on one of his bad days."

Echo grinned, and she was also amused.

"Mr. Echo was first my master for many years during my training as a youth," she said.

"You're an augmented human?" I asked.

"There are many terms, but that one is the same as the others, and correct. I am the property of the Hiero Corporation."

An "augmented" human could truly mean many things. From genetic engineering, bio-synthetic implants, and mental conditioning to bionics, nano-tech, and secret tech straight out of science fiction. The megacorps had it all, but more important to them than having such soldiers was that no one knew anything about them, especially the governments of the world.

"What is it that you think I can possibly do for you? I'm only a street detective."

"There's much you can do for us," Echo said.

"I've already had a gun battle with fake digital samurai sent by Voodoo Child, whoever or whatever that is—"

I saw the looks of shock on their faces. They looked at each other, as if speaking telepathically. They quickly exchanged words in Japanese.

"How do you know this?" Echo asked me.

"One of them told me by mistake. He wanted to show off that he worked for someone I should be afraid of. He realized his mistake, then he committed suicide."

"Suicide?" Echo asked.

"How?" she asked me.

I recounted the whole incident for them. The man biting his own tongue almost in half to release a poison to kill himself.

Echo looked at her. "We have less time than we thought."

She nodded. "Here is not safe."

"His office is being watched," Echo said.

"We have to go elsewhere. A place they would never attack, but we're not ready," she said.

"I know a place you could use," I said.

"Where?" Echo asked.

"I know lots of places. When I was on the illegal hovercar racing scene, you'd have to find places to hide fast when the police were after you."

"You do work for the police," Echo said.

"Not back then. Do we stay here or do we go?"

She looked at Echo and spoke in Japanese, then looked at me. "Your alternative hideout may be of use in the future, but we will prepare another place. You'll ride with us and we'll return you home until we're ready. We will need a day. Your vehicle may be compromised," he said.

"I'm not leaving my classic hovervehicle on the roof of this warehouse."

"Pro will drive it back to your office."

"Better he drive it someplace else, just in case. The fake digital samurai hit me at my office building in the parking area. It's already gotten damaged. I'd like to get through this case without my vehicle getting blown up."

"You worry about unimportant things, Mr. Cruz," she said.

"Possibly. I am just a Metropolis street detective."

"I'm a global enforcer for a centuries-old Metropolis megacorp. I worry about very important things, but Mr. Echo feels you can help us. We leave now."

"The Macro Corporation cannot get control of the society," The Digital Samurai said to me.

"What society?" I asked.

The hoverlimo we sat in was much larger than the previous Hiero craft I'd been in. Echo and she sat across from me. Judo and the other men were in the middle closed section in front of us. We had the rear section to ourselves.

"We hired you, Mr. Cruz," Mr. Echo began, "to observe how you'd handle yourself. We've been making inquiries about you for many months to prepare. Your test with me was more than acceptable, as was the one with my understudies. Your test against Mr. Glyph and the Macro Corporation exceeded expectations. We had to be sure. The stakes are too high. What do you know of digital samurai?"

"Criminal samurai soldiers who existed before the Modern Analog Age, when Earth was in its digital age. They were known for their unique laser-edge swords and digital technology. Neon tattoos on their bodies and digital tattoos on their uniforms. The neon tattoos and laser sword-weapons remain, but the digital tech that made them so formidable back then was abandoned by Earth."

"It was much more than that," Echo said. "Before the modern analog tech age, everything was digital—vehicles, homes, even weapons. Digital samurai of the time could hack into any device and shut them off or use them against their user, all without cable, wire, or touch. That was their power, not their laser swords. They could turn the very digital world against us all."

"Then the Crash," I said.

"Yes, that digital world of Earth is gone, and the one off-world is beyond them. All that remains are the laser swords and neon tattoos," she said.

"But you are The Digital Samurai," I said to her.

"Call me D.G.," she said.

I liked the nickname. "Okay. What's this about? What do you want to hire me for now? And that's a lot of money for Hiero to pay me just to observe my work habits, though I'm not complaining."

"Your work for Hiero is over, yes, but not for us," Echo said.

"I'm hiring you," D.G. said.

"To do what?" I asked.

"Retrieve some people for us and get them to safety."

"Is that what Hiero wants?" I asked.

"No, it's not," D.G. said.

"You'll need to explain. I didn't think megacorp soldiers at any level could act counter to the interests of their company."

"I need you to help me destroy the society," she said. "Five megacorps control it. With the Hiero and Macro merger, one entity will become more powerful than all others. They will control a society of elite enforcers used by Earth and off-world megacorps to assert their will on all others—weaker megacorps who threaten their interests, governments who overreach or investigate where not wanted, gangsters who don't know their place, and much, much more."

"What on earth could I possibly do to help you?" I asked.

"You already have if Voodoo Child sent those men."

"Sent those men to kill me."

"They were no match for you. If she wanted to kill you, she would have done so herself. She sent them to make you do what you did and force my hand. We are accelerating our timetable before we are ready, but we have no choice anymore."

"Who is she?"

"She's an assassin. Their best. There are others, but she works for the other three megacorps who co-own the society."

"Another assassin?" I asked.

"Yes," D.G. replied.

"I still don't know your motivation."

"Grab my hand," she said.

Reluctantly, I did and squeezed. Her hand wasn't metal. It felt more like tightly wound fiber.

"I told you, Mr. Cruz. I'm the property of the Hiero Corporation. I may be the best, but I'm one of many and I want to be free for the first time in my life, no matter how short of a time that may be, and I want to make sure no one else is made property by them ever again."

"You have many questions, Mr. Cruz, but time is limited," Echo said. "We hire you to do simple 'missing persons' work. We find them and you retrieve them. Simple transactions that you'll be paid for."

"This will help you destroy this society of assassins?"

"Yes," D.G. said.

"Why now?"

"Once the merger is complete we will have no power," Echo said.

"No power—"

"We will have no power because we will all be dead, Mr. Cruz," Echo said. "Myself, Judo, Pro, all my men, all thousand of them. Then they will hunt D.G. down to the ends of the earth until they kill her. Once that happens no megacorp on this Earth, nor the Council of Corporations itself, will be able to stop them. We have only twenty-four hours left."

DELPHI

I was back at the Metropolis Municipal Court Building on my way to the seventieth floor and Room 80 at the far end of the hall. Same small office and same man sat at his station behind a big terminal. He looked up at me.

"Mr. Delphi is on his way."

"Thanks."

"You can wait in the conference room."

I sat in the same conference room, but my wait was short. Delphi came in, dressed similar as before, and closed the door. He was glad to have gotten my call.

"What do you have for me, Mr. Cruz?"

"Mr. Delphi, for all I know you're working this case by yourself like the Lone Ranger or the lone gunman. Hub vouched for you, but he's not directly tied into Cybercrimes. Maybe you've gone rogue. Why should I trust you?"

"The Lone Ranger or the lone gunman? I don't know the first reference, but I know the last. Okay, Mr. Cruz, follow me."

We returned to the main lobby and took a back entrance. Delphi was in no hurry, and we casually walked to another, smaller tower. I could see the Metro PD megatower—Police One, the Feds tower, City Hall across the street.

The main lobby of the building was fairly empty. There were guards at the reception station but only a few. We reached the elevator banks, stepped in, but Delphi pressed the button to go down.

When we stepped out it was like I entered a new dimension. There were both human guards and robotic sentries. I had to show ID, my photo was taken, my fingerprints and palm prints taken, retinal scans, my mobile was taken. Then I had to walk under several scanning arches, in addition to a scanning tunnel.

"Delphi, what the hell."

"Cruz, this was your idea, remember?"

Once cleared I was able to follow Delphi through the doors of the Cybercrimes Division. The layout inside was very similar to Metro PD. A waiting area, a bull pen of dual cubicles for field agents, single cubicles for higher-ranking agents, and beyond were the offices with glass walls for the higher-ups.

As we walked down to the offices my eyes locked on one of the whiteboards on the other side of the room. One agent was at the board, saw me, and he slowly reached to the side of the board to tilt it. I veered away from Delphi.

"Mr. Cruz," I heard him say but ignored him.

I joined the other agent at the whiteboard. I saw my picture, my wife, my parents, her parents, PJ, Phishy, Run-Time, his wife, his VPs, including Mr. Mick, their families. Delphi joined us at the whiteboard and pushed a button on the side and the entire board went black.

I looked at Delphi. "Well, look at that."

"Mr. Cruz, what did you expect?"

"You have me and everyone I know on surveillance. Oh, you forgot a suspect." I reached into my jacket for my wallet. "We can't forget Cruz Jr. He's very dangerous, especially with his bottle. I believe him to be a trained ninja. Got to get him up on the white board too." I showed them my son's picture. "Don't you need to take a picture?"

"Mr. Cruz, we were walking to my office."

"Yeah, we were, until I saw my mug on your board wearing my tan fedora."

"You have 20-20 vision. Good for you, Mr. Cruz. Follow me."

I followed Delphi back to the aisle then to his office. Delphi was a senior agent in charge.

"Have a seat, Mr. Cruz."

He closed the door as I sat in the chair in front of his desk. I could see through the glass walls other agents standing up from their chairs, looking at me, and talking to each other. Delphi walked around and sat at his cluttered desk. For a cyber-geek, he did seem to have a lot of paper.

"As I began to ask before: What do you have for me, Mr. Cruz?"

"This is Cybercrimes. Never got to visit it when I was a police intern."

"Back when you were in high school?"

"Yeah."

"This must be a dream come true for you then."

"Before I tell you anything, I need to know what you know."

"That's not how it works, Mr. Cruz, and you know that.'

"You said you were here for me."

"And we are."

"The full resources of Metro PD's Cybercrimes Division."

"That too."

"The Hiero and Macro Corporations. What's Cybercrimes investigating them for?"

"Mr. Cruz, this is my office, so I don't have to go anywhere. You, however, if you don't have anything for me, you'll be escorted out, and you'll have a long walk back."

"Mr. Echo."

Delphi watched me, emotionless.

"Mr. Ming."

Delphi sighed.

"Mr. Glyph."

Delphi looked bored.

"D.G."

Delphi stopped reaching for a cup on his desk. "What's D.G.?"

"Voodoo Child."

Delphi grabbed the vid-phone on his desk and pressed a button. "Come in here, and bring the team." He pressed it again. "And notepads!"

The door opened and the same man from the whiteboard entered, along with three other men. The others looked like they were all just out of high school. They came in and closed the door. Two of the men had electric notepads. The first man stood with his arms folded. The other men leaned against a long file cabinet against one side of the wall.

Delphi looked at me. "What's D.G.?"

"The Digital Samurai told me to call her that."

Two of the men jumped up and hollered like they had witnessed the winning goal of a soccer match. The first man started smacking the sides of his own face, he was so happy.

"Gentlemen, there's more. He said Voodoo Child too."

More jubilation.

I sat there realizing I was the only one in the room unaware of what was going on.

"Delphi, I'm not saying anything else until I get some answers," I said.

Delphi pointed to one of the junior agents. "Go."

"Mr. Cruz, we've been working this case for...years. It's big. Really big."

"Do you know what the Ghost Market is?" the first agent asked.

"Of course," I replied. "The Net version of the Shadow Market. It's the online shopping bazaar for criminals. Mostly, stolen data."

"Stolen data, secret communications, secret transactions, including contract killings for hire, and shadow currency vaults," the same agent said.

"Okay," I said.

"You don't know who they are?" one of the agents asked me.

"D.G. and Voodoo Child? Enforcers? Tell me."

"No," Delphi said. "They're assassins for the Hiero and Macro companies. Enforcers guard execs and beat people up. Assassins do neither of those. They kill people."

I wasn't naive about the world of megacorps with their corporate and samurai soldiers. I knew they employed assassins too.

"How did you find out what she did for Hiero?" Delphi asked me.

"She told me," I replied.

"Told you?"

"Yes."

All the agents looked at each other, puzzled.

"If someone can tell me what's going on, I can start piecing all this together. I don't have much time."

"What does that mean?" Delphi asked.

"They hired me—"

"Who?"

"D.G. and Mr. Echo. And I'll be done with their work in twenty-four hours."

The agents looked at each other again. Delphi jumped from his chair. "Get the others in here."

One of the agents bolted out of the office. In moments, he returned, but six more agents filed into the office and the last closed the door.

"Everyone, it's all going down in the next twenty-four hours," Delphi announced. "This is what we've been preparing for."

"Preparing for what?" I asked. "You haven't told me a thing yet."

"Cruz, most of these megacorps are involved in criminal activity, many using one or both of the illegal markets. Five years ago, the Hiero Corporation began talks with their rival, the Macro Corporation, about a merger. Later that year, the talks broke down. Beginning the following year, there were half a dozen hostile takeover attempts by Hiero of Macro, then it all stopped. About a year ago, it was announced that Hiero would be acquiring

Macro, with the board being a 50-50 even split of both companies for the new entity. All that is the public story for the business newsfeed."

I kept a complete poker face. Cybercrimes told me that Macro acquired Hiero, but I knew Hiero owned fifty-one percent of the new company, which at the time, when I saw the numbers, made me take notice. Companies that acquired other companies didn't own less than the new company. Even a high-finance novice like me knew that. But I decided to keep the fact to myself.

"Where does Cybercrimes come in?"

"The megacorps have their own security forces—corporate soldiers, samurai soldiers, cyborg soldiers, using all the cybercrimes tools in the toolbox: stalking, extortion, warfare, and terrorism. But often many go much further, employing their own assassins. The Hiero and Macro Corporations are at the top, rumored to have the best assassins of all the megacorporations."

"Wouldn't assassins and contract killers fall under Major Crimes or Organized Crime?" I asked.

"We handle cyber-assassins."

"Cyber-assassins?" I asked.

"The Digital Samurai is said to be able to travel via the Net to find and kill her targets," an agent said.

"Do you honestly believe that?" I asked. "Sounds like a bunch of sci-fi to me."

"How much of science fact started out as sci-fi?" an agent challenged.

"However she does it, she's done it many times before," another agent said.

"This Voodoo Child?" I asked.

"Created by a rival megacorp to stop The Digital Samurai. She kills targets by casting cyber-spells on them."

I smiled, trying not to laugh.

"You may not be convinced, Mr. Cruz. But we are," Delphi said.

"Why?"

"Because she killed an informant of ours years back. I saw it," another man said.

"The Digital Samurai?"

"Yes."

"How?"

"Sliced him in half and escaped through his computer screen."

I stood from my chair to look at the agent. "That's impossible."

"I saw it!"

"In person?"

"No, on the surveillance monitor of the room."

"It's not scientifically possible."

"I saw it, and what do you know about science? You're a detective."

"I built a working hovercar when I was a kid in high school. Did you? Can you? I know plenty about science. Matter dematerialization is the stuff of science fiction, like time travel and warp drive."

"Doesn't change what I saw, and others saw it too."

"Gentlemen, we can have the science versus science fiction debate later. The facts are she has killed people and can kill people and is an assassin on the payroll of the Hiero Corporation," Delphi said.

"And Voodoo Child? Who does she work for?" I asked.

"Macro. They wanted their own counter to The Digital Samurai," Delphi answered.

"Are there other assassins?" I asked.

"Many more," an agent answered. "But these two are rumored to be the best."

"Do you have the names of the other assassins at the top?" I asked.

"Yes, why?" the agent asked.

"I'd like to know."

"What we do know is if there is a one-day countdown, either Hiero plans to wipe out Macro, Macro is going to move against Hiero, or another megacorp is about to move against the new merged company," Delphi said with trepidation. He looked at me. "And it all begins within the next twenty-four hours."

"Why is this all happening now?" I asked.

"We're not sure," an agent replied. "Something happened about a year ago within the companies."

"Why does Cybercrimes care if one criminal megacorp wipes out another?" I asked. "I would think that's something you'd celebrate."

"Collateral damage, Mr. Cruz," Delphi said. "The one thing worse than a new company bigger, more powerful and more lethal is two smaller ones at war. The attacks will not be confined to the boardroom, but innocent people will be caught in the crossfire. It always turns out that way. No one wants this. Not us, Metro PD in general, City Hall, and neither does the Council of Corporations."

"You're working with them?" I asked.

"They've been feeding us intel for years," an agent revealed.

"I'm sure they have."

"Mr. Cruz, we don't have the luxury to only work with angels. You know that. But they've fed us intel not just on Hiero and Macro, but many companies they feel threaten the business universe. However, we don't share any of our ongoing investigations with them, of course. What we do is strictly confidential, and the Council has no knowledge of our activities."

"What do you want from me then?"

"Keep us informed," Delphi said. "You've filled in a few holes for us. We're grateful for that. Two cyber-assassins in play. Their two megacorp controllers ready to make their final moves. You're the man inside, Mr. Cruz."

Cyber-assassins? I thought. I'd heard the term before, but that was as a kid playing video games. Cybercrimes was telling me they were real.

"Sounds like I'm in the middle of a corporate war again."

"A different animal and the stakes are higher. I'm going to brief Chief Hub and have Metro PD on standby."

"Delphi, I don't think you should be so eager to go into battle with these people."

"If we can avoid it, we will, but it may come to that. If so, we'll have the full force of the Metro police in our pocket," Delphi said.

Metro PD was good at blasting criminals to bits, their vehicles, even whole buildings if needed. They were not, however, good at surgical strikes, quite lousy, in fact. Metro PD arrived with blaring sirens, flashing lights, thundering police cruisers. We were dealing with people adept at quietly disappearing into shadows without a trace.

The giddy agents called in one of their sketch artists, rendering tablets in hand. They wanted a full composite picture of The Digital Samurai. I had no problem with that because I doubted they'd ever see her in person, and even if they did, she wouldn't look anything like her picture.

Regardless of my disagreement with their overall strategy, there was the little matter that Delphi and his unit really didn't have the full picture anymore than I did. What I did know, and didn't tell them, was that the Digital Samurai wasn't getting ready to do battle against some arch-nemesis called Voodoo Child. She and Echo were acting completely on their own, against even their own megacorp. Such a thing in the megacorp criminal world was unheard of. Mr. Mick had already warned me that I would never be told the full story by my clients as an "outsider," but it was essential I find out somehow. I needed the truth behind all of it.

CAVEAT, COUNCIL OF CORPORATIONS MAN

L iquid Cool, the Detective Agency, was my company. I'd already built up a good reputation and had a diverse clientele. With my high-profile, mass-media exposure I had the kind of name ID that major detective firms would kill for, but I'd gotten mine for free. Very impressive in a few short years, but I'd never be a major player among the Metropolis business elite. My company didn't have the gross profits. I'd never be a megacorp. Thank God!

I did trust Echo—to a point. I liked Judo. I wasn't sure about D.G. yet. After all, she told me she was an elite enforcer—but Delphi said she was an assassin. I needed more information. I was tempted to contact Mr. Mick again, and I was sure I would before the case was over, but I needed a different perspective. He wasn't a criminal and Let It Ride Enterprises wasn't a criminal megacorp. I needed to speak with someone or an entity that would have that kind of insider information. Any full-scale corporate war, even behind the scenes in the shadows, was bad for everyone's business in the megacorporate world because it could attract the unwanted attention of the Metropolis Police Department. Metro PD wasn't above arresting everyone at a company "suspected" of criminal activity and seizing megatowers and everything inside. They'd done it before and would do so again.

Delphi gave me the law-enforcement, "outsider" story. I need an "insider" point of view. I needed to speak with someone at the Council of Corporations, the membership organization of all megacorps on Earth. The only membership organization I'd ever be part of was the Metropolis Business Association. For the Council of Corporations you needed net profits of at least one billion dollars annually.

The Council of Corporations occupied a massive monolith pyramid tower in the center of Silicon Dunes. Its megacorp members didn't need snazzy benefits like my Metropolis Business Association. Megacorps wanted an organization to lobby for their interests on Earth and Up-Top. They needed an entity separate from the government, as ruthless as they were, to keep the peace by being the ultimate referee of all business disputes between all megacorps. Public corporate wars had to be avoided at all costs. War hurt business. War diminished profits.

As a non-member, no one would normally take my call but my best friend's company, Let It Ride Enterprises, was a member. Mr. Mick made the call for me after I promised to meet with him later.

Mr. Caveat met with me. A slim, bald Caucasian man in an Asian-themed black suit—Japanese symbols sewn into the sleeves. He wore ice-blue tinted round glasses.

I entered the lobby and checked in with the female receptionist, who I swore was an android. She had me take a seat as she called up. Her high reception desk and the waiting area were the only pieces of furniture in the bubble-designed room with a ceiling a good five or more stories high. Then a large man appeared, likely a corporate soldier, took me to the elevator, and up to one of the "lower" floors—floor one hundred fifty.

Mr. Caveat handed me a card that had only his name, then sat. It was another Japanese custom—exchange business cards. I reached into my jacket to hand him mine. We both sat in transparent chairs made of a cool-to-the-touch, leather-like material. There was no other furniture in the expansive white marble conference room. The walls were glass too, but turned opaque white when Caveat had arrived and sat.

"No need, Mr. Cruz. We bumped into each other at a previous Christmas party hosted by the Council. You made quite the impression with your performance with the Orochi Corporation."

"Yes, I've been trying to forget."

"It was the talk of the town for months. You should feel proud. Many important people took notice of you. Probably sent you some business."

"Then I don't feel so bad. Thank you again for meeting me, Mr. Caveat. I need some Council advice."

"You, advice? I'm intrigued. What can the Council do for you?"

"I don't expect you to answer my questions, but I'm hoping you can give me some guidance as to what I've gotten myself into. The Hiero and Macro Corporations."

"What about them, Mr. Cruz?"

"Will this conversation remain confidential?"

"It can be."

"I need it to be confidential. I'm sure you'll talk to your bosses, but neither Hiero nor Macro can know. I was hired by Hiero but there's more basic private investigation work to complete. Nothing major, but I get the distinct impression that I may have stepped into a secret battle between both of these megacorps for control of the new company. I don't want to be used and I don't want to be targeted by anyone."

"If you fear for your safety, then you shouldn't take their case."

"I already have, and I'm not necessarily afraid for my life. I want to know what's really going on, so I can maneuver accordingly. That's all. Do my work and move on with my life. If people want to battle it out for control of the company, it's none of my business. Can you tell me anything to help, Mr. Caveat? I can't ask them."

"No, you couldn't."

Mr. Caveat sighed and thought quietly for a moment.

"Here's what I can tell you, Mr. Cruz. The Council is very interested in the merger of Hiero and Macro, as are many of our members here on Earth and off-world. We are also aware that the Metro Cybercrimes Division has heightened interest in these companies. The Council's position is that we'd like this merger to go through without bloodshed."

"Bloodshed?"

"The Council would also like to keep Cybercrimes and any other government entity out of the business of our members. If your involvement can, in any way, aid in a smooth merger of the two companies, we'd recommend you continue your services for Hiero. That is as much as I can say, Mr. Cruz."

"I have one more question," I said. "Which phrase do you prefer—elite enforcer or cyber-assassin?"

"My, my," Caveat said. "You do know a bit more for a one-man detective shop. You've met one."

Caveat pressed a button and his chair floated to mine. He leaned forward to me and we seemed to be engulfed in a force bubble of heat.

"Digital Samurai and Voodoo Child are assassins, not enforcers, Mr. Cruz. They are the last remaining members, as they have killed all other samurai masters like them. These cyber-assassins are walking, fighting, killing computers in human form."

"Cyborgs," I said.

"No, Mr. Cruz, definitely not any cyborg you've ever seen."

"I've seen a lot of cyborgs no one has ever seen, here and Up-Top."

"You are right, Mr. Cruz. You have. Soon you'll get to meet another."

"I did shake her hand."

Caveat backed away from me. "You touched her? I'd have your hand and clothes thoroughly micro-scanned. Check everywhere you've been. Any device you had on you at the time, I'd immediately destroy."

I looked at my open right palm with a concerned expression.

My meeting with Caveat didn't last much longer. I left the Council of Corporation's building but stood outside the building still staring at my right hand. Then all hell broke loose—

hovervehicles descended from the sky, filled with armed corporate soldiers and people in gray bio-suits. They weren't after me. They locked down the entire headquarters, moving me and other pedestrians back. The Council of Corporations was officially quarantined. (A concept I'd learned much more about than I'd ever want to in my entire life in my Biopunk Blues Case.)

"For how long?" I asked.

Security told me, "Indefinitely, until further notice."

I wasn't going to get into my Pony now. But too late. I already had.

However, my visit to Mr. Caveat was very revealing. He knew about my visits to Metro Cybercrimes; Delphi did say they were sharing information. But of special note was the fact Caveat knew all about my two cyber-assassins. That meant the Council of Corporations knew too. Who knew how many of their members that included? It made me want to be a Council of Corporations member too, so I could be brought in on all the dark megacorp secrets.

BUGS, VETERAN TECH SWEEPER

My right hand was fine. My Pony was fine. The Liquid Cool office and my Concrete Mama home were fine. As a recovering germophobe, my mind had conjured up the possibility I was infested by microscopic, self-replicated nano-robots on my skin. When I was given a clean bill of health, as were with all my possessions, work place, and home, I felt stupid.

"What did you think happened?" Bugs asked.

"Honestly, I don't know."

Bugs was a "sweeper" and security tech guru. He reminded me a lot of my posthumous mentor, Wilford G. Bugs was old-school but the best. Listening device detection, motion detection security, intrusion defense security, video surveillance, door and wall defense security, door and lock augmentation, trap door and panic rooms. My best friend, Run-Time, had introduced us when I first got into the detective business.

I don't think I'd ever seen him wearing anything other than his standard uniform—dark overalls over his purple suit, holding his custom-built contraption with one hand and a long telescoping wand with the other. He arrived at the Concrete Mama with his team of two college-kid-looking workers. He'd cleared me, my Pony, and they finished my apartment.

"Did you think your hand was going to fall off or she infected you with nanites?"

"Nanites?"

"Microscopic robots—"

"Bugs, I know what nanites are. I'm anti-robot, no matter the size, and my family is anti-humanoid robot too."

"Android."

"What?"

"Your anti-humanoid robots. Those are androids."

"Them too."

Bugs laughed. "I still want to know what you thought shaking someone's hand would do to you."

"I don't know. It's how he described her. Then when I saw them shut down the headquarters and the bio-suits land..."

"Nothing more than precautionary," Bugs told me.

"Ever heard of cyber-assassins?"

"Yeah."

I'd washed my hands like twelve times using all my decon gels I bought from my CDC supplier.

"What can you tell me?"

Bugs joined me in the kitchen. "You don't want to meet one."

"Too late."

"Serious?"

"A client."

"Client? Why would they hire you?"

"It's complicated."

"You'd better stay away from them."

"A paying client."

Bugs chuckled, shaking his head. "What do want to know?"

"How do you beat them?"

"You can't."

"So if I ever did battle with them—"

"You'd be dead. Even running away might not save you."

"Let's rephrase the question. If I were to encounter a hostile one, what would I do to ensure I escaped unharmed, knowing there's no way I could beat them?"

"That's the main thing. You can't beat them. Only the best samurai soldiers could challenge them offensively. Your strategy would have to be defensive and evasive. Defend and run away, fast."

"How do you know about them?"

"We tangled with one—once."

"Run-Time?"

"Not Run-Time directly, but security at Let It Ride. This was many years ago. Run-Time was new to the world of expansion in the corporate sphere. A megacorp didn't like it. His company had dealt with corporate and samurai soldiers, every kind of gangster and thug imaginable, every kind of cyborg enforcer, digital samurai, but then we tangled with a cyber-assassin from Up-Top."

"Up-Top?"

"Yeah. But we had some weapons from Up-Top. Kind of like you with your Up-Top gun. We learned a lot about cyber-assassins that day, that long day. We locked down the tower, but he got in still. Got in, even with the lock down. He was invisible to video surveillance, motion sensors, infrared sensors. Digital samurai were scary when Earth was digital; not so much when new analog came in. Cyber-assassins remained scary because they could manipulate machinery."

"How?"

"Don't know how. They did it."

"Can you walk me through the encounter and how you defeated him?"

"We didn't defeat him. We escaped from him."

"You were there."

"I was head of security back then. We escaped. He ran off. Run-Time found the people who could track him down. We blew his hoverplane out of the sky as it left its rooftop landing pad. He wasn't able to beam himself out of that."

"The Council guy called them walking, fighting, killing computers in human form."

"He was downplaying them. Long time ago they used a word *transhumanism*. Transforming the human being with sophisticated technologies to enhance human intellect and physiology."

"Is that when they thought you could download the human mind into a computer?"

"Yeah. Early cyberpunks and the rest weren't too bright. Like most things, the idea came before the ability to do it for real. But the reality never matched that original idea. Evolving the human race beyond its current physical and mental limitations through technology. Evolving, no. Creating test-tube slaves, yes."

"Cyber-assassins are cyborgs or bio-gens? And slaves?"

"Both. The property of the megacorp that created them."

Property was the same word D.G. used.

"Don't you want me to sweep your office too?" Bugs asked me.

"Yes. I'll drive you and you can walk me through how you escaped that cyber-assassin."

"Your client."

"I'm not worried about my client. I'm worried about the other one."

"Two of them! Cruz, you're involved with two of these things?"

"We'll talk on the way."

VOODOO CHILD, CRAZY MANIAC ASSASSIN

I never played games when it came to criminals and death. The second after my first encounter with Echo, I knew I'd entered a realm of operators far above the street punks I usually dealt with. I had no problem dealing with adversaries I knew I could beat. I had no problem running away like a chicken or having others fight my battles with those adversaries I even suspected could beat me or worse. However, I was dealing with people I might not be able to run from and Metro PD couldn't get to me fast enough before my body was riddled with bullets or throwing stars. I'd already been carrying weapons and attachments for my omega-gun that I'd never used before. As a result, I wouldn't be doing much running at all, since I'd added about fifty extra pounds to my person.

Bugs told me my Liquid Cool office was all clear after he did a full sweep. PJ said she could have told me that without us spending all that money. I told PJ to behave herself since we'd likely need many more upgrades to our office security as time went on.

I headed out in the Pony to my one outstanding "cheating spouse" case. Of all the places to go, I was headed to the Whiskey Way district. Good people did live and work there too, but it was a criminal hot spot. As a working street detective, it was a part of the city I'd been to before and would visit again.

On the way I did call Mr. Mick, and all he said was, "Bugs and I spoke. He knows more about cyber-assassins than I do. He had to devise the company's security measures against them. Do whatever he tells you." I knew that already. Bugs was a gold mine of information when it came to security.

The other thing I kept going over in my mind was my meeting with Caveat. He knew about these cyber-assassins. I'd never heard of them, which meant nothing. I was sure there were lots of things behind closed doors that neither the public nor I knew about.

That first client that day—the middle-aged woman with a pale complexion and short dark hair—looked a lot like the woman coming out of a megatower. That's because it was her. She and her husband worked together in the same office. Her husband's mistress apparently also worked in the office. My client was not supposed to be at their office. She was supposed to be on a quick vacation to see her mother. It wasn't the first time, nor would it be the last, that a client wanted to hang around to see me work. I strictly forbade it, but sometimes they did it anyway.

The client hopped into a hovertaxi and was gone. She and her husband ran an import-export like most of the businesses in Whiskey Way, which meant it was shady too. However, I wasn't here to do the police's job. PJ had done the standard background checks on the wife and husband. Nothing came up.

Fortunately, the Way had many secure parking lots. I found the biggest one with the most lights and the scariest cyborg guards. The walk to the husband's office tower was about two miles, but walking never bothered me. Having something happen to my Pony would bother me.

At the corner of the office tower were three sidewalk johnnies, chatting it up and smoking. There were sidewalk sallies nearby too. They were harmless street hustlers, scamming and scheming for cash. Homelessness had been eradicated long ago, like polio and cancer. Housing was mandatory for all, even for those without a legacy. But sidewalk johnnies all had a "turf." For most, it was a street, street corner, or alleyway. Many never ventured beyond it.

My opinion of them had changed dramatically over the last few years. Partly because of my associate, Phishy, and because sidewalk johnnies were my own network of street informants. They kept me up-to-date with what was happening on the streets and did small jobs for me. All they wanted was some fun to break up the monotony of life, and of course a little cash for their time.

"Hey!" They saw me approaching and started to wave.

"Hi guys," I greeted when I reached them. "Are they both up there?"

"Domestic case?" one asked.

"Yeah. I'll get my pictures and go."

They laughed.

"If it's anything racy, please share."

"Sure, guys. Catch you later."

Though out of the way, Whiskey Way was their "turf" district. As my three sidewalk johnny friends walked off, I entered the main entrance of the office tower—a one-hundred-story grimy building with no lobby security, no cameras, no guards. There was no directory listing, so maybe that was their form of security.

I reached into my jacket for my enhanced glasses. Time to prepare for battle.

The main reason I excelled at the detective biz was my attitude. I didn't trust anybody, even my own clients. I was better than most at sizing up people. There were those I trusted implicitly and those I didn't from the second I saw them. But then there were those I wasn't sure of either way. In those cases, my fall back attitude was to trust no one. Paranoia in this trade made for a long life.

I hadn't gotten much sleep the night before because I was studying all the tactics the stealth soldiers megacorps employed. In fact, The Mick had given me one of the better books I'd collected. He'd probably forgotten he lent it to me since he had it memorized from beginning to end. Most of their tactics were my own standard tactics, except for one—disguises. They liked using disguises to spy on, follow, and attack their prey. At no time, from my first encounter with Hiero, did I not know I was now the prey. The Digital Samurai and Echo had enemies. They told me so. What would those enemies do? Get at me to get to them. It's what I'd do.

Maybe I was wrong. Maybe Ms. Lean was a legitimate client with a legitimate case. But she called every day to update me on her husband's schedule. She gave PJ great intel—her husband's schedule morning, noon, and night. All so I could figure out the best time to catch her husband and female employee at the company "in the act." She told me their "favorite places." Tonight was the perfect night for me to snap my pictures and wrap up the case. I had no intentions of going where I was being herded to. I knew the layout of the building. It was the same as every other megatower on the boulevard. You couldn't take cover or hide in an elevator. Step out into a hallway and there was no place to take cover or hide. Emergency exits in these old buildings were like playing the lottery—door open or door welded shut. I entered the building but I went straight through to exit out the back.

But there was always the possibility that that was exactly what they wanted me to do. I reached into my jacket again as I stepped from the light into the shadow just before the exit door and stood quietly to the side.

How peculiar, I thought. I'd been standing like a statue in a nice cul-de-sac outside the rear doors of the building for over two hours. Not a single person came through the front entrance or out of the elevators. The odds of such of thing? It was impossible for an office megatower of this size. In Whiskey Way, nighttime was showtime; it was when street activity increased not disappeared. My instincts were right.

My mobile was vibrating in my pocket. I tilted to my shoulder to activate it.

"Hello."

"Mr. Cruz?" It was Ms. Lean, my client.

"How did you get my mobile, Ms. Lean, when I didn't give it to you?"

"Your secretary gave it to me. I desperately had to give you more details about my husband. I think he knows I hired you."

"Have you figured out where I am yet?" I asked. "When are you coming out so I can see you?"

"Coming out?"

I hung up. My only question was just how many others were in the building. They had three ways to me. The rear doors were thick, but even a laser blast would pass through like they weren't there.

My mobile vibrated again but I didn't answer it. My hands were at my side—omega-gun in the right, a device in the left. Hopefully, I wouldn't have to wait long.

Something moved near the front entrance doors.

"Cruz!"

An Asian man stood there in a black suit and tie, with a white shirt.

"Come with us!"

I said nothing.

"There is nothing you can do," he said. "Come with us quietly and you will not be harmed. We do not want you; we want her."

I still said nothing.

"If you do not approach me, we will come for you."

I didn't look directly at him, more to the side. I had my left arm extended out and my right arm at my side, armed.

"Answer us! We do not want to harm you! What is your answer?"

It seemed very important to him that I speak, which is exactly why I wasn't going to. He yelled the same thing to me, and his body began shaking. He was so agitated.

He flung something at me so fast. The device in my left hand fired a laser so fast that it blew away whatever projectile it was. I shot the man with the gun in my right hand, but it wasn't a clean shot because my device then erupted in a volley of laser fire so fast that it jerked my arm and put me off balance. I'd shot the man in the arm, so I had to shoot him again in the chest. Projectiles came at me in a shower of metal from the front. My hand robot shot everyone out of the air.

I heard war screams as samurai soldiers ran at me from around the corner, maybe coming out of the elevators. I gunned every one of them down.

I saw them. Corporate soldiers rushed in from both the front and rear doors. I shot twice and explosive rounds from my omega-gun blew them back the way they came, crashing down on the pavement in glass.

They couldn't kill me. I knew it. They had orders to capture me, not kill me.

All I had to do was stay in my defensive position and wait for the police. They'd be here soon. I flicked the switch on my omega-gun and fired another explosive round out the rear door. It exploded with a thundering boom. The police would get here even faster now!

I made a gagging sound. Then I felt myself flying through the air toward the front entrance over the pile of samurai and corporate soldier bodies. As soon as I crashed, I recovered and started firing. The figure in the shadows was gone.

Slowly, I rose to my feet. I was completely exposed and I'd dropped my laser robot from my left hand. My omega-gun alone would not help me.

The figure stepped out of the shadows. A woman's body wearing a full, tight black body suit. The black material seemed to change in appearance, some type of illegal cloaking suit.

"You will come with me," she said.

"No, I won't, Voodoo Child," I said.

She remained silent.

"No kidnapping me tonight," I continued.

I heard her low laugh.

"When did you know?" she asked me.

"I never really knew, but I suspected. You did what I expected."

"You did what we expected," she said.

"And here we are."

"You're not fast enough to stop me," she said. From behind her back, she held up a tiny doll of me! I instinctively swallowed hard. "What would happen if I were to crush it in my bionic arms?" she said.

She dropped the doll to the ground. Someone was behind me. I knew it, but if I took my eye off her, it might be the last thing I ever did in life. From my left side Echo stepped forward with his sword in hand. Judo and Pro appeared to my right. The men kept their eye on the cyber-assassin.

I felt the presence of another. Another person appeared to my side.

"Hello, Voodoo," The Digital Samurai said. She had a samurai sword in each hand teeming with electric light. "Looks as if someone killed all your men. I wish I could lend you some of mine, but I won't."

It was safe enough for me to at least glance back. There was an army of corporate soldiers with laser machine guns behind us.

I felt larger than life, standing tall, chest pumped up, my own army with me. Then Voodoo dropped the entire megatower on us!

FREE CITY FUGITIVES

In my Blade Gunner Case, the late Monkey Baker, the head of the late Animal Farm Crime Syndicate, planned to drop a building on me...or blow up my residential building with me in it. Now some crazy maniac named Voodoo Child, carrying a creepy doll that looked exactly like me, with a tan fedora and slicker too, did drop a building on my head. And of course, she escaped.

The whole thing happened in slow motion. The explosions all around at key points of the lobby, then I felt I was either spontaneously rising up or sinking down into the ground. Quickly I realized it was the upper levels of the building itself coming down on us to turn us into human pancakes. I'd never seen people move so fast. All the corporate soldiers flew out of the lobby; they must have had hidden jetpacks in their suits. Echo somehow threw a volley of throwing stars at Voodoo Child as she faded back into the shadows. She was gone and the throwing stars flew past. My eye caught something fly from The Digital Samurai's hand. Something on the ground had exploded in a blue flame. It was the doll of me! But it was ashes. Judo grabbed me, as if to keep me from running.

However, it was The Digital Samurai who did something I'd seen in movies, usually the comedic kind, but what I saw was real. With her two glowing swords, she sliced at the building as it collapsed around us. She moved faster than the levels came down, creating a perfect cylindrical hole around the four of us. The ground beneath our feet shook under the weight.

Time moved normally again. I saw spots of red in the cement then heard laser gunfire. The corporate soldiers cut their own hole for us to crawl though. Well, I crawled; they jump-flew (my new word) through. I came out, one of the soldiers in a suit helped me out, and I looked up. The building was still there. Voodoo Child had tried to crush us with only the second level, which would have been enough.

I remembered. "That doll," I said. "She had a doll of me."

"Hold still," Pro said as he forcibly stood me up straight and gestured for me to lift my arms up and out.

"What's going on?" I asked.

Pro scraped the back of my jacket with the blade of his sword.

"Look forward," he chastised after I tried to see what was falling to the ground.

When he finished I spun around. "What are those?" I bent down and the ground was littered with tiny metal objects shaped like starfishes.

"Don't touch them," Judo told me.

He gestured to the men and they wildly stomped them with the heels of their shoes.

I stood up and looked at D.G.

"Yes, Mr. Cruz. If she had crushed her cloned mech of you, she would have killed you."

Centuries ago the landmark Jarvis Laws created what was now called Legacy Housing and changed the world forever; only the introduction of the hoverengine and off-world colonization was more profound. Once a mortgage was paid off, it could be passed on to family and descendants forever. The politics and legal battles became which descendants would get it next, but the ancient real estate market disappeared with the dinosaurs and Dodo birds. Housing for the rich, poor, and everyone in-between was essentially free. But nothing ever turned out to be as it was intended in this world. We were on our way to Free City.

The hoverlimo I sat in looked identical to the other Hiero ones. I sat in the same spot, but this time Pro sat on my right and a new man sat on my left. Echo, D.G., and Judo sat across from me in that order. We were one of seven hoverlimos racing in sky traffic away from Whiskey Way. With the lights dim in the compartment, The Digital Samurai's eyes had a distinct green glow.

"You seem upset with me," I said.

"What you did was foolish. Mr. Echo said you handled your encounter with Glyph brilliantly and Ming professionally. But you did this. You knew your client was her."

"I didn't know my client was her. I suspected it. I took every precaution in case it was her."

"You knew, but you came anyway—alone."

"I wasn't alone. I knew either you or Mr. Echo was nearby. That I knew."

"And if we didn't get to you in time?"

"You would. All I needed to do was buy time."

"She threw the attachments on your back when she was in the hovertaxi."

I could have slapped myself. That's why she was at the building leaving in the hovertaxi. She'd been waiting for me and timed it perfectly. She knew exactly when I would have turned my back to walk into the building. Voodoo Child had profiled me so well that she even knew where I'd stand in the lobby. She probably mapped out every possible action I might have made, and was ready for all of them.

"We would have heard the devices cut through the air and fasten on to clothes," D.G. said.

"You can hear silent things flying through the air?" My question was rhetorical.

"She could have easily thrown a dagger into the back of your skull," D.G. said.

"I was in no danger from her. She wanted you."

"She came to kidnap you," Echo told me. "Hold you for ransom. She knows we need your services."

"I find it hard to believe that you need me for anything. What services exactly? You've spoken in general terms but no specifics."

"We will speak once we get to a secure base," D.G. said.

"Free City?"

"Yes. The new hideout is prepared."

As districts go, Free City was the dumps. It was government housing for the unlucky five percent of the population without legacies. The district didn't have sidewalk johnnies and sallies loitering around. Free City had street punks. It wasn't until my NeuroDancer Case that I learned it also had a commercial section. I'd known it as a sea of slender residential towers. I assumed we were going to the commercial area but though the darkly tinted windows I noticed we were flying into one of the apartment towers, maybe around the 100th floor. Already I could see heavily armed corporate soldiers in suits.

Our passenger door opened and Echo gestured. I followed him with Judo and Pro behind me. The entire top levels of the apartment has been turned into a parking bay.

"Where are the residents?" I asked.

"They have all been given an overseas vacation for a few months. They did not object," Echo said.

"When you have no money, I'm sure you wouldn't."

We walked through double doors to the interior. A long gray commercial-size hallway. Echo led us to the end and around the corner.

"Could that Voodoo Child really have killed me with that doll?" I asked.

"Normally, the attachments would simply rip through your flesh, but with the body armor you're wearing under your clothes they'd have crushed you to death. Each node has its own hoverengine. Powerful enough to lift a hovercar," Echo said.

I made a mental note. Now I had another cyber-assassin "trick" to design a countermeasure for.

"Do not concern yourself, Mr. Cruz," he added. "It would take you a lifetime to study every secret weapon at the disposal of a member of the society and you would still not know them all. That is why we study and train daily all our lives. You cannot gain this knowledge in a few days."

"That means I'm staying close to you," I said. I glanced back to Judo and Pro. "And when he's not around, both of you."

"Our base is secure," Judo said to me.

"Are there any others that I should know about besides this Voodoo Child?" I asked Echo.

"Others?" he asked.

"Other crazy maniacs who would want to harm me."

"You have already met them."

"Who?"

"Mr. Ming. Mr. Glyph."

"Why would Mr. Ming want to harm me? You work for Mr. Ming."

"We *used* to work for Mr. Ming."

"Used to? I thought you meant you were freelancing, not that you resigned."

At the end of the hall was a door guarded by three corporate soldiers armed with laser machine guns. They were cyborgs too, at least their arms and hands were all metal. They stepped aside as we entered the room and one closed the door behind us.

Inside the room was like any normal apartment. It reminded me of my own, though it was decorated in a Japanese motif. Clearly, it was far below the standards they were accustomed to in the ultra-wealthy Silicon Dunes.

"This is our base," Echo said. "Please be seated."

I sat on the main living room couch. Judo sat on a side chair. Pro walked into the kitchen and I heard him opening cabinets.

"You say Voodoo Child was trying to kidnap me for ransom. Why?" I asked.

Echo sat at the dining room table viewing the screen of a mobile computer.

"You do not need to concern yourself with her anymore. We will deal with her. You will focus on the new case."

"What new case?" I asked.

"Locate a person." The Digital Samurai came from one of the back rooms with a portfolio. She approached and handed it to me.

She sat on the carpeted floor, legs crossed, never taking her gaze from me. Echo joined me on the couch. I opened the portfolio. It was filled with files.

"No data disk or file?" I asked.

"We know you prefer physical paper," she answered. They'd profiled me too.

I scanned the files. "Who am I locating?" I asked.

"A criminal," D.G. answered. "A very evil man."

"Name?"

"He's known on the streets by the alias Hackasaurus."

"A hacker cyberpunk."

"You know of him?" she asked.

"No, but the name fits for a hacker cyberpunk. They like those kind of street names. Why would you need me to find a hacker for you?"

"Because we no longer have the resources of the Hiero Corporation at our disposal," Echo answered. "And we would not have been able to begin the search from within the company without their knowledge."

"They? Have you really left the company?" I asked.

"Yes," D.G. replied. "We have, and that is why we needed to hire you. You will find this hacker. We will deal with Hiero. We will be your bodyguards."

I scanned more of the documents. "Why do you want this hacker?"

"He is more than a hacker," Echo said. "He is a criminal broker on the Market."

"Which Market?"

"The Ghost Market."

I nodded. "What kind of criminal activity?"

"Stolen corporate data. Weapons transfers. Money transfers. People transfers."

"People transfers?"

"Yes. People are transferred via the Market. Ordered on the Ghost and delivered through the Shadow for all kinds of reasons. You can use your imagination."

"Why do you want him?"

"He has my child."

I stopped looking through the documents. "Your child?"

"Yes."

"You want me to believe that you, Mr. Echo, all your men have left the Hiero Corporation, which means that you have signed your own death warrants, for a child?"

"You have a child," Echo said.

"I do, but I'm not a samurai soldier or an assassin. This is your plan? I find this hacker, you get him, you slice a piece of him off to find your child, slice him to pieces after he tells you the child's location and you confirm it, and fly off into the sunset."

"Our plan exactly," she said.

"What's wrong with the plan?" Echo asked.

"If you've left Hiero for this, they know too. This Voodoo Child will know too. They probably have a better profile of you, than you have of me. They know what you're going to do."

"But they don't know what you will do," D.G. said.

"You're counting on me being unpredictable for us to be successful."

"Is that not a good calculation?" Echo asked. "Our encounter with both Ming and Glyph proves you are what we need. You can improvise for any situation. Be unpredictable to any adversary to achieve your end. You've done so many times."

"In strategy and tactics, maybe yes, but physical confrontation?"

"We will be your bodyguards," she said.

"We will deal with any physical threats as we did today. You focus on the hacker. We focus on your safety."

"The entire resources of the Hiero Corporation after us?"

"We know all the resources they have. We have both been those resources and used them," Echo told me.

"How old is your child?" I suddenly asked her.

"She's seven." The Digital Samurai had answered but in her split second delay, I suspected that she made-up the gender and age on the spot.

"These files have everything I need to know about this Hackasaurus?"

"They do," Echo replied.

"I can use that computer?"

"It is for your use," Echo said.

"When will Hiero know that you all have officially resigned?" I asked.

"They may already know," Echo replied.

"I need complete quiet while I review the files. I'll need a secure phone."

"You'll have more than one, and Mr. Pro is preparing your dinner."

"Good. I'll start now. I'll need to make a lot of calls. I wish we had the confidential files from Cybercrimes if you say he works the Ghost Market."

"Those files are included," D.G. said.

I looked again at the pages I had. The last page was from Cybercrimes.

"I won't even ask how you were able to get this, but one page? That's no help at all. This will be a long night."

"Your fees have already been paid," Echo said.

"Never doubted otherwise." I stood from the couch. "I have some nighttime reading to complete."

"How many days do you anticipate you'll need to find this person?" D.G. asked me.

"Days? I need to find this person tonight. I'm operating under the assumption that if you know this hacker, your former bosses do, and your fellow cyber-assassin does. We find him tonight or not at all, because Cybercrimes may not be able to find him, but the Hiero Corporation certainly will."

D.G. and Echo exchanged looks. I'd surprised them. Neither believed I could deliver what I said as fast as that. The fact that they had Cybercrimes private files meant, as I suspected, the Metro Division had been searching for the hacker for them. My new clients had access to the Cybercrimes headquarters or, with the vast monetary resources of Hiero, had one or more moles.

"Before I get started, what does D.G. stand for?" I asked.

"Digital Gal, of course. My nickname."

"Of course."

The Digital Samurai had a child? Good con. I was a new father, so invent a child to appeal to my fatherly instincts. Make it a girl to really appeal to my inherent father-protecting-daughter mythos. Hint at kidnapping and all kinds of venal crimes. Yep, they'd checked all the boxes. A cyber-assassin having a child, seemed far-fetched to me, but then they would know I'd be suspicious. However, they also knew I'd ignore it all to find that hacker—and I would.

Hackasaurus was a complete mystery to Cybercrimes. Their file, all one page, was a whole lot of nothing. All the file told me was they knew "he" was based in Metropolis and mentioned some 57, 677 times on the dark Net in the last two months. He was a major hacker, who came onto the scene a decade ago with more requests for "his" services than he could take on. No details of his specific hacks were available, and no mention of any crimes related to people smuggling.

The Hiero files were the opposite; there was too much specificity. Everything D.G. stated as his crimes was listed individually—corporate data hacks, weapons transfers, money transfers, people trafficking—by hiring client, most of which was Hiero, dates, going back how many years, and even, in some cases, how much he was paid for each job.

I didn't know much of anything about the illusory net world of the Ghost Market, but I did know something of the underground hacking world. Cyberpunks. The term cyberpunk had all kinds of meaning throughout history, but nowadays, it was used to describe the geek subculture of mostly youth, who lived most of their life in VR (virtual reality). All of the best hackers in the world came from this world, even better than governments and megacorps.

But I had to work with the information, or the story, I was given. My favorite beverage was my silk coffee, and Pro had made some of the best cups of it I'd ever tasted. I skipped dinner, but he had it on the kitchen stove for me for later.

Once I finished and digested what I'd read about this Hackasaurus, time came to figure out how to get to him. I had a dedicated mobile computer and ten different mobile phones on the glass table for me to use. Judo sat on the same couch, fast asleep. Echo was curled up on the bigger couch sleeping. Pro sat in the kitchen on a stool at the counter, wearing big headphones and watching TV on a mini-computer screen. The Digital Samurai had returned to the back rooms.

The apartment was so quiet; it was eerie. My mind's eye imagined that outside our Free City fortress, the forces of Hiero were searching for us. That Voodoo Child woman with her devil dolls was out there. So was the Macro Corporation. I was a prisoner.

PJ

With my reading and computer research done, I grabbed one of my disposable mobile phones. Pro had earlier showed me that the dining area had a privacy zone. Ready to make my calls, I hit a button and a light went on above me from the ceiling. The apartment was already quiet, but now there was no sound whatsoever and no one outside the zone could hear me. However, I assumed that D.G. or any of her men were watching everything I typed on the computer, would listen to my conversations, and watched my every move. I didn't care; I had work to do.

The first person I'd call was going to be PJ. She'd update me on what was happening at the office, and I had plenty for her to do as well.

Her tiny face appeared on the screen when it connected.

"I was about to call Missing Persons."

"Hello to you too, PJ. What's new at the office?"

"I can't delay clients forever. Business is flying out the door."

"I'm sure you're handling it. I have more tasks for you."

"Where are you?"

"I'm with Mr. Echo."

"Oh, good. No one can do anything to you with him around."

"I want you to call Dot. Lots of people may be looking for me. These are the kind of people that hide in shadows, and when they're not in the shadows, they're standing next to you, invisible."

"Like Mr. Echo did."

"Yes. I don't want these people near my wife."

"I don't want those people near me."

"Call whoever you need to. I'll call Prima too."

"Eye Candy may be an image salon, but it's safer than Metro PD."

PJ wasn't exaggerating. My wife worked at Metro's premiere high-end image salon, Eye Candy. It was located in the upscale Paisley Parish, and the police working that beat had no sense of humor and were everywhere. My wife's boss, Prima Donna, had been in the business for ages, and knew plenty of gangsters herself since her place did the hair, skin, makeup, manicures, pedicures, styling, etc. of all their wives, girlfriends, and mistresses. Between the police outside, their security measures, and the weapons in Prima's walk-in safe, I wasn't worried—as long as Dot was inside.

"Your wife drives like a maniac so no one can follow her."

"These people can follow anyone. Besides, they know where we live. But they want me, not her."

"I'll handle it. I'll call Mr. Post at the building too."

"Good. That'll save me a call."

Mr. Post was the doorman and security manager at the Concrete Mama—my residential tower. PJ lived there too.

"Before I forget, do you remember that first client call you set up after Mr. Echo visited us? The three client calls."

"Yes, the spousal surveillance job."

"It was a set up. Ms. Page was actually another corporate assassin."

"What?"

"She tried to kill me, but Mr. Echo and his colleagues arrived. Long story that I'll tell you when I see you."

"Why not tell me now?"

"It's too long a story. Corporate soldiers came after me. But I took care of them. Our Ms. Page turned out to be an assassin named Voodoo Child. She planned to kidnap and hold me for ransom."

"Ransom you to who?"

"Mr. Echo and his colleagues, but we got away. After she tried to drop the building on us. But she got away too. I'll tell you later."

"No, tell me now. Drop the building on you? I didn't see that on the newsfeed."

"It was in Whiskey Way."

"Oh, a crime district. We don't care about it then."

"There are some regular folks who live there too, PJ."

"Whatever. What about this Voodoo Child? What did she do?"

"PJ, that's not why I called you."

"What did she do? Did she put some voodoo on you?"

"PJ, what does that even mean? No, but she had one of those little voodoo dolls of me."

"No way! That's real?"

"Not real, but in this case it was real."

"So if she stabbed the doll, you'd be stabbed."

"If she crushed the doll, then all these metal bug things, they looked like tiny starfish, that she secretly threw on my back and body would have crushed me."

"What!"

"PJ, this is not why I called."

"You're the one telling me the story."

"Oh, the reason I mentioned her was to tell you that she likes disguises."

"She's like you then."

"I rarely use disguises."

"Says you."

"So be careful. Anyone who comes in could be her or her people trying to find me."

"I put that together already when you told me she pretended to be a regular client."

"I need you to find B.B. I mean Bubble Baha."

PJ laughed. "That's such a stupid name. Why?"

"He knows the Ghost Market."

"Couldn't he or she be—?"

"Yes, B.B. could be this Voodoo person. I already thought of that. But not likely. Besides, he's a true Liquid Cool fan. I can tell these things."

"Is that so? You and B.B. are best friends after one visit."

"We are. Track him down again through those Pixel Posse people."

"Another bunch of stupid people. Why don't you talk to cyberpunks who know the Ghost Market? It's safer."

"We don't have any trustworthy contacts in that world yet. Do you?"

"No."

"We have our Sidewalk Johnny Brigade for street intel. We actually have no trustworthy contact for either the Shadow or Ghost Markets, which I'll remedy in the future."

"What about the police? You have like five hundred thousand friends there."

"Not them either. We need a free agent who works in it."

"A criminal."

"A good criminal."

PJ chuckled. "Okay."

"And you know how to secret message me."

"I think I do," PJ said with sarcasm.

"So who are you calling?" I asked.

"Cruz, I know my job and who I'm calling. You do your job and make your calls. And you'd better call your wife to say where you are, or give a good lie. I don't want her calling me."

I laughed.

THE NEW BUBBLE BAHA

The banter between PJ and me could go on for hours. When I hung up with her, I called Dot and spent almost thirty minutes on the line. I reluctantly called the HellSpawn, since they were babysitting, but it was to say hello to Cruz Jr. who just giggled and tapped the screen. I called Prima Donna, the queen of Eye Candy, just to let her know that there may be nasty people floating around. She told me she'd handle everything as far as Dot's safety.

I would never type as fast as PJ with her bionic fingers and I never liked voice-typing, but I was moving fast on the keyboard. As I worked, a notification popped on the screen. I checked the secret email account. PJ had already heard back from Bubble Baha, which was good but was also suspicious. A fact that PJ made sure to repeat and type in all caps. B.B. wanted to meet me again at the same place.

I was back in Tokyo Town at the same dark bar with no name signage. Like the last time, I gave my name at the front counter. A different female waitress checked my ID and another male thug-in-a-suit led me to a table. The same clientele—slimy, thuggish, ne'er-do-wells—filled the place in enclosed booths on three levels.

The thug showed me to the booth, which I was almost positive was the exact same one as before.

"Can I choose another booth?" I asked.

"No," he said and left.

The man who arrived wearing a tight-fitting hoodie, gloved hands, and a white mask covering his face from his forehead to his nose, was clearly *not* the same man as I'd met on the previous night. He sat and pushed the button that made the tinted glass privacy shield come down on the open side of the booth.

"Where's B.B.?" I asked, annoyed.

He noticed two men appear and sit in the booth across the aisle opposite to us—Echo and Judo.

"I told you to come alone," he said.

"Relax, they're my bodyguards."

He seemed very nervous, too nervous.

"I'll ask again. Where's B.B.?"

"I am Bubble Baha."

"You're not the guy I met last time."

"I'm the new Bubble Baha."

"What happened to the old one?"

"I'm sure he told you that Bubble Baha is a collective. We are many people."

"You can give the same name to all the people you want. I was expecting the other guy. Where's the other guy?"

"He's unavailable."

"What does that mean?"

"You talk to me or no one."

"Seems you're the one who wants to talk. You responded to our message pretty fast. Is the other guy dead?"

"No. Why would you say that? He's taken some time off."

"Why?"

"I'm not here to be interrogated by a wannabe cop."

"Wannabe? I'm a wannabe nothing. I'm a detective. How do I know you didn't kill the other guy to take his place?"

"You don't, and he's not dead. What do you want? You called me."

"I called the other guy."

"I can leave."

"I don't like surprises."

"Neither do I," he said, pointing to Echo and Judo at the other booth.

"The other guy knew the Ghost Market."

"I've been in the Ghost Market longer than him."

"The Hiero and Macro Corporations are players in the Ghost Market."

"Did you really call me to ask questions about companies your cop friends can answer for you?"

"Why are you so jumpy?" I asked. "It's like you're trying to goad me into saying something that you can use as an excuse to run away."

"Why did you call me?"

"Tell me about a player called Hackasaurus."

He laughed. "You'll never get to him."

"Why do you say that?"

"Never in a million years."

"Why?"

"People are always looking for him, but some new people have been really looking for him hard lately. Far more dangerous than you."

"What people?"

"Your two friends from Hiero across the way."

"Why are my friends looking for him?"

"Ask them. They're your friends."

"I'm asking you."

"Ask them."

"Who's Voodoo Child?"

"I don't know that one."

"The Digital Samurai?"

"Don't know that one either. Hiero soldiers?"

"Maybe."

"I see you wasted my time."

"The other guy was so helpful and friendly, unlike you."

"Sorry to disappoint."

"Why did you agree to meet me? You're not going to tell me anything."

"You're asking far too many questions and looking for very bad people. You look for them; they'll look for you too."

"What does a cyber-gremlin do? The other guy was a cyber-gremlin."

"I'm one too."

"What do you do?"

"We get into a system and cause as much chaos as we can."

"Why? There's no profit in that."

"Because we can."

"That's dumb."

"Cyber-anarchy isn't dumb."

"Oh, you have a name for your dumbness. Do you have a manifesto too? Am I doing okay?"

"Doing okay?"

"Yeah, stalling. That is why you agreed to meet me but tell me nothing. You're setting me up for someone. Who's coming? Is it the Voodoo woman?"

"I don't know who that is and I don't know what you're talking about."

"Mr. New Bubble Baha, you're about to be the ex-New Bubble Baha."

"I don't know what you're talking about."

He went to touch his hands together, and that's when I blasted him with my omega-gun from under the table.

The blast shattered the privacy shield. Echo remained seated quietly, but Judo stood up as all hell broke loose in the bar. People jumped out of their booths and ran for the door. The bar's security—more thugs in suits—came at us with long guns. Guns weren't allowed in the bar, but my omega-gun was made off-world so it was undetectable to most Earth sensors. In the case of Judo and Echo, they were better than guns.

Judo took a karate stance in the aisle. Suddenly there an explosion of black smoke. Someone grabbed me out of the booth, and I couldn't see a thing. I heard yelling and cursing, then we were outside the bar. Echo was the one who'd grabbed me. Where he came from I didn't know. Judo had the wounded B.B. over a shoulder. A hoverlimo descended, we piled in, and the vehicle shot away into the sky. That was one dark bar that I'd probably never be able to set foot in again for the rest of my life.

The partition between the middle section opened up. The hoverlimo had its own hover bio-bed. The new B.B. was lifted onto it, he was strapped in, and his mask was removed. Normal face, nothing unique about it. He was in his thirties at most, so I doubted he'd been Bubble Baha for decades as he said unless he began his crime life within the womb.

I hadn't noticed D.G. until she leaned over him and waved her hand under his nose. The man jolted awake. Stunned, he tried to sit up, until he realized he was strapped in.

"Where am I? Where are you taking me?"

I sat in the seat closest to him and leaned over. He looked at me.

"Listen to me good. I want the other guy. I don't trust and I don't like you."

"I told you. He's not available."

"I'm about to tell my friends to set this vehicle down, let me out so I can take a stroll for a few hours. Whatever means they deem necessary to get the info we need..."

On cue, and we didn't even rehearse beforehand, D.G. flicked her arms and her electric swords were in her hands.

The guy swallowed hard. He laid his head back down and looked up at the ceiling.

"I want to go home."

"Where's the other guy? That's the only way you're getting out of this."

He closed his eyes. He opened them, tears welling up.

"I'll tell you what you want to know."

"Not you. Tell me how to call the other guy!"

"I'll give you the number but I have to call."

"No. I'll call. I know how to dial a number. Assuming it's the real other guy and not more stalling tactics."

"I'll give you the number."

He did. I called from another disposable mobile. The number connected but instead of a face appearing on the screen, there was a flickering blue pattern.

"Isn't this a surprise, Mr. Cruz," a familiar voice said.

It was him! I smiled and said, "The real B.B. at least."

"The real one that you know."

"I don't like your friend."

"Why not? I sent him."

"I don't trust him."

"His people skills suck, but that's why I sent him. He won't learn if he's not out there interacting with people."

"He needs more training."

"I need you to let him go."

"We can't talk first?"

"How do I know your friends will let my man go after? No. We're breaking all kinds of protocol here. You need to let him go now. When I know he's safe, we can talk."

"How do I know you'll call back?"

"You don't, Mr. Cruz, but Bubble Baha hasn't survived this long without adhering to our protocols. We don't do any business if there's danger. If I were you, Mr. Cruz, I'd listen. I was the one who had us call you back as a favor to you."

"What favor?"

"We'll talk when my man is freed."

I made a gesture for us to land. Echo shouted something in Japanese. The hoverlimo descended.

"Can you help me find this guy named Hackasaurus?" I asked.

"I can, but you have much bigger problems. The Hiero Corporation has all its personnel looking for you and a Mr. Echo."

"EE-KO," Mr. Echo corrected.

"All of you are in serious trouble. A lot of money is out on the streets to find you. Corporate soldiers everywhere."

Judo and another man released the imitation BB from his restraints. "You promise to call me back?" I asked.

"When my man is free. Also, do you know someone named Blur?"

It was as if someone announced that we were sitting on top of a hydrogen bomb and we had ten seconds to live. Even D.G.'s face looked concerned. She and Echo exchanged looks. Whoever or whatever Blur was, it was not good news.

BLUR, CRAZY MANIAC ASSASSIN KILLER

The second we touched down on the ground and the door opened, the imitation B.B. bolted. The rain had started again and he was out of sight into the crowds in seconds. The passenger door closed.

"Who is Blur?" I asked.

"Will this man call you?" D.G. asked me.

"I believe he will."

"Why?" she asked.

"He's a fan and wears Liquid Cool T-shirts."

My answer caught her off-guard and she began to laugh. Her hand covered her mouth as if she was embarrassed, or hadn't laughed so hard in a very long time. The men were not shy at all. They laughed.

"Blur is an assassin killer," Judo replied.

I gave him a double-take. Did he really say what he said?

"Yes, an assassin killer," Judo replied.

"Then they're after D.G.," I said.

"Yes," Echo said.

"What about Voodoo Child?" I asked. "We have her and this new person, Blur after us?"

"They're after us, not you," D.G. said.

"Us. I'm with you."

"We encounter them, you take cover. You are not to involve yourself in any fighting. We fight. You don't."

"Then that's what I'll do. You're the soldiers. I'm just the hired detective."

Echo gave the signal to another man. The hoverlimo rose back into the sky, heading for sky traffic. I kept quiet as a heated debate in Japanese broke out among them. I had no idea what was being said, but it seemed like four factions were arguing: Echo, Judo, one group of samurai soldiers, and another group. D.G. listened, her eyes cast down to the floor. She held up a hand and the men quieted down.

"We have no choice," she said.

That was the end of the debate.

We didn't return to Free City and Bubble Baha didn't call back. I looked out the tinted windows and we seemed to be circling Downtown Metro in traffic. City Hall, Metro PD, the Court Building were all distinctive landmarks.

"If he hasn't called, there's a good reason," I said aloud. I knew what they were all thinking.

"Or he will not keep his promise," Echo said.

"Maybe, but I think there's a reason."

"We have no choice but to wait then," D.G. said. "Is he your only contact to the hacker?"

"I have more but no matter how long we have to wait, this is the fastest way," I replied.

"Then we wait," D.G. said.

We didn't have to wait long.

I'd been on some of the wildest illegal hovercar racing courses on the planet. I'd never been scared in all that time. When the hoverlimo suddenly dropped, I was terrified. My stomach was in my throat, the same sensation as one of those psychotic roller coasters, which was why I didn't go on them. But this was real, and dropping in a vehicle of this weight twenty or more feet in the air meant there'd be nothing left of us to scrape up into a little baggie, let alone a body bag.

Gunfire erupted all around me. I heard one loud bang outside the hoverlimo. Rapid yelling of Japanese from the men inside all around me and from the unseen driver's compartment.

My entire body seized up as the roof of the hoverlimo flew off. We were now a falling hoverlimo convertible. Convertibles were only legal in museums on the ground and inoperable. The hovertraffic was above us, but multiple hovercars were racing straight to us. Machine-gun and laser-fire exploded around me from all the corporate soldiers. The chasing hovercars fired back. Their shots were precise. Pro reached over to me and a shield popped out both ends of his forearm, glowing red around the edges. He covered me just in time. I ducked, but the shield blocked all the gunfire. All the soldiers activated their shields, except Echo and D.G.

There was a loud click. Multiple lasers fired from the side of our hoverlimo, shaking the craft. All five of our pursuers were blown apart. The debris rained down after us. I felt our momentum slow a bit, then it blasted forward. None of us were wearing seat belts. My hand had been in a death grip on the front of my seat the whole time.

Unfortunately, they had vehicle laser cannons too. My eyes didn't even have time to react as our hoverlimo was blown apart too. What I perceived after that was in flashes—dust, debris, someone grabbed me, sounds of metal crashing to the ground. I felt weightless. But my feet did touch the ground softly.

"Cruz!"

I don't know who yelled at me. I was in shock. External sensory overload, a cyberpunk would say. My senses were being bombarded with too much stimuli to process. I was moving, floating, or being carried. Lasers rained down. We were in a shadow between two buildings. I was sitting on the cold, damp ground. Damp ground meant isopods! I came to my senses and jumped up from the ground.

It looked like all of Echo's men and D.G. were fine. The men fired their weapons in unison into the sky at other hovervehicles. Pro stood next to me with gun in one hand, sword in the other. Judo, the same, stood in front of us. Echo and D.G. stood watching the sky, calm and emotionless.

A huge hoverplane glided above us. Judo was yelling in Japanese. A drone floated next to us from out of nowhere. Robotic arms threw one plasma blaster after another to the men. They dropped their machine guns to the ground; they had laser hand-cannons now.

As Pro pulled me closer to the wall in the alleyway, I looked up. Descending from above were corporate soldiers on our side wearing jetpacks. I'd seen Metro police do the same many times before. As our corporate soldiers fired, more and more hovervehicles veered out of sky traffic to attack us with their own machine-gun and laser-fire.

There was nothing for me to do but watch. For all the madness of flying bullets and lasers, I wasn't concerned. The average Metro resident would have been, but I'd been in worse before. I might have been the only living civilian to see all five hundred thousand Metro police engage the combined gangster army of the Animal Farm Crime Syndicate. That syndicate no longer existed. This battle was bad, but not as bad as that. But I wanted to be useful. Pro was protecting me, so what could I do?

Blur. Who or what was an assassin killer? They never answered me.

Everyone else was occupied, so I scanned the surroundings where they weren't watching. We were in a narrow alleyway by Metropolis standards, between two commercial towers. We were in Silver City, Metro's center of robotic production. It was not a coincidence that we were hit here. Very few people worked here, so there'd be no bystanders to kill and no one to call police. With megacorps involved, they probably were creating chaos elsewhere in the supercity to occupy the police.

I stared at the far end of the alleyway. The end was, maybe, five miles away. Lights lined the wall every few feet about eight feet up from end to end. I squinted again. I saw it again. When I glanced at D.G., she was looking back at me. The two of us were the only ones looking down the alleyway.

Suddenly, I was on my back on the cold, wet, nasty ground again. I dry-coughed and grabbed my throat. What was happening to me? I jumped to my feet. Pro was lying on the ground on his chest; he wasn't moving. I looked around and Echo, Judo, all the men were also laid out on the ground unconscious. Why I was conscious I didn't know.

I heard the sounds and turned. Digital Samurai was fighting a living shadow! It was different from Voodoo Child's ninja-like costume. Blur's outfit alternated between black and invisible. It was more than that. Her image wavered and jumped from point to point. I assumed Blur was a woman too from her build. Both fighters attacked and defended with dual swords.

Because Blur shifted from place to place, D.G. swung and missed more than she hit her target. The assassin killer, Blur, always blocked the sword attacks. D.G. couldn't even anticipate Blur's moves because of the shifting. There was no pattern to where Blur appeared.

Our corporate soldiers hovering via jetpack in the air above us couldn't help. They were now barely holding off the increasing numbers of attacking hovervehicles from the sky traffic. This was why first B.B. didn't call me back; he knew this was coming. The new B.B. probably set it all in motion, or aided them.

The battle wasn't going D.G.'s way. She couldn't land one blow. Blur kept shifting from place to place. D.G. cried out; Blur had thrust her sword through D.G.'s thigh. Blur sliced D.G.'s arms, her legs, then abdomen. D.G.'s face was covered with so many cuts, dripping blood. The Digital Samurai was losing.

I looked up at the sky, and our hoverplane above now found itself underneath an even larger arriving hoverplane. I heard gunfire. We were out-manned and outmatched. We were losing.

I was being ignored because I was viewed as an insignificant insect. The second I engaged, they'd try to kill me, and these were not the people you wanted trying to kill you.

"Enough of this," I said to myself.

I reached into my jacket for my new weapon. Bugs gave me the weapon. It was for cyber-assassins and the like. I aimed it at Blur and fired.

The blast knocked her into the wall. Her shifting effect stopped. The Digital Samurai sliced off both arms before Blur could attack again. Blur kicked; D.G. sliced off the foot. A laser blast hit D.G. in the back from above.

My reflexes did what they always did—respond. In less than a second I drew my omega-gun from my jacket, fired a laser at Blur, hitting her in the face, fired an explosive round above, blowing up the laser gun from the enemy hoverplane, dropped to one knee and rapid-fired laser rounds at the hovervehicles from the sky traffic. I hit what I fired at.

There was a flash. I turned and what was left of Blur was flying up into the sky to the enemy hoverplane.

I jumped as plasma blasts erupted around me. Pro, Judo, all the men were conscious again, back on their feet, and back in the battle. Half were firing at the enemy hoverplane and half were firing at the enemy hovervehicles.

Echo had run to D.G., who had collapsed to the ground. With one arm, he did the same thing he did with me. He swatted laser blasts away to protect her.

Again, I was a fifth wheel and didn't know what to do. But it didn't last long. The enemy hoverplane blasted away, then all the other hovervehicles that hadn't been blasted out of the sky. We had destroyed close to two dozen; mangled piles of metal littered the ground all over. In the distance, we saw the police lights. Corporate soldiers dove, grabbed one of us, and, once inside our hoverplane, we blasted off too.

SHOT CALLER, DARK NET TRAFFIC CONTROLLER

When the Metro PD had you in their sights in a chase, nothing would stop them. They'd get you. On the illegal hovercar racing scene, I'd done "in-motion jumps" before. That's what we called it, but it was actually the most dangerously dumb thing someone could do. Jumping from one moving hovervehicle to another—no safety line, no parachute, no jetpack. If you mistimed it or lost your grip, you'd "return to surface," to use another euphemism that involved little plastic baggies, spoons, and coroners. However, that's what we did now, but on a far grander scale.

Another hoverplane came alongside us, and all of us jumped from one to another, two miles up. My man Pro jumped with me. They all moved like they did the maneuver every day. I was a bit more nervous about it but did it. Echo carried D.G., who was wrapped up in a blanket from the plane. She was in bad shape. When the side cargo door closed, the planes blasted away from each other. The other ascended but ours dove toward the city. As we all took our seats, all the windows went black. Only when I was in my seat did I realize that it wasn't the windows going dark; we were a plane within a plane. Our small craft dropped out of the larger one. Both planes went in different directions.

The plane was like any other private jet in layout. Clean and functional. It had one row of seats on either side with a large aisle. The rear of the jet had bunk-style, fold-down beds, which was where Echo had set an unconscious D.G. A soldier was with them. He wore a suit, had a gun in a shoulder holster, but it was clear he was also a medic. He passed a device that looked like a small tablet over her body.

"Are we going back to Free City?" I asked Pro, who sat next to me.

Pro shook his head.

"Then I need access to a computer," I said.

Pro reached over to my seat and pushed a button in the right armrest. A computer terminal rose from the floor.

"I need to keep checking my messages constantly. I assigned tasks to my own people," I said. "Bubble Baha didn't call me because I think he thought we might not survive."

"You think he will call?" Judo was seated next to me on the left.

"I do. I know I have no real reason to believe he will, but, wearing Liquid Cool T-shirts aside, I believe he's a person who does what he promises."

"But you have other means to find Hackasaurus?" Judo asked.

"I do, but B.B. can get us there much faster. I'm sure you agree that the longer we're out here on our own, the worse things will get for us."

"Yes."

"We go to medical facilities," Pro told me.

"Is D.G. Mr. Echo's daughter?" I asked.

"He raised her from her childhood, trained her in her early years, until she surpassed his teachings. Then others took on that role. He, however has always remained as a father to her," Judo said.

"Her battle with Blur reminded me of Greek mythology. There was a giant who could defeat any man as long as he stood upon the Earth. He was invincible. Then he met Hercules, who picked him up off the ground and crushed that giant to death in his bare arms," I said.

"Very astute. That is a good story," Judo said. "The Digital Samurai is invincible to things she can touch. Blur cannot be touched."

"I touched her," I said.

Judo smiled. "You always do the unexpected."

I looked up and Echo was standing next to us.

"Yes, our desire to retain your services has borne more fruit than we could have ever anticipated."

"The only fruit we need now, and fast, is this Hackasaurus," I said. "I hope I'm not wrong about B.B."

"Your instincts have not been wrong so far," Echo said, reassuringly.

Oh no! The one district in all of Metropolis that made the hair on the back of my neck stand up was Mad Heights, more commonly known as Mad City. The Hiero Corporation fugitives flew into a neighborhood of maniacs. Mad City had a much higher profile in the low-life, high-tech underworld when the Animal Farm Crime Syndicate was around, but after Metro PD wiped them out, no other gang could amass that much power again. One massive gang was replaced by a million tiny gangs.

I breathed a sigh of relief. Our hoverplane was not landing anywhere near the ground. We set down on the roof of one of the towers. The architectural design of Mad City was no design. The neighborhood was old and existed before the building codes were formalized in the city. It looked like a crazy group of builders had put the town together. There were skinny towers next to monolith towers, twenty-foot towers next to two-hundred-foot ones. It all looked...mad. If a construction crew was high on drugs and did whatever popped into their minds, Mad Heights was what they would have come up with. Adding to the madness were the neon signs of all sizes and shapes—no standard like other districts.

The building tower was a clinic. I'd been in one of those too in Mad City. A slimy sewer of a facility with flies and jumbo roaches and isopods. The thought alone made my skin crawl and made me want to run all the way to the Centers for Disease Control to jump into a decon gel pool. But what we entered was far different. We descended from the roof stairs into a state-of-the-art medical ward on the penthouse level. Medical staff in white clothing were waiting, and there was plenty of corporate soldier security.

As Echo attended to D.G. with the medical staff, Judo gestured to me.

"We can have you work in our offices," he said.

"Will she be all right?" I asked.

"We have the best doctors. They will repair the damage."

"Has she ever been beaten before?"

"Not by a single person. However, she is strong and will adapt. The same thing will not happen a second time. What was that weapon you used?"

"I call it a pulsator."

"Did you create it?"

"A friend did. He encountered cyber-assassins in the past. I actually brought it to use against that Voodoo woman, but I was happy to use it against Blur."

"Fortunate for all you had it. You may have saved us all."

"You would have done the same, Mr. Judo, if you were able. Are there any other people out there besides Blur and Voodoo Child that I should know about?"

"You must not think of them as the same group. Each are different. Voodoo works for Macro. Blur was sent by Hiero. There are others from other megacorps, but we are dealing with them."

"But Blur and Voodoo Child are the most dangerous?"

"Yes."

"More like them."

"Many, but you will not encounter them."

"I'll get back to work, but I want to talk with D.G. when she's conscious and able."

Judo nodded.

The business offices and conference rooms were very much like what I'd seen at Hiero, but normal size for normal people like me, not the size of any entire stadium. I had access to a computer and disposable phones. The first thing I did was check email, and I had several from PJ.

I'd been working at a single desk computer for not even an hour when Pro appeared.

"D.G. will see you," he said.

I followed him down a winding, curving hallway. We passed the hospital ward section to one large open space. Corporate soldiers were stationed right at the entrance with large plasma rifles. We passed them by as we walked to the other side. Halfway down were more soldier sentries. I saw a bio-bed within a neon circle. Echo stood at the foot of the bio-bed with Judo and a few doctors.

D.G. lay there in a sleeveless white gown under a blanket. An array of I.V. lines connected bags of liquid, some colored, to her neck. Her cyborg arms were of a design I'd never seen before. They reminded me of muscled arms without skin, but the muscles were like wound copper fibers. Her hands were made of black material, with multijointed fingers. The Japanese ruled bionics, with America and China fighting for the distant number two spot. In Metropolis, ninety percent of the cyborgs had the bio-tech from Japanese megacorps. Everyone knew that the megacorps kept the best tech for their own cyborgs, and I was seeing it for myself.

"Are you feeling better?" I asked her.

"I have you to thank for that," she answered.

That green glow of her eyes was far dimmer. Her face looked gaunt; she looked tired and weak.

"My loaner weapon did all the work."

"My men told me you did considerable damage to our adversaries."

"I bought us time. You took care of Blur; Mr. Echo and the others took care of the rest."

"I wish I had dealt with Blur as you say. She is a far more advanced cyborg than I. I am the assassin. She is the assassin killer. They will have already rebuilt her."

"You are all unique cyborgs."

"Yes. Each of us is a unique model."

"My employee is a cyborg too. Both arms."

"Yes, we know that and that you were the cause."

I smiled. I couldn't forget they'd done full profiles on me and every person associated with me—just like Cybercrimes.

"What's the material?"

"Too technical. You wouldn't be able to pronounce it," D.G. replied. "Steel alloy skeletal structure, carbon steel fiber-weave musculature, micro-bionic implants. As I said, I am the property of the Hiero Corporation. I was their property."

"Is it a coincidence that you, Voodoo Child, and Blur are all female?"

"Perceptive of you."

"I noticed it because I've seen very few female corporate soldiers, but all the cyber-assassins are women. Not that I'm an expert."

"Our scientists find the creation and conditioning of assassins better suited for the female of the species."

"Cats make better assassins than dogs."

She grinned. "Something like that."

"I'm glad you're better."

"Please find my daughter, Mr. Cruz."

The glow in D.G.'s eyes seemed to switch off. A tear ran down one cheek. I wondered if her eyes were bionic too.

"I contacted my secret message exchange. I may have a lead," I said.

"Hackasaurus or Bubble Baha?" Echo asked.

"Neither. Someone new. PJ checked him out and I think I should meet him."

"You think it wise to meet him?" D.G. asked.

"No, but we don't have a choice."

"Judo will take you," Echo said.

My cases took me to the ritzy districts, the seedy ones, and everything in between. However, as a recovering germophobe, I refused to deal with filth—but it was never an issue because those that lived in those districts would never wander into my detective office. The street I found myself on was so filthy even the rain couldn't wash it all away. The ground had an oily residue that I didn't even want to guess what it might be. The scummiest of sidewalk johnnies hung around on street corners wearing slickers and clothes so dirty that the rain was the only washing they'd ever seen.

Different groups noticed me and their loud talking changed to hushed tones. Smoking cigarettes and drinking from bottles, the neon and lighting was scarce. I stuck out like a screaming police siren the way I dressed. They probably thought I was some booshy hood meandering onto their turf to hire a few of them to do some kind of unmentionable crimes.

I ignored them, but kept my hands in my pockets. I had nothing to worry about. My bodyguards were close, and they could hit a target with their throwing stars from any distance. I walked down the middle of the empty pedestrian street to avoid any of the johnnies.

I was to look for a neon eye and it was ahead. The small tower loomed, but it was only fifty or so stories. All the buildings in the district were not megatowers at all. I wondered if Metropolis even considered this area a district at all, more like a space between districts. I reached the neon symbol on the wall of the unlit building. I had my enhanced glasses on, so I could see in the dark fine. My eyes never left the different groups of congregated sidewalk johnnies. I didn't want to wait any longer than I had to. What I was doing was dangerous, but whoever my potential contact was had convinced PJ that it wasn't a trap, and he wasn't one of the cyber-assassins.

There was a light. It startled me. A door opened on the side of the wall and a figure came out. The man approaching me wore a hooded slick poncho. He held an umbrella over himself. He had on dark glasses and his face wasn't perfectly clear under his hood.

"I didn't think you'd come, Mr. Cruz," the man said.

"How did you convince my office manager?" I asked.

"Easy. We have mutual acquaintances. Six degrees of separation."

"Good thing for you. Why did you pick this place to meet?"

"Why do you think? Would you ever meet in a place like this? Even the roaches avoid this place. Besides, the people out there looking for the people you're working with wouldn't even know to search here."

"I wouldn't. What should I call you?"

"Shot Caller."

"Well, I'm here. Based on your conversation with my office manager, you know quite a bit about my recent activities. What do you want? You paid a big retainer too."

"I needed to talk to you privately."

"Why?"

"I need you to leave my business alone."

"Business?"

"The Market."

"Which one?"

"The only real one. The Ghost Market."

"Some would say the Shadow Market is the real one."

"The Ghost Market is endless. The other one is finite. My market is the real one and you're upsetting business."

"Why did you want to see me? You said you had important information for me."

"I want to make a trade."

"Trade what?"

"I give you information you need. You stay out of the Market."

"I don't know what you mean."

"Mr. Cruz, do you know what I do? The Ghost Market is an endless cyber-universe and is so vast that without people like me, the people who need it wouldn't be able to use it. I'm like a traffic controller at the intersection of a freeway with many lanes. I'm the person they trust. I safely direct the traffic of trade to where people want to go."

"Trade? You mean crime."

"Business. I connect buyers with sellers. You're bringing a lot of heat to the Market."

"Me? How am I doing that?"

"Metro Cybercrimes. The Council of Corporations. The Hiero-Macro Corporation. Dozens of megacorporations on Earth and Up-Top. Hundreds of gangs. All those users interested in your case. That's too much heat, even for us. That kind of attention hurts business, grinds things to a halt."

"I'm sorry to be complicating your criminal life."

"You do know The Digital Samurai is lying to you."

"I know that. But how do you know my business?" I asked.

"I know more about your business than you'll ever know."

"I need Hackasaurus."

"Never will find him. He knows you're looking for him."

"You met him?"

"I'm the Shot Caller. I've met every player in the virtual world."

"Virtual world of crime."

"No one cares about morality in my business. But I'm not here to debate you. I'm here to trade. I need you to be done with your case so the Market can go back to normal."

"I told you what I want."

"You do know that Hack is hiding from The Digital Samurai because she wants to kill him. Hack's worked for Digital Samurai and the Hiero Corporation for a long time. Whatever Digital Samurai told you is a lie."

"I need to contact this Hackasaurus or Hack to end my case."

"You shouldn't be so eager to find Hack because the second you do, Digital Samurai won't need you anymore."

"If he worked for The Digital Samurai, what happened?"

"Partners fall out all the time."

"I told you what I need. That's what I need, and we don't have a lot of time."

"You got that right. I can't help you with Hack. Maybe Bubble Baha can."

"How do you know B.B.?"

"I'm the Shot Caller. I make the Ghost Market possible."

"Then what do you have to trade if you can't get me to him? Sounds like I came to this filthy place for nothing."

"Not nothing. I'll give you another name instead."

"I've already met the cyber-assassins."

"Which one did they send?"

"Voodoo."

"Voodoo Child. There's many more. You kill one and there's five more to take their place. I'll give you a name but it'll cost you."

"I thought we were trading."

"Free? I'm not in the charity business. I'm in the business business. Besides, I'm a criminal. You said so."

"My clients will pay your fee."

"The Digital Samurai's society of samurai soldiers? They have money; you don't, so that's a deal I can do. I'll send the amount of my fee to your office manager. Make sure the society pays promptly. As of tomorrow, your main problem will no longer be Hiero-Macro."

"They're officially one company?"

"They finalized the merger yesterday when they confirmed your clients ran away from their masters. I heard about a big battle in Silver City. Heard you were there too."

"What this name you're trading?"

"Brain Shark. Forget about Hiero-Macro. He's the enemy. You have a head start. Don't blow it."

"I don't understand what you told me."

"You will, and remember I'm the one doing you a favor. Tomorrow, pay me my money and you, your clients, and everyone after you can stay away from the Market and let us get things back to normal. You have the name and plenty of friends well-versed in megacorp high finance to tell you what to do with it. I'd call them tonight. I helped you; you help me. If you want to panic a market, panic the Shadow Market. I don't care about those criminals. The Ghost Market is the only real game in town."

BRAIN SHARK, GANGSTER CORPORATE RAIDER

On the mean streets of Metropolis amoral people were like specks of sand on a vast beach. I didn't really mind them because they were so predictable. I was costing Shot Caller and his clients money, so he helped me. If he could have made more money not helping me, he would have. The Ghost Market was his cash machine and that was all he cared about. The problem was who the heck was Brain Shark.

The name sounded like another refugee of the VL world, but no one knew who he or she was. I'd given the task to PJ. She searched and she had others searching too but nothing so far. Shot Caller spoke of high-finance, so with my best friend, Run-Time still out of town on business, that meant another call to Mr. Mick.

I hated detours in a case, especially now, but had no choice. Shot Caller did send a bill for his fee. A ridiculous amount of money that was probably normal in his criminal world at his level. But he didn't seem worried about getting paid for his information. He knew who'd be paying it, and ex-Hiero samurai soldiers never paid for services from a stranger they couldn't verify. If they weren't legit, those samurai soldiers would come after you. That's why I felt Shot Caller was legit. He wanted the heat to go away, not to increase it. We had to find out who this Brain Shark was.

With so many people looking for us, I couldn't go anywhere near the Let It Ride corporate headquarters. Mr. Mick replied to the message I had PJ send him. He offered another place I'd never been to.

I felt I was trapped in a repeating time loop because, once again, I was doing an in-flight jump from one hovercraft to another—our hoverplane to another—wearing an oxygen mask. We were miles above the surface in dark clouds. Mr. Mick's corporate soldiers grabbed me when I jumped and the cargo hatch closed. My bodyguards would fly in tandem with us for my meeting.

Security led me from the rear of the hoverplane to the center area where Mr. Mick waited in an office. He sat in a plush chair and I sat in the one across from him.

"That's a Hiero Corporation jet," he said.

"You know megacorp aircraft by sight?"

"I do. What do you need help with this time, Mr. Cruz?"

"Are the Hiero and Macro Corporations officially merged?"

"Merged? No. Hiero acquired Macro."

"But Hiero owns fifty-one percent of the company."

"Who told you that?"

Mr. Mick took out a palm tablet from his jacket and began typing.

"An informant. He also referred to the companies as one. Hiero-Macro. My informant also talked about someone named Brain Shark."

"Sounds like a hacker."

"It does. So you've never heard of him?"

"No. The record shows a fifty-fifty distribution."

"I was at the megacorp myself, Mr. Mick. I saw the financial records."

"You saw the public records, not the private ones. I wouldn't believe what your informant said. Companies at this level would only do a fifty-fifty split. Otherwise, one company would be superior to the other. Neither one of these companies would agree to an inferior standing."

"Even so, my informant told me to contact friends well-versed in the world of megacorp high finance."

"I'm glad I'm a friend. Why? Why not give you the information directly without the riddles?"

"I don't know, but can you look into it? Both companies or the new company, and Brain Shark. I wouldn't know what to look for."

"I'll contact you."

"Thanks."

"How are your new megacorp clients?"

"Keeping me busy."

"Anything exciting occur?"

"All boring stuff."

"Boring. If that's so, I don't need to give you what I was going to give you."

"What were you going to give me?"

"Another weapon."

"Weapon?" I'm sure my face looked exactly like Cruz Jr.'s when being offered sweets or new toys.

"But all you're doing is boring office work."

"Yeah, but why don't you give me the weapon anyway. Just in case I'm in a big gunfight with corporate and samurai soldiers, and attacking hovercraft and planes, and cyber-assassins."

"Just in case, right?" Mr. Mick said. "Not like that scenario could ever happen."

"Better safe than sorry."

I returned to my fugitive Hiero hoverplane the same way I got there. Jumping from one moving plane to another, high above the ground; I was beginning to enjoy it. If Cruz Jr. could only see me now. As long as he didn't tell his mother.

We returned to our tower hideout in Mad City. Back in my same modest office, I logged on to check messages—nothing from PJ. For a few moments I stared at a blank screen. There was nothing more for me to do, other than wait for my contacts. The detective business was often one of highs and lows, hurry up and slow down. I had to wait and rely on others because I couldn't do the footwork myself. However, I had to keep myself busy. I stood from my chair, forwarded the feed to one of the disposable mobile phones, and put it in my pocket.

When I stepped out the door, Pro was there, standing guard on the opposite side of the wall.

"Mr. Pro, does this building have a shooting range?" I asked.

"You want to play golf?"

I chuckled. "Shooting range. As in guns."

"Oh."

"I'm waiting for my contacts, so I can take a nap or I can do something more constructive. I'm not a samurai soldier like you. I'm only a mere mortal."

"You saved D.G."

"Maybe, but I'd rather practice on some targets with my new weapons. If I see that Voodoo woman with another doll of me, or what did Mr. Echo call it, a mech-clone? Two shots. One for the doll. One for her. I won't have to worry about Blur. I know D.G. wants her rematch. We need to practice, practice, practice for the future battle. Doubtful the police will save us the trouble and pick them up for reckless driving anytime soon."

"We have a virtual shooting range on the floor below."

"I wonder if I were to challenge you, who could shoot a hundred targets first," I said.

Pro smiled wide, showing his gold teeth.

The firing range was the entire floor of the level below us. My weapons were modified for target shooting and we all had our special holo-augmented glasses. We were ready. We moved through the virtual back alley mean streets of Metropolis, congested with people and hovercars above. With open building windows and rooftops, plenty of spots to be attacked from.

Somehow word had spread that Pro and I would be having a holo-shooting match. Behind us was an observation area behind a glass wall. Everyone was crowded in there: Echo, Judo, lots of men.

"Begin!" the overhead speaker sounded.

Our surroundings were so lifelike. Pro walked down the left of the street; I was on the right. The simulation launched every kind of bad guy at us it could. Hovercar gunmen shooting laser rifles, corporate soldiers attacking us from the crowd, with laser swords or guns. Gunmen from windows, the rooftops, and behind us. It was all like a holo-video game to me. In fact, that's how I learned to shoot better than most policemen.

Pro was an excellent shot too. We were virtually even after fifteen minutes. I didn't like to lose. Instead of walking through the streets, I bolted forward. I needed to speed up my encounters with virtual corporate soldier attackers. Pro realized my strategy and ran too. My shot count pulled ahead.

The phone in my pocket began vibrating. Under no circumstances was anything going to stop me from getting to one hundred shots first.

I had to get crazy. We each had one gun, but I pulled my second gun. Shooting with two guns was stupid. Such things were seen in movies but professionals never did such a thing. Unless you had two heads, two guns split your focus and your effectiveness. Unless you got crazy, which I did, and I really pulled away.

Pro panicked and did the same thing but missed a few shots. Then he got shot. So the computers deducted some points from his shot count. I was using people as human shields, which I'd never really do, ran into stores for cover, sprinted ahead to draw out my attackers. 85. 90. 95. I saw a parked hovercar on the ground. I knew the computer put it there for me to run to it for cover. I did no such thing. I didn't even wait for them to jump out. I fired at the hovercar nonstop. The corporate soldier attackers jumped out but were cut down before they could shoot me. 100! Pro had 87.

I looked at him, grinning.

All the people, vehicles, and landscape disappeared. I shook Pro's hand.

"If I were competing against an average man, I'd be at 100 and they'd only have 20. I've never beaten someone so poorly in a shooting game than against you."

Pro laughed.

"Oh, my phone." I reached into my pocket.

The message was from The Mick. I was elated. I bent down and laid my weapon on the floor and messaged him back. The phone rang again.

I answered it immediately. There was no image on the mini-screen. I put the mobile to my ear.

"Mr. Cruz."

"Mr. Mick."

"Something major is happening."

"What's happening?"

"A new megacorp has purchased all the outstanding shares of Hiero-Macro."

"Mr. Mick, you know I don't know anything about stock market stuff. I'm a street detective, not a broker."

"It's the only story on the business newsfeed. It's a hostile takeover of both companies by a megacorp no one has ever heard of."

"What's the name—?"

"The CAD Corporation."

"Why is this important?"

"The CEO and chairman is a man named Brian Shrak."

"Oh my—Brain Shark!"

"You did crossword puzzle games as a kid too."

It wasn't just Pro watching me closely as I spoke on the phone. The entire group from the observation room had joined us. Echo's face was especially concerned. They could hear Mr. Mick's voice.

"What does this mean?" I asked him.

"This new CAD Corporation will run the new Hiero-Macro if they can't be outbid. This is normal for smaller companies, but never happens with megacorporations, especially ones like these."

"Mr. Mick, you know I don't speak foreign languages. That's what high-finance talk is to me. I know it's bad but I don't understand what this means. He didn't give me the real name because if he had we would have made inquiries and tipped him off."

"Who are you talking about?" Mr. Mick asked me.

"The guy who gave us the name Brain Shark. But what does it mean?"

"It means that Hiero-Macro doesn't have the financial means to fend off the hostile takeover," Echo said aloud.

I looked at him.

"He's right," The Mick said in my ear.

"No money," I said.

"Yes," The Mick said.

"Isn't this company a multi-trillion-dollar megacorp?" I asked. "How can they have no money?" My eyes stayed on Echo. "What do you know?" I asked Echo.

He didn't answer me.

"Who is this Brian Shrak?" I asked Mr. Mick on the phone.

"Everyone is trying to find out to confirm, but the rumor is that he's a crime boss."

"A gangster?" I asked. "A gangster is about to control a multi-trillion-dollar company."

"No!" Echo yelled.

A torrent of Japanese erupted among Echo and all the men. One of them ran out of the room through the door. I knew he was going to inform D.G.

"This cannot happen!" Echo yelled. "We must go there."

I stepped away from their yelling. "Mr. Mick, what is going to happen here? When this CAD Corporation comes in to claim Hiero and Macro."

"Mr. Cruz, there is no way that those companies will allow a second-rate crime boss to take them over. Legally, if they can't counteroffer, there's nothing they can do. But they won't care about legality and laws. There's going to be a bloody war over this. He's already called in the Council of Corporations to make sure Hiero-Macro complies."

"The Council will protect the CAD Corporation?"

"Yes, but Hiero-Macro won't comply. If Hiero-Macro goes to war with the Council, the Council will obliterate Hiero-Macro from existence."

"No!" Echo yelled.

The samurai master was always cool and reserved. But he'd turned into a raving madman. All the men were frantic and screaming. The door opened and two doctors pushed D.G. in her hover-bio-bed into the room. Everyone informed her of what was happening in Japanese. On her face too I saw the panic and anger. Their plan, whatever it was, was unraveling.

"We must go there in force and attack!" she yelled.

"Mr. Mick, I gotta go," I said. "Thanks for calling."

"Simply make sure you return the weapons we lent you, Mr. Cruz."

I disconnected and ran to the crowd.

"You will do no such thing!" I yelled at them.

Everyone turned and looked at me. D.G. watched me from her bio-bed.

"If you storm the Hiero Corporation building, or Macro, whichever, we'll all be wiped out. Blur is out there, and the Voodoo woman, and the combined corporate soldier armies of both megacorps. It would be suicide."

"We cannot allow this CAD Corporation to gain control of Hiero," Echo yelled.

"And they won't," I said.

"What is your plan?" Echo asked.

"I will go. Send a few men with me. Maybe six. But not you or Judo or Pro. Send me your most junior men."

"I have to go!" D.G. yelled.

"You have to go nowhere," I interrupted D.G. "You are where you're supposed to be. In bed, resting and recovering, with your doctors looking over you. Give me six men. They need to look young and deceptively harmless."

"Seven men?" Echo asked. "Against an army?"

"Mr. Echo, they will be waiting for your army to attack. On the lookout for you and all your senior men. None of them care about me, and they probably don't know your junior men."

"They know all of us," D.G. said to me.

"Maybe, but only six of them. They'll be confused. 'Where's the rest of them?' they'll ask. 'Where's Digital Samurai? She must be outside somewhere hiding. We haven't found her. Leave those seven inferior men and go find D.G. and her senior fighters.'"

"Who's speaking of a suicide mission now?" D.G. asked me.

"This is how it's going to be. Pick your men and I'll lead the mission."

"I thought you were only a street detective," Judo said.

"Yes, but today I'm leading the mission."

"Why are you doing this?" D.G. asked.

"It's the only move they won't expect," I replied.

"It will not work, your plan," Echo said.

"It will. Pick your men and make sure one of them knows how to pilot a hoverplane, because I don't."

Like all Metropolitans, I had a love-hate relation with the supercity. We all complained, but it was home and we'd never live anywhere else. When I become a bona fide private detective, it was perfect. I'd work the biggest supercity on the planet and would always have more work than I could handle. With a new wife and, now, Cruz. Jr., it was perfect. Never did I have to go anywhere. I'd work local cases and be home at the end of the work day. Twice I did leave Metropolis on cases, but that was the exception. I didn't like to be away from home for extended periods, even with being paid. This case was turning out to be the longest I'd ever been away. Hopefully, I was closer to wrapping it with Mr. Mick's call and information.

Echo assigned the six men I requested. I'd already met them. They were the same junior corporate soldiers who drove our hovercycles when we visited the Macro Corporation headquarters. We raced out of Mad City on three anonymous larger hovercycles.

My plan was solid, but only if we didn't deviate from it. There were only seven of us, so we had to make sure none of us encountered any of Hiero's or Macro's people. The responsibility was on me alone to make sure we accomplished the task for all of us to return alive and well.

But we had to make one pit stop for some quick clothes shopping.

Even from the sky lanes, we could see them above the cluster of megatowers that included the Hiero building—galaxy-class hovercruisers hung above them all. I couldn't tell exactly how many there were, maybe three, but the craft were in a tight pattern.

When parked a couple of miles away in a swanky public bay, we didn't look like ourselves. I replaced my standard attire of tan fedora and slicker with a standard dark slicker like most Metropolis pedestrians wore. I had my six new friends ditch their corporate suits for standard attire too. We blended into the street crowds heading to Hiero on foot. The view of the hovercraft was more clear; Hiero had *seven* super-cruisers hovering above them. Their design didn't give me any clues as to who each one belonged to—Hiero, Macro, the Council of Corporations, or the new player, CAD.

From the streets, one couldn't pick out the Hiero Corporation headquarters building from any other. We were like ants looking up from the base of a mountain. In Silicon Dunes and every other super wealthy district, signage was meant for upper-class people arriving via hover-transport, not riffraff from the ground. We entered the ground lobby and it was as Echo told me—a combination receiving dock and two-person security reception desk. The space was more of an afterthought. Here security would be nonexistent. That would change once we wanted to take the elevators to the main floors. My new six buddies quietly followed behind me.

"Hello, sir," I greeted.

The two guards at the counter, typing on touch screens in terminals, wore standard Japanese-style suits. Neither one looked up when we entered, which meant they were watching us on their terminal screens rather than simply look at us directly.

"Delivery or media?" he asked.

Standard question offering two incorrect answers. Answer either one and they'd tell you to go away.

"We're here to see Council of Corporations representative, Mr. Caveat," I answered.

I poured glass after glass of Japanese whiskey at the bar. I had a new uniform and so did my buddies—that of waitstaff. While we were waiting for the Council hoverlimo, I could tell they were scared—seven of us against armies of corporate soldiers. The only emotion I wanted beaming from every pore of my person was confidence. They'd feed off that reassurance.

We were in the Hiero tower's main ballroom dressed as servers. We were here courtesy of the Council of Corporations. I'd called Mr. Caveat before we arrived.

"Why should I let you insert yourself into this matter?" he asked me.

"We both know there's going to be an all-out corporate war if CAD takes over Hiero-Macro. Maybe I can make it all go away with words. But if you prefer to be in between the shooting match, go for it."

"I don't trust you, Mr. Cruz."

"I don't trust you, but I won't be armed so what do you have to lose."

I gave him my plan. He agreed. We'd play at being servers, waiting for the CAD CEO, Mr. Shrak.

The Hiero Galaxy Lounge Room took up half the level. The elevated ceiling was ten stories up, painted black with simulated stars flickering. Security was out in force, lining the edges of the room. A crowd of corporate dignitaries and staff chatted away, while an army of waitstaff, including my six new buddies, served appetizers and drinks.

All was going well until I spotted Mr. Able staring at me from within the crowd. I was one of five dozen or so other bartenders. I was no bartender, but all I had to do was pour and stack glasses on trays. No skill involved. I didn't see his boss, Mr. Glyph, but Able slowly walked to me. He stopped at the counter and placed his open palms on it.

"Before you shoot me or do something stupid, I'm here as a guest of the Council of Corporations. Go ask Mr. Caveat if you don't believe me," I said, continuing to do my work.

"Do you normally work events as a bartender for them?"

"I got bills to pay and mouths to feed. I'm not picky."

"Where is your client?"

"Mr. Caveat?"

"The Digital Samurai."

"We parted company."

"Where is she?"

"I don't know, Mr. Able. I'm not working for her anymore. But since we're chatting, what insider information can you share about this CAD Corporation?"

Able gave me a dismissive look and walked off. He signaled one of the security men, spoke to him, and the guard ran off for the main entrance. Able moved into the crowd. My eyes stayed on him and now I saw Mr. Glyph, who stared at me. My time was running out.

There was a commotion at the main entrances. Everyone in the room stopped what they were doing and watched the doors open and another contingent of people come in. Two men led them in. Mr. Caveat was one; the other man I'd never seen before. The contrast between him and everyone else was dramatic. He had a cigar in his mouth, overly slicked-back hair, a suit that looked like it could do with a bit of tailoring. Another group approached them, led by Mr. Ming.

A big smile came across the new man's face. He extended a hand but Ming didn't respond.

"Mr. Ming," he said with a chuckle. "When CAD owns your companies I swear, I'll keep you on. Shrak always keeps his promises."

Ming turned his attention to Mr. Caveat. "The Hiero Corporation will not stand by for this."

"Mr. Ming, as I've already said, does Hiero-Macro wish to make a higher bid to regain its shares?" Caveat asked. "The rules are the same for everyone. The Council of Corporations will not interfere in normal transactions in the market."

"How did this crook acquire such resources?" Ming yelled.

"Guess I'm better at saving than Hiero-Macro is," Shrak said. "You want control of your company back. Pay me!"

"Drinks, sir?" I asked, holding a tray of beer.

From Ming's expression, it was like I'd spat in his face. Corporate soldiers began gathering behind him, all glaring at me. Mr. Glyph and Able strolled over too with their own group of corporate soldiers. I glanced back and my six buddies had my back, each holding trays of food or drinks.

"Mr. Cruz, what are you doing?" Caveat asked.

"Ming, your boy doesn't seem to know his manners." Shrak puffed on his cigar. "Who are you?"

I said nothing but handed a white card to Mr. Caveat.

Caveat read it. He looked at Ming, then Glyph.

"Gentlemen, excuse me for a moment," Caveat said as he turned to Shrak. "I need to take a call in the corridor."

Caveat left us, and took three-quarters of the corporate soldiers in the room with him.

Shrak tried to put on a brave face, but his Council security had just vanished with the snap of a finger because of me. Ming and Shrak were in a staring match.

"You try anything, Ming, and I'll do more than fire you when we take ownership."

"Sir, may I ask you a question?" I asked.

"Who are you anyway?"

"I'm a private detective. The name's Cruz."

"Never heard of you."

"I'm the guy who brought down one of your colleagues."

"Who would that be?"

"Monkey Baker and the Animal Farm Crime Syndicate."

"You're that guy."

"That's me. Mr. Ming asked an important question that you ignored. How did a crook like you acquire the resources to buy a multi-trillion-dollar megacorps like Hiero-Macro?"

Shrak had seen it too. Ming moved to my side with all his corporate soldiers. They were all focused on him now.

"It doesn't matter how. What matters is the money."

"Why do you call yourself Brain Shark?" I asked.

Shrak's eyes darted around.

"It's very important that you answer my question," I said.

"Are you a cyber-cop?"

"Do Mr. Ming and Mr. Glyph need to involve the police?" I asked.

Glyph stood next to Ming and both men watched Shrak closely. Able directed Macro's men to surround Shrak from the rear.

Shrak was sweating. "I'm not answering anything. Where did the Council go? What did you say to them? I'm leaving."

"That would be a smart thing to do, Mr. Brain Shark," I said.

"Stop calling me that!"

"Why? It's your street name, or your cyberpunk name."

"What are you talking about? I'm not a cyberpunk, I'm a..."

"You're a what?"

Shrak said nothing.

I turned to Ming and Glyph. "Mr. Shrak is known as Brain Shark in the dark Net. He calls himself Brain Shark because he's a hacker who specialized in draining all the information from a megacorps mainframe, then extorting the company for their own data."

"That's a lie!"

"The note I gave Mr. Caveat was to tell him that the word on the street was he also wants to acquire Hiero-Macro, not only to consolidate power among all the criminal gangs. His scheme is bolder. He wants to use Hiero-Macro to burrow into the Council's secret data centers to blackmail them and all their members."

"That's a lie!"

Shrak rushed me, but my buddies jumped to my defense and kicked the man, dropping him to the floor. He lifted himself to his feet with a bloodied lip.

"I'm going to get you, Cruz," he sneered.

"Are you?" I asked. "I think you have much more serious problems than me because the Council is going to want to know exactly where your money came from. Exactly. Otherwise, you won't be acquiring Hiero-Macro or any other megacorp."

I set my tray on the floor. My buddies did the same.

"Gentlemen, we're going to leave you all here to converse privately with Mr. Brain Shark."

"Stop calling me that!"

"Oh, Mr. Able, after your conversation, please send out the press release to the media that the CAD Corporation has withdrawn its bid, I believe that's the fancy financial term, to take over Hiero-Macro. Have a good day, everyone," I said.

I led my team out of that room and the building without looking back once. Brian Shrak of the CAD Corporation, Brain Shark, was on his own.

Before we reached the main entrance, I heard Ming say, "Tell us or I will have your fingers cut off."

Yep, it was time to go.

HACKASAURUS, CYBER-EXTORTIONIST

In the detective business the unexpected was to be expected at all times. Shot Caller gave me the name and I took it from there. But the wild card, Brain Shark, had only taken us off track temporarily. He was that random element that popped up, but wasn't part the real story. I'd brought us back and bought us some time. We hightailed it out of the Hiero headquarters as fast as our legs could move. Above the megatower all the hovercruisers were gone, which meant all of them had belonged to the Council—a show of force to keep the corporate peace. My six buddies were all laughs and good cheer. They saw me work and we got out of the building alive, but we weren't out of danger yet.

"Is there somewhere else we can go?" I asked. "We have to assume we're being followed."

They all agreed. I ran to a hovertaxi station and called one. One descended from the hovertraffic and we piled in.

"Address?" the driver asked.

"Two miles down. A parking building, but we want you to drop us off on the roof."

"I can do that."

"I'm sorry. I'll rephrase. When you get there we'll jump out of your cab."

"Jump?" he said.

In this case I was jumping from hoverlimos, jumping between hoverplanes, and jumping from hovertaxis. My buddies were corporate soldiers, but I'd never done so much combat jumping in my life. We reached our parking building and all he did was slow down. Out the passenger door we went. They jumped and landed on their feet. I landed and, ungracefully, fell over, but I hopped back up. We got to the stairs and descended to our level as fast as we could. Moments later, we blasted out of there on our three hovercycles.

I told them it was a race. We had to be at our secure location before the Hiero-Macro press release went out.

We hadn't gone far when they suddenly exited traffic and headed to a Jamaican takeout place. There was covered parking next door and we parked but we didn't go inside. We got in the elevator and instead of going up, it went down, even though there was no indication there were any lower levels. When the doors opened the design was identical to our Free City hideout. Corporate soldiers, on guard, filled the hallway. My buddies ran to one of them and there was that rapid-fire Japanese.

"Is there a business office set-up here too?" I asked.

One of the men gestured to me and I followed him down the hall. He took me to a room that was similar to the one at the other place with a desk computer and multiple disposable phones. Quickly, I logged on to check my email service, then connected my notification to a new phone. I was taking every precaution possible. People knew that mobile phones could be hacked, but most people didn't know that auto-notifications made one more vulnerable to hacking. Blur, Voodoo Child, and many others were still searching for us and I wasn't about to be the weakest link. Next I went to the business newsfeed. At that point, all I could do was wait.

Suddenly a message notification popped up on my email. Cruz Jr. had left me a message. Funny. Cruz Jr. was a smart little child, but I didn't think even he had mastered how to leave a message himself. Who called me?

The message was a phone number. But it had a strange prefix and letters at the end. I hadn't seen numbers configured like that before, so I researched it. It was some kind of hacker-cyberpunk secure forwarding number. I'd call and be transferred to another. Even using a disposable phone didn't reassure me because these super hacker types had all kinds of cyber-tricks up their sleeves. To be safe, I completely shut down the computer and took out the power cards from all the other disposable phones. Then I called the number.

My eyes saw it immediately. The vid-cam indicator light on the computer turned on.

"Mr. Cruz."

"Hi, Cruz Jr. What do you have to tell your daddy?"

There was laughing on the other end.

"Who do you think it is?" he asked.

"I'm not going to guess. I'll let you tell me."

"I hate the name Hackasaurus. Sounds like a kid's name. I'm trying to get people to call me The Hack, but it's not sticking."

"People don't like change."

"Tell me about it."

"I heard you're in hiding but I don't know why."

"First, what did they say about me?"

"Who's they?"

"Everyone knows you're working for The Digital Samurai."

"How would anyone know that?"

"Everyone knows."

"I thought Digital Samurai's existence was a secret."

"A secret to who? You're on the inside, Cruz. Everyone knows her."

"Maybe I can get some answers from you. What's this all about?"

"What did they say about me?"

"She said you're an evil kidnapper."

"That's a good one."

"Who did I kidnap?"

"Her daughter."

"Strange to kidnap what doesn't exist. You do know she's lying."

"Of course. That's why I asked what's this is about. They seemed very upset about this Brain Shark character."

"Hoods shouldn't try to be hackers. It gives us all a bad name. He used cyber-tech to bludgeon his way through. No real skill at all in his hacks. He won't be around long. I heard you turned the tables on him."

"How did you hear that?"

"My sources are everywhere, Cruz. That's what makes hackers like me so good. We always know what's going on everywhere at all times. Know the people. Know what they need."

"What did Digital Samurai need?"

"She wanted her freedom from the corporation that created her and needed the money to do it."

"How much did she need to buy her freedom?"

"Assassins like her are never free. They remain as property of their company for life. Born and bred for the life. Death is the only escape."

"The money then."

"Her plan was to blackmail them for her freedom. She stole their money."

"How much?"

"You don't get it. She stole *all* their money."

"You're that good that you could hack into their bank."

"Companies like Hiero store their illegal assets in shadow wealth."

"Digital money? That's crazy."

"Aren't credit cards digital money?"

"No."

"Yes."

"No."

"Digital money is as real as real money."

"Storing money on the Net so it can be stolen by people like you."

"Lots of people and companies, not only criminals, prefer their assets in shadow wealth to be beyond the prying eyes of the government or the Council of Corporations."

"You stole all of it."

"Yes. She was able to get me the codes. I did the rest."

"I understand now. Hiero-Macro couldn't stop Brain Shark's takeover of their company because you stole all their money."

"But you got Brain Shark to go away."

"How did he find out about Hiero-Macro's money troubles?"

"I'm not the only one with sources everywhere."

"I made Brian Shark go away and you lost a big payday, so you're trying to get back in her good graces through me."

"Cruz, that's a very unkind thing to say. My feelings are hurt."

"I'm surprised you didn't steal the money yourself."

"If I did something like that, I'd be dead in a day. No one steals a megacorps' money. No one. Not even her. I told her that. I couldn't get away either if I stole it from her. I only want a fair fee for my work. Brain Shark made a better offer but since he's out of the picture, I'll go back to her."

"So there it is. The double-cross. I'm starting to wonder if the things about you are true."

"I deal in data only. There's endless fields of data for me to harvest. When you trade in physical things, that's when the danger quotient skyrockets. I'll leave that to others."

"She said she was hunting you because you kidnapped her child, which I never believed. You tell me you two were partners in stealing all of the Hiero Corporation's money from the start."

"To return to them when they promised to let her retire from the life."

"But you double-crossed her to a bigger fee from someone else."

"I'll deal only with you. Tell her I'll return control of the Hiero's shadow money for a fee, but it has to be what Brain Shark was going to pay me. Double the original amount. She agrees to those terms, we have a deal."

"If not?"

"There are lots of people like Brain Shark out there, Cruz, who'd kill to get their hands on Hiero's total shadow wealth. You have the honor of negotiating with her on my behalf. You even have my number."

"Double-crossing a cyber-assassin doesn't seem to be a wise move at all."

"I hear she has bigger sharks to worry about than me."

"I thought you were hiding from her."

"Hiding? I didn't want to return her calls anymore. Cruz, she'll never get her freedom. She's a dead woman and I think you know that too. Assassins are never allowed to walk away from their company, never. All the bio-modification, bionics, training the company put into her from birth. A billion-dollar woman. And the term is cyborg assassin; that's what she is. The cyber-assassin thing is more myth than reality. Long time ago cyberpunks were into the fiction of downloading a human consciousness into a computer or onto the Net. There's only one person I know of who was able to kill people through the Net. You killed him."

"The Ripper."

"That's when you came to my attention."

"I'm glad you're a fan."

"I'm not. I'm all about the money."

"Like everyone else."

"Just like you, Detective. After you talk to her, get back to me. But don't wait too long. Offers are finding their way to me and I may see one that I like. In fact, I'm talking with a new prospect tomorrow."

"Why don't you give us some time?"

"Why should I?"

"Why? Because they had a deal with you and you're the one who double-crossed them. Give them a day or two."

"Cruz, you do know these are killers you're dealing with. I did to them what they probably planned to do to me. Get back to me when you talk to her and have the new offer. In the meantime, I'll conduct my business life as normal. Nothing personal. That's the life."

The line went dead.

Hackasaurus was a bum. D.G. and Echo probably planned their escape for years, maybe decades, and one greedy hacker ruined the plan. Whether the deal went through now without any more problems, he was dead. Double-crossing assassins and samurai masters didn't make for a long life. My hope in the case was to see it to the end with the least amount of casualties. I knew that was almost impossible now. Lots of people were going to die in this case before it was over. Hiero-Macro was after D.G. She was after Hackasaurus. And with the total illegal digital storehouse of wealth from this new megacorp for sale, potentially every megacorp, government, and criminal from Earth to Up-Top would be after all of us if they found out. When we left the Hiero headquarters building, I felt sorry for Brain Shark; now I envied him. I wanted to go away too.

BRAIN SHARK, CRAZY MANIAC WITH A GRUDGE

I wanted to get back to our Mad City hideout. I wanted to hear the truth from D.G. and nothing but. Silence was all I heard beyond the door—too quiet. At first, it wasn't anything I could pinpoint, but I felt something was off. I waved my hand in front of the panel and the lights went off, but it was one of those rooms with a strip of dim neon molding lining the wall, near the ceiling. I wanted it completely dark inside the room but it would have to do. The normal hall light was on outside on the other side of the door. I moved my body to the side of the door.

"Hey, Pro, I have news for D.G.," I called out and turned the doorknob.

A laser blasted through the door. I would have been cut down and dead if I weren't on the side. Some thug kicked the door in, and that was the last thing he'd ever do in his life. I shot him dead in the head; his laser machine-gun dropped to the floor and so did he.

I heard running toward the room. I threw his gun out to distract whoever else might be in the hallway. Immediately, there was a blizzard of gunfire at the weapon, then it all ripped through the open door.

Another thug tried to sprint across the open doorway to the other side. I shot him dead mid-stride, and he dropped to the floor too. I heard cursing in hushed tones.

"Hi ya, Cruz!"

The voice was Brain Shark's!

"That was some bind you put me in. Nice job. I'm glad I have a chance to return the favor. If I can't have Hiero-Macro, the least I can do is kill the guy who prevented me. What do you think of that?"

The entire front wall exploded into the room. Several gunmen rushed in and began firing. The cloud of dust made it too thick to see, even with enhanced glasses, so they shot everywhere in the room I could be. They didn't stop firing. It went on for a seeming eternity as the dust started to settle.

"Do you see him?" Brain Shark's voice echoed from the hallway.

"No, boss. Too much dust."

"Turn on the light!"

"The wall is gone, boss. There's nothing to turn on."

The men used their hands to try to wave all the dust away.

"What do you see?" Shark asked.

"Nothing, boss."

Brain Shark wasn't going to come into view. I hovered above them all in the shadows. You couldn't fly with a hoverbelt, but it could keep you floating. They were mostly used by construction crews doing work on megatowers.

I fired once. The explosive round blew all the men into the hallway. I jumped down and fired again around the corner in the direction I heard Shark's voice.

"Go!" I heard him yell.

Another explosion.

It was my turn to sprint. As the dust cloud blocked the view, I ran down the hallway in the opposite direction. Where was everyone? I didn't get the full tour by my new buddies, but I couldn't imagine there wasn't serious corporate soldier security in this hideout too. But where were they? How did Brain Shark and his people get in?

When I turned the corner, there were elevators and stairs. My decision had to be quick. However, I never had the chance. Something hit me in the head, dropping me to the ground.

"Hi ya, Cruz."

My eyes were closed but the fact that his voice was close, calm, and conceited meant my situation was bad. The fact that my arms were tied behind my back and I was on the floor meant it was really bad.

I opened my eyes to see I was among dozens of men—all bound like me. My six buddies were among them. Most of them were young—barely into their twenties, a few older ones like me. Corporate soldiers, but tied up and sitting on the ground flanked by Brain Shark's gunmen, as many of them as us. The man himself stood near me, gloating. We were in an open space—an empty conference or storage room.

The question remained: how did he and his men get in and take D.G. soldiers by complete surprise?

"You didn't think you'd see me alive, did you?" he said.

"Why am I alive?" I said, almost annoyed at him.

He didn't know what to make of my attitude.

"You're alive because I need you to undo what you did. That money is mine, and you're going to see to it that it's mine again."

"How am I going to do that?"

"You're going to call the Hack and make it happen."

"Who's the Hack?"

"Cruz, I have no time for it. We both know who the Hack is. You were speaking to him on the phone. He told me you two talked. When I was on my way."

"He told you?"

"Yeah, he did. So, are you going to do what I say or do I need to give you an incentive?"

"No, you don't need to do that."

I knew he wanted to start shooting captives.

"I knew you'd see it my way," he said with a big grin.

"You are a brain after all."

"If I wasn't, I'd just be Shark, not Brain Shark. Whether in the real world or the virtual one, I go after what I want until I get it. Never stop and no one stops me. Mega-top snobs think they're better than the crime world. They're no better. Definitely no smarter. If I can come out of nowhere and take all their wealth from them, centuries' worth, how powerful can they really be?"

"Untie me and give the phone," I said. "It's a good thing I memorized his number before your men blew up the room."

"Sure, Cruz."

He signaled to his men.

"I don't have to tell you that if you try something, my men will laser every last men in the room dead."

"Obviously, you don't have to tell me because you just did."

"Cruz, I have to say this is a nice piece you got," he said with a bigger grin, holding my omega-gun in his hand. "Very nice beauty here. How did you get an Up-Top gun? You couldn't afford it if you worked every second of every day your entire life. Low-end street detective like you, without your gun you're as helpless as a kitten. Low-end street detectives should learn a thing a two from your soldiers-in-suit comrades and learn to kill people without a gun. Isn't that right? We had to tie you all up extra tight."

"Well, Mr. Shark, as you say, I'm a street detective not some kind of martial arts ninja commando. I'll stick to my guns and leave the throwing stars to them."

One of his men untied me and lifted me off the ground.

"Give the man a phone," Brain Shark directed him.

One of his thugs lowered his gun in one hand as he extended another to give me a phone.

"Thanks."

Brain Shark never knew what hit him. I threw my shuriken so fast, so hard; it embedded itself in his forehead like a dart into a dartboard. The thug giving me the phone was the lucky recipient of my second shuriken. It hit him in the neck. As he fell, I grabbed his gun and then the fireworks began.

I rapid-fired Brain Shark's men as I ran to Brain Shark's body. Then I had my omega-gun back! I shot bullets, lasers, explosive rounds. I ran to my six buddies—they quickly turned their backs to me—and I blasted their hand restraints off. That's all I had to do. They did the rest—grabbing weapons, freeing their men, firing at Brain Shark's men.

I'd hidden my shurikens in secret compartments in my clothes. I don't know where they hid theirs, but soon bullets, lasers, and throwing stars were flying.

The battle didn't take long. The Shark was dead and so were all his men.

"How did they get in?" I yelled at one of my buddies.

I could see the distress in his face at my question.

"We don't know."

"We have to leave now!"

"But it's not safe."

"Now!" I said. "The hideout is compromised. We have to go now."

That's what we did. We abandoned our Silicon Dunes-adjacent hideout near the Jamaican Japanese takeout for Mad City. Who knows how many were following us and lurking in the shadows? But there was no other choice. We survived a very, very close call.

TRUTH

Hackasaurus had told me that my clients were killers. I knew that already and had never forgotten it. Corporate soldiers of any kind were not and would never be pacifist monks. There was no telling how many—even my baby-faced buddies—had killed. The dark world of the megacorps required security far more deadly than all the mean streets of Metropolis. I was about to see a bit of that brutality for myself in person.

Anything that couldn't be carried, like furniture, was ripped up and thrown into piles and set ablaze. While one group of ex-Hiero soldiers dragged all the bodies of Brain Shark and his men into a corner of the wide open room, more entered, each carrying machetes.

"Oh my God," I said, noticing a man pushing a dumpster. "This is the part where I leave the room."

I immediately marched out of the room, followed by four of my buddies.

"Please close that door," I said to them.

I heard chopping and decided I wanted to move away further.

"Are we leaving on hovercycles?" I asked.

"We will use hovertrucks. We leave when they arrive. If we are attacked, we will have better defenses."

I pointed up. "The roof?"

"Yes."

"I'll wait there."

The hallway was busy with corporate soldiers scrambling in every direction. I saw brooms, mops, men with spraying devices. When all was done, there would be no trace that any of us had ever been in the building.

I'd thought I'd escaped from anything that could shock my sensitive sensibilities, even though I was plenty capable of shocking behavior to save myself from a crazy maniac. We exited onto the penthouse floor from the elevator and walked right into a full-blown Japanese yelling-fest in the hallway. Three men were surrounded by other corporate soldiers. One of the three men saw me and yelled even louder as he pointed at me. Someone in the crowd smacked me on the top of the head. Blood spilled out. The three men attempted to reach for weapons, and swords came out of the crowd and sliced the men apart before I even had time to close my eyes.

When I re-opened them, it was like every soldier in the crowd took one piece of the three men and walked single-file to the stairs of the roof. As the last man, I followed the blood trail after them. I stepped out onto the roof to see the corporate soldiers throw the body parts off the roof. I'd thought littering on the streets of any kind was illegal.

I thought it best to keep quiet. It was a matter of honor and brotherhood with these men. They'd killed three of their brothers who they felt disgraced their clan. I was an outsider and I needed to stay out of it. They were also sending a message to the outside world. Brain Shark and his men vanished forever. Metro PD, whenever they were called, would shut down the entire area, and all would know what happened to those three men who they believed had betrayed the society to Brain Shark. However, I didn't believe that they would betray their brothers to that gangster slob. It was someone else, and they sent Brain Shark to do the dirty work.

It was as my instincts had predicted. Everything was going to get much more violent. Was this the fate for D.G., Echo, and all the ex-Hiero men too? What about me? Surrounded by all the forces of Hiero and Macro to be sliced to pieces and dumped onto the streets to be eaten by bugs, rats, or whatever critters were out there. I'd thought Brain Shark was the one who'd gotten away. But he hadn't. I wanted to get away. But would I?

Not until we were out of the parking building next to the Jamaican take-out did I see how many of us there were. We were an army and loaded into dozens of hovertrucks. When we were in the air, we stayed in the sky lane closest to the ground, which was the designated lane for heavy hovervehicles. Each vehicle carried about fifteen of us. Everyone kept long guns and machine-guns ready, including me. If Brain Shark was led to our hideout, who else might me waiting for us out here?

Even though they were all professional corporate soldiers, I didn't want to get blown out of the sky. Then my mind went to that Voodoo woman and Blur. Though Blur was more dangerous, it was Voodoo Child that scared me. The doll. That creepy doll of me.

"If we come across that Voodoo woman again, if she has another doll of me, can I just blast it?" I asked.

"If it's not linked to your body," one of them answered.

"Linked to my body? What would happen if it were?"

"You would be shooting yourself," he answered.

"Her tech transfers energy," another corporate soldier added.

"I don't care. I'll risk it. I don't want to see another one of those creepy dolls of me again. I see one and I shoot it before I see her."

They laughed. One of my buddies patted me on the back.

"You will be okay."

At least, I could lighten the mood a bit. Until we got to the Mad City hideout we were nothing but giant floating targets in the sky.

Through the tinted passenger windows, I kept my eyes on the sky traffic. If something came at us, I wanted to have as much time as possible to react. Some said that Metropolis was as vast as the universe with all its many streets, establishments, and sites. But I knew much of it and recognized where we were. One of my least favorite neighborhoods in that universe was coming up fast.

"Get ready," one of my buddies said.

"More jumping from moving vehicles?" I asked.

He nodded.

"You do know I've done more of this in this one case than my entire life."

He smiled.

Our specific hovertruck was in the center of the procession. Before I knew it we were diving for the ground. All of the men stood up and neared the passenger doors. They gestured for me to do the same.

"We move fast. Follow," one said.

As soon as I nodded, they shoved the doors open and jumped. Once again I was jumping out of a moving hovercar without knowing where I was jumping.

We landed on top of a hoverlimo and I was pulled inside through open doors. I saw what they were doing. Each hovertruck would act as a shield for each hoverlimo. We blasted off for Mad City.

Every stretch of the way I had convinced myself we'd be attacked, but we never were. We entered the airspace around Mad City with its population of criminals and degenerates with no incident. When we landed in the parking bay of our hideout tower, I breathed a sigh of relief. For now we were safe.

When we descended from the roof stairs of our clinic tower home away from home to the penthouse level, D.G. and Echo were waiting, with plenty of security, which included Judo and Pro. They saw the annoyed expression on my face.

One of my buddies started speaking Japanese to them. They watched me as they listened.

"Your plan worked," D.G. said.

"Barely."

"You're here, so that is all that matters," she said.

"Do I get to hear the truth now?" I asked.

223

"What is truth?" Echo asked.

"Truth is that thing opposite of the story you told me about Hackasaurus, the evil kidnapper, snatching your imaginary daughter. He's no kidnapper. He's a blackmailer."

"He also happens to be one of the best hackers on the planet and in the employ of the Hiero Corporation for years," she said.

"And your partner," I added. "A partner who double-crossed you."

"Yes," D.G. said.

"I think I can guess what part of this is about. You wanted him to call me, but it had to be his idea."

"We will speak privately," Echo said.

The office I was led to was on a level I hadn't been on before. Four floors down, and when I stepped out of the elevator I entered a hallway coated in a shimmering black substance—floor, walls and ceiling. Mr. Echo led the way, D.G. walked alongside me, all the other men followed.

"You kept your other talents from us, Mr. Cruz. Killing Mr. Brian Shrak, alias Brain Shark, with a throwing weapon," D.G. said to me.

"I didn't like him touching my gun."

"We'll remember that for the future."

We entered a Japanese-style office typical to Silicon Dunes rather than a Mad City office tower. It told me that they'd had this hideout for a long time, likely with many others throughout Metropolis.

Only Judo entered after us. The other men waited in the hallway as Judo closed the door. Echo sat behind the main desk,

D.G. sat in a chair on the side. They motioned for me to take a seat in front of the desk.

"Hackasaurus, your partner, told me his side of things," I said.

"Our partner?" D.G. asked. "You believe him?"

"I don't believe what you told me, if that's what you're asking. I knew it wasn't true the moment you told me. You didn't know if you had a kidnapped son or daughter. Of course, you picked a girl."

"You'd put yourself in great danger rescuing a kidnapped girl."

"My first ever case," I said.

"We thought you needed an incentive to work for us. I'm not as gifted at lies as yourself or my men. As assassins, we don't speak much. We also didn't care if you believed us. As long as you took the assignment."

"Then tell me what it's really about."

"We will tell you then," Echo said.

"What about the breach of security at the other hideout?" I asked.

"We handled the situation," Echo said.

"Our men were saved twice by you," D.G. said. "It's becoming a habit, Mr. Cruz. You're supposed to be the civilian; we're the soldiers."

"Think nothing of it. You'll have your chance to return the favor, I'm sure," I said. "But the breach. Brain Shark was no brain. Are we certain we know how he found it? Someone led him to us."

"In our clan, everyone knows their task. We are within the company of our brothers at all times. We know where each one of us is at all times. When there is a breach, we all know who is responsible," D.G. said.

"As when you left the employ of Hiero," I said.

"Hiero knew within minutes of what we had done. The order to kill us was made as quickly," Echo said. "The matter of Brain Shark has been handled, as his conspirators were handled."

"Yes, I'm trying to forget about that," I said.

"We will deal with the main person at the appropriate time," Echo continued.

"If you aren't worried, then I'll drop it. Tell me why you really hired me. Why did you really want me to find this Hackasaurus? Since he's no evil kidnapper."

"Mr. Cruz, it is as we said. He's one of the best hackers on Earth, employed by Hiero. I hired him to steal the entire shadow vault of the Hiero Corporation to buy my freedom and the freedom of our clan."

"Steal their money? Hiero doesn't believe in banks?"

"Banks are for profits for their legitimate businesses. Most of Hiero's business is illegal."

"What happened? Why did your partner turn on you?"

"We misjudged him," Echo said. "We thought he would remain loyal to us. He did not."

"He told me that he did to you what he thought you'd do to him."

"Do you believe him?" D.G. asked.

"I think he's a very bad person. Only you know all that he's done, but I would never have trusted him no matter how genius of a hacker he is. But I guess you decided better the devil you know rather than one you didn't."

"Yes, that was our calculation," Echo said. "Our miscalculation."

"We should have paid more attention to his words. He has always called himself a cyber-anarchist. Hiero, and by extension, we became his target," D.G. said.

"Will you pay him the money?"

"There is nothing to decide. We will pay whatever he wants," Echo said.

"It all makes sense now with Brain Shark's attempted takeover."

"Hiero spent all their physical bank money to keep majority control of the new Hiero-Macro company," D.G. said.

"But Macro really has control since they didn't spend all their money," I said.

"They do. Their reserves are still intact, but Hiero will never allow Macro to gain ultimate control," Echo said to me.

"Another corporate war to come," I remarked.

"Mr. Cruz, you'll be happy to know that you have concluded your work with us."

"I have?" I said to her, surprised.

"Yes," she said. "We know how to directly contact him."

I nodded. "My disposable phone. You were listening in."

"Always," Echo said.

"I'm glad I was of service then."

"You will receive a bonus for your service, of course," Echo said.

"We may have chosen unwisely with the hacker, but not so with you," D.G. said.

"I hope it all works out for you," I said to them. "That you get your freedom to live a peaceful life."

"Thank you, Mr. Cruz," The Digital Samurai said.

I stood from my chair and Judo led me out. Was it really over? I asked myself. Judo led me to an actual hotel room on another floor. I would rest and then have my own corporate security force take me home.

That was the plan.

I lay on the bed with my eyes closed, but I wasn't sleeping. How could I? I was on my back on top of the covers. My hand on the trigger of my omega-gun at my side. I'd sleep when I was home.

The peace and quiet of my room lasted only a couple of hours. I heard commotion again and I immediately assumed we were under attack—again. Judo burst into the room. He looked as if he'd been crying.

"You must come with me."

"What happened?" I asked as I jumped up from the bed.

"Mr. Hack is dead!"

"Hackasaurus?"

"Yes!"

"How do you know?"

"His body was dumped in the street."

"Where?"

"At Hiero. The police have it. The police are there."

Judo took me back to the meeting floor. This time the hallways were jammed with corporate samurai soldiers. All of them had the same expressions on their faces—distress, panic, tears in their eyes. When Judo led me into Echo's office, the samurai master stood in front of his desk, deeply distraught. D.G. paced back and forth nearby. She looked like she was on the verge of a nervous breakdown.

"What happened? Who killed Hack?" I asked.

"We do not know," Echo replied.

"How do you know he's dead? Maybe that's not the real him. He could be hiding or faking."

"We know. We know his true identity because we've been protecting it all his adult life. The police authorities have his body. They call him a John Doe, but we know who he is. All who knew his true identity will now know he's dead."

"He said he had another offer for this shadow vault."

Suddenly, all of them looked at me.

"What did he say?" Echo asked.

"You know what he said. You were listening."

I saw their faces. "I see. You couldn't listen into his call. But you recorded the number I dialed when I called him. He confirmed what I already knew. He told me that you'd have to pay him whatever Brain Shark had offered him, but we had to hurry with the offer because he had another offer. How could he let himself be killed? Be so careless?"

"They found him somehow," Judo said.

"Who killed him?" I asked.

"It does not matter. To know changes nothing for us," Echo said.

"This man!" D.G. yelled.

I saw the carbon-weave titanium muscles tense as her fists clenched. She held back from striking the wall but she wanted to.

"All I wanted was to escape from this life. Is that too much to ask?" she yelled. "It is a life I couldn't tolerate for another day. This man has taken away our only opportunity."

"Depending on a cyber-anarchist was never the best thing," I said softly.

"He was our cyber-anarchist. He was well-paid and would continue to be well-paid."

"Maybe he thought you'd cut him loose from your employment. Or Hiero would."

"Someone of his talents always has someone who will pay the bills," she said.

Echo said something to her in Japanese.

"It would appear that our situation worsens each day. After so many years of planning, our perfect plan becomes a disaster."

"What will you do now?" I asked.

"We only have one more chance," Echo said. "We must appeal to the Disk Keeper."

"Who's he?" I asked.

"Access codes to shadow vaults can be hundreds of alphanumerical symbols. You cannot memorize it or write it down. You must store it. Password depositories. They are run by gatekeepers. Disk Keeper is one of them and the only one the Hack would have trusted," Echo informed me.

"Could someone steal it?" I asked.

"No. It is like a safe deposit box at a physical bank. Both parties must open it," he said.

I asked the obvious question. "What happens if one of the parties is dead?"

Echo did not answer right away. I saw him holding back the tears.

"We must appeal to him. It is the only way," Echo said to me.

In the real world, if the party died, only a registered will specifically transferring ownership to an heir or heirs would allow that box to be opened. Otherwise, the standard was it would be quarantined for a century or more before ownership transferred to the bank. That was the law. But that was the legal world. This was the shadowy, illegal world of the Ghost Market. It sounded like if the party was dead a shadow vault filled with digital money could never be opened by anyone ever again. Neither Hiero, Macro, nor my ex-Hiero clients would ever see it.

THE DISK KEEPER

The homicide was all over the newsfeed. Such things weren't supposed to happen in upscale districts like Silicon Dunes. Metro PD also cordoned off a few other places for investigation. The area around our Jamaican takeout hideout and the parking lot was shut down when pedestrians realized they'd actually been hit by body parts from the roof. One woman found a piece that dropped into her purse. I felt sorry for the business owners whose entire livelihood was on hold due to police investigators. Hopefully, the media attention would bring more people to their places of business after the yellow police tape was gone.

At the Hiero Corporation, the unidentified male, who we knew as the Hack, was dumped at the building's ground floor steps. That meant a message, but from who? His face was all over the newsfeed. Eurasian guy, average face and build, nothing significant or unique like tattoos or piercings. No other details were released by the police.

With the media out in force, Hiero media relations had to give a statement on camera. The Asian female did a lot of smiling, answering all reporter questions, but said nothing. The company didn't know who the man was. He had no connection with the company. The company was cooperating fully with authorities. When questions moved to the aborted CAD Corporation acquisition, she quickly wrapped things up.

"I'm sorry, but this press conference is to address the poor, unidentified man found in front of our megatower. We are here to ascertain who he was so that any next of kin can be notified and he can be buried with honor and dignity. It is inappropriate to discuss business matters here," she said and excused herself.

Men in suits blocked the reporters from following her into the lobby.

I reached out to PJ via email to get all the details on who he was. She shared with me all the news. I also had to contact my wife. We hated communicating to each other over the computer, but that's all we could do. My case wasn't over. I thought it was, but it had become something else. They wanted my help in communicating with this Disk Keeper.

"What can I do?" I'd asked them.

"If he communicates in Japanese, Mandarin, Cantonese, your work is done. But if he speaks English, we will want you here to observe," Echo told me.

"You speak English as well as I do," I said.

"It is not my native language and this is not my native country. We know the language but not the common slang present in all languages that only true natives understand fully. Our business is too important to leave anything to chance."

I nodded. "I'll do it."

I almost felt bad for them. They were paying me every step of the way but I knew their resources were dwindling fast, if it hadn't already all been spent.

We were going into the field again. They fitted me with new body armor to wear under my clothes—thin, sheer material but strong as steel, and super-expensive. I packed all my weapons on me, both old and new. I wanted to be ready for Voodoo Child and her creepy dolls, Blur, or anyone else.

Judo came to get me when the team was ready to depart.

We were a small air armada. Flying out of Mad City, our forces were anything but inconspicuous. The corporate soldiers wore their standard suit and tie but all had body armor too. The total firepower was enough to give Metro PD pause. They carried guns and rifles I'd never seen before. I expected we were about to storm a megacorp office tower; instead we landed in some grungy, drug-smoke filled, flashy neon lit, cyberpunk district. I thought it was a joke. I followed them into a virtual game arcade filled with kid and adult gamers. Their reactions were to be expected. What was an army of samurai soldiers doing in an arcade?

Like a lot of places, there was the legitimate business in the front and the illegal stuff in the back. We went to the back. I'd had my fill of the virtual reality world in my Electric Sheep Massacre Case, and I was not eager to be anywhere near it again. The back room was an illegal bar filled mostly with what looked to be teenagers. There was a man—not a teenager—standing in a corner chatting with some of them, mostly girls. He wore a red suit, white shirt and had crazy white hair. I saw the neon tattoos on his neck and wrists.

He saw us enter and got nervous.

"Officers, everyone here is over eighteen," he said.

"We are not police," Echo said to him.

"We need an introduction to the Disk Keeper," D.G. said to him.

"Disk Keeper, Officer. I don't know who that is."

"We are not police," Echo repeated.

"You look like Vice to me, but I'll play. I don't know any Disk Keeper and if I did, I wouldn't tell you."

"I will ask one more time," D.G. said.

"You can ask—"

I wanted to jump in and say something, but this wasn't my show. I was happy to stay quiet and observe. D.G. didn't have to reach for any knives; they popped out from her fingertips and she slashed the man's face. He yelled as he fell back. "Cat claws"—the retractable metal finger claws of the illegal cyborg world—were not as plentiful as they used to be because even the criminal world had begun banning them; they were too dangerous. If caught by the police, they'd take your arms and put you in jail. Everyone in the room screamed as they got out as fast as they could.

The man touched his face and looked at all the blood on his hand. He stayed on the ground but glared at them.

"Yeah, you're not the cops. I said I don't know no Disk Keeper. I said that because I don't."

"Then refer us to someone who does," D.G. said. She knelt down and her eyes began to glow green. He leaned away from her, nervous. "This is not the time for false bravery. You cooperate and we go. You never see us again. You don't and we will stay for awhile. You will not like that."

"He's a code keeper for shadow vaults?"

"Yes."

"I know someone. If he doesn't know him, he will know who does."

"Call him and tell him to expect us. I'd prefer nice conversation rather than violence. Do you agree?"

"I agree," he said.

In the criminal world, it was often hard to get to talk to the person you wanted without a referral. People had to know you or someone they knew. However, corporate assassins were plenty scary enough to jump to the head of the line. We still had to go through intermediaries and found ourselves at another arcade.

Just like there were dark bars, the word dark meaning criminal, it seemed the same rules applied to arcades. I thought all of them were filled with hackers, druggies, gamers, virtual life addicts, but there seemed to be a whole underground for the criminal class too.

There were all kinds of cyborgs in the world and Up-Top. I'd seen truly the scariest of them, including D.G., whose full abilities hadn't been displayed yet. The pair of cyborgs in front of the arcade we approached were of the type most gangsters didn't like—they were too cyborg. Two large, barrel chested cyborgs with oversized arms and metal fingers, wearing dark shades, with cigarettes in their mouths.

They immediately blocked us from entering the arcade.

"What do you want?" one asked.

"We're here to play games," D.G. said.

"You look like you're here to cause trouble."

"If we were, what could you do about it?"

"We wouldn't do anything about it, but our associates might."

He pointed, and across the street were about a dozen thugs loitering around a few parked suped-up hovercars. In the blink of an eye, all of them were cut down in a burst of throwing stars. They barely had time to scream. I heard a horrific sound of metal behind me and turned. D.G. had ripped apart both cyborgs. Armless and legless piles on the ground. She kicked them away from the door.

Large screens hung on the walls with the feed of the establishment's surveillance cameras outside the entrance, so everyone knew what had happened. They saw us and most decided to run the hell out of there. But not everyone had run out of the building. A groups of kids, all in hoodies and wearing glowing blue shades, stood around one retro game pod. They watched us.

"Disk Keeper!" D.G. yelled to them.

"If we talk, will you go away? We're about to set the world record on this game, been playing for three weeks straight and we don't want you ruining our chance for the universal title. We want to beat those no-talent Martians for the title real bad, and it's a big payday. But if you're going to be throwing things and destroying our game pod, we're going to have a big problem with you," one kid said. They were very focused on the game.

"We have no desire to interfere in your business. Tell us how to contact Disk Keeper, and we're gone. You'll never see us again."

"We hired those cyborg bodyguards to keep people out of here. Why did you do them like that?"

"Compensate the gentlemen for their loss," D.G. said to one of our corporate soldiers. "Next time they'll know to hire either more intelligent ones or ones who can actually fight to win."

"Disk Keeper isn't here, and no one here knows him. I don't know why that other place keeps doing that. Sending people to us. You know they did that on purpose. He's betting on us losing. You know that's why he did that."

"Who should we talk to?" D.G. asked.

"We'll give you the address and the name to ask for. This is a Shadow Market joint. Ghost Marketeers don't hang here. You need to go to one of their joints."

"Thank you," D.G. said as one of the corporate soldiers pulled a digital card from his jacket.

"Give it to them," one of the kids said. "Our bathroom break time is almost up. We got to jump back in."

That's all they cared about. Playing their game. Team tournament for the last three weeks, straight play 24-7. Giant meteors crashing to the Earth, a 9.0 earthquake, a giant shootout in the street outside their arcade. None of it would have mattered to them. The next generation that would be running Metropolis when my wife and I were old and gray. Good grief! We'd have to make sure Cruz Jr. grew up right. The kids gave us the information we needed and we were gone.

This was ridiculous, I thought to myself. The next place we went to was also in walking distance. Immediately, I could see the change in clientele. The pedestrians looked more dangerous. One of them had a dog that looked dangerous. The bouncers at the door of the establishment looked plenty dangerous, but they were more intelligent than the last bunch. There was no telling what weapons they had under their jackets. The exterior looked like another arcade, but I wasn't sure. Would thugs really frequent an arcade to play virtual games?

"We're looking for Introduction," D.G. said.

"You can go in. But take only five. Your army waits out here with us. Look for the one with the big flashing 'I' on his jacket," one bouncer said. His face was scarred up and one of his eyes had a dim glow. "Don't cause any disturbances like you did at the other place. Might not go as easy here," he said.

They moved away from the door. Judo grabbed me and D.G. led five of us in.

If hoodies hadn't been invented, what would these people wear? Even the bouncers outside had them, but they at least had nice jackets over them. The place wasn't an arcade. It was a bar—very loud, filled with smoke, alcohols being consumed by the gallon. The only games in the arcade were holo-darts, which seemed to be the star attraction. However, the holo-darts in this place were throwing knives.

We didn't have to look for Introduction in the crowd. He found us. He pulled down his hood. She found us. A middle-aged female with piercings in her nose, multiple ones in her earlobes, hair cut close enough for her to look bald.

"Tell me here what you want," she said. "We'd rather you not stay too long."

"Why is that?" D.G. asked.

"We know who you are, Digital Samurai, and your colleagues from the Hiero Corporation. There's a bounty on all of you. This is a Ghost Market affiliate establishment. Did you believe you were walking incognito onto our turf? No outsider sets foot here unless we allow them to be here."

"Then you know why we're here," D.G. said.

"He'll see you. It's the least we can do. Hiero has been a historic supporter of the Ghost Market. We believe in helping those who've supported the goal for humanity to recognize that the virtual world is more real than the flesh world."

"As long as no one turns off the electricity."

Oops! Did I say that out loud? She was looking at me with a sinister grin. Introduction walked right to me.

"Mr. Cruz," she said.

Then she started to lift up her top. What was she about to show me? A Liquid Cool T-shirt!

"Please, don't tell my wife you showed me that."

The Introduction woman laughed. She returned to D.G.

"Here."

D.G. took a plastic card from her.

"I wish you all the luck in the world, Digital Samurai. But remember no matter what we do, we cannot escape fate."

Introduction lifted her hood back over her head and disappeared into the establishment's crowds. I didn't know exactly what she meant by what she said to us, but I didn't like it. I didn't know what she meant then, but later I would.

Disk Keeper appeared as a disembodied giant head floating in the air. We were all seated in the room—D.G., Echo, me. Everyone else sat at the outer edges of the room, in the shadow.

Echo had been speaking in Japanese for a good ten minutes. I had no idea what was being said. When the samurai master was done, he leaned back in his chair. We waited for Disk Keeper to speak. I prayed that he'd respond in a language other than English. If he did, I was free from the case.

"I understand your predicament," Disk Keeper said in English! "However, you must understand mine. These rules were not created by me. They've existed centuries before all of us. There are rules we must all follow no matter the circumstances. Those rules keep the order of things. I'm not speaking of business. The rules allow us live. Shadow vaults can only be opened by two parties simultaneously entering their access pass codes. Not by one party alone. You know this. If one party dies, then—"

"There must be another way," D.G. said. "We'll pay any amount. We can come up with a solution."

"What solution? Breach the shadow vault? Even if you could locate it on the dark Net, there is no way to open it without both codes. They are programmed to erase all digital contents if an unauthorized attempt is made."

"But arrangements must have been made," Echo said.

"I'm surprised by you. No arrangements were made for Hackasaurus. He stole the vault from the Hiero Corporation for you and he stole its control from you. Now he's dead."

"We must get access to the vault," D.G. said. She said it with feigned control of her emotions. Actually, I feared she might explode. Good thing all of us were actually meeting in a virtual world.

"I will do this, Digital Samurai," Disk Keeper said. "I will consult the regulations to see if there is any contingency for such a situation."

"Yes," Echo said, nodding.

"I make no promises, but this must have come up before."

"Thank you," D.G. said.

"Give me a day. I understand the urgency. I'll review and contact you."

"Thank you."

"How would you like me to reach you?"

Echo reached into his jacket and produced a business card. The card turned into a dove and flew into Disk Keeper's mouth.

"I will be in touch."

Disk Keeper's image disappeared.

We all disconnected too. I sat up in my VR recliner and rubbed my eyes after I lifted off the visual interface glasses. I looked at myself. At least I didn't have to wear any helmets or black pajamas covered in nodes.

Pro was at my chair and helped me get out. I glanced over at D.G. and Echo speaking to each other in Japanese.

"I will take you back to your room while we wait," Pro said to me.

I nodded and followed him. As I glanced one more time at D.G. and Echo, I wondered what would happen when there was no more hope. I saw Judo watching me. Was he thinking the same thing?

Officially, it was the longest I'd been away from my wife, Dot. And what about my son? I was getting irritated. However, after an hour video-call with PJ, I was back to my normal self.

PJ reported back to me what was being said about the late Hackasaurus. Low-life cyber-anarchist hacker by night, stockbroker by day. Ultimately, it told us nothing. He could have had any of a million other professions. In his case, he was a bad guy who worked for badder guys and got himself killed trying to play at blackmail.

Mr. Mick also left update messages for me. The last message confirmed what I knew was coming. The Macro Corporation was making its move against the Hiero Corporation. Glyph would soon be announced as the new CEO of *Macro-Hiero*.

I also had a message from B.B.—the good one, not the jerky one. I read the message and my stomach tightened. He told me, "Cruz, get away from all your clients as fast as you can. You're not one of them. The Hiero ship, and everyone connected to it, is about to crash into the giant iceberg."

I'd learned awhile ago that in the criminal world, when a deadline was agreed upon everyone had to stick to it. Meeting and sticking to deadlines kept all involved out of jail and alive. Someone was late, it often spelled trouble. If someone was early, it definitely meant trouble. Pro knocked on the door to my room and entered.

"Disk Keeper has contacted us," he said. "We call him now."

I looked at the digital clock on the wall.

"He's early," I said.

Pro said nothing.

We were back in the VR room of our new hideout. D.G. and Echo were already connected in their recliner. When I was connected with Pro's help, I joined them all in the virtual environment.

Disk Keeper's disembodied giant head floated in the air. He was already speaking in Japanese.

"All have arrived," he said. "We shall begin."

"What news do you have?" Echo asked.

"I've been in this business a long time. I've made a fortune offering my services in the Ghost Market. Confidentiality. Impartiality. Reputation. Without those traits I am nothing. I have no clients, no business, no money. Digital Samurai, you hatched a plot to escape from your owners, you convinced your clan to conspire with you, but you made one critical mistake. You enlisted the aid of a man who knew nothing about loyalty. Life isn't fair, and it's less fair for people like us. When Hackasaurus was killed, he killed you, your clan, your owners, your former megacorp, and me.

"I, too, wish I had never met the man Hackasaurus. He took the secret of his access pass codes to the grave and there is no possible way to retrieve them unless we could bring him back from the dead, which we can't. However, like you, there are so many people out there: Hiero, Macro, countless other megacorps, countless syndicates, the Council of Corporations itself. They will never stop until they find out my identity, track me down, torture me to repeat the same thing over and over again. They'd kill me and nothing would change. There is no way to open a shadow vault without both parties and their codes. The trillions upon trillions of digital currency will remain in that vault until, maybe centuries from now, those impenetrable digital walls will be brought down with new tech, new hacking techniques. So this is my last communication as the Disk Keeper. My vocation has ended because I can't trust a single client who ever contacts me again.

"With so many people chasing me, I also needed to give myself as much of a head start as possible by helping bring down my chief pursuers—Hiero. I called them and told them what you already know. Hiero's entire wealth is gone. I told them, Macro, your society, even the Council, even the authorities. I want the whole world to know so others will do what I can't: destroy all of you.

"I'm sorry. It's not personal. As I said, whoever killed Hackasaurus killed us all. It's not the decision you wanted, but in your heart you knew it was the only decision that there would be. Good luck to us all. We'll need it."

Disk Keeper's image flickered away.

TECH-JACKS

The control of one's emotions was the first thing samurai soldiers learned as children, then, as one matured, to control those emotions in the face of horror and distress that no average person could withstand. The panic gripped my ex-Hiero clients so completely I felt obligated to stay with them, as I was the only rational adult among them.

Everyone ran to the parking bays, jumped into hoverlimos and hovertrucks, and shot out of there. No one was left behind. I don't even think any security measures were activated. We were never coming back. *They* were never coming back.

I might as well have been invisible. I was in one of the hoverlimos, but had to jump in because I would have been left behind. Men were screaming madly, crying, hitting themselves. All I could do was stay quiet. I focused my attention out the window as we wildly raced along the sky freeway to confirm my suspicions. It didn't take too long to see that we were back in Silicon Dunes, and I saw the Hiero headquarters building rapidly approaching. The one place we needed to stay as far away from as possible was where we about to land. I was the only sane man on an insane ship. But I was on the same ship too.

The vehicles landed haphazardly, dropping to the ground, screeching to immediate stops. Men jumped out of the hovervehicles, not even closing doors. When I wanted to run, I was faster than most, but I strained past my limit to keep up with them. I barely made the last elevator, throwing myself in.

The elevator capsule reached our floor. As soon as it opened, we were overcome with loud yelling and howls of crying. They rushed out. If I had known what I was walking into I wouldn't have accompanied them. But I wasn't about to be left behind in our hideout to run into Voodoo Child or some other assassin.

At the elevator bays were crowds of armed corporate soldiers, but they let us past. D.G. was on her knees, weeping. Echo was jumping up and down in crushing despair. Everyone was mad; their backs to me. Once I stepped past them I saw why. Beyond us were bodies. The entire level was filled with corporate soldiers slumped over on the ground in pools of blood. Small katanas were at their sides. With some I could see piles of guts too. There were too many of them to count. I didn't want to know how many dead there were. We hadn't made it in time. Hiero's entire corporate soldier society that hadn't rebelled with D.G. had committed ritual suicide.

I stepped away and walked back to the elevators. There, waiting, was another virtual army of corporate soldiers—all belonged to Macro. They paid no attention to me. I guess I was invisible to them too.

"It's a shame, isn't it?" I heard Mr. Able's voice. He was among them.

"I hear your boss got a big promotion, so that means you move up the ladder," I said.

"Why are you here, Mr. Cruz?" he said. "You're not a society member."

"Neither are you," I said.

"We've extended a one-time courtesy to them. After today, if they don't join their brothers in the afterlife, our forces will be authorized to kill them on sight."

"Where's Mr. Ming?" I asked.

"Mr. Ming is nothing. Do you have any openings at your agency? Maybe he can work for you."

"I don't think so. He has poor references."

"No matter. Someone will take him on, or kill him. You should also know that the authorities raided this building earlier. Metro Cybercrimes. Physical agents came in through the front doors; their hackers came in through the Net. I don't think there's a file or piece of data left."

"Why would Cybercrimes raid Hiero? Hiero is your company now."

"A company with no assets. A company with no assets is not a company. We reported them to Cybercrimes ourselves and told them of their multiple criminal improprieties. They had to raid them or risk losing evidence or data being destroyed."

"Criminals calling the police on other criminals. It's been done before."

"I'll ignore your slander. Macro finds itself in an undesirable position. The acquisition was supposed to have elevated our organization. But we're making the best of it."

"Mr. Able, you talk all nice with your fancy suit, but I've met crooks in the gutter with more class than you and your boss. I know about you."

"Mr. Cruz, you know nothing and are nothing. Macro is an eternal empire that floats far above all who exist in Metropolis."

"Be careful how you treat people, Mr. Able. You may meet them again on the way down."

"Have a nice life, Mr. Cruz. Our two worlds will not cross again. The time of mourning is over. Take your associates and get out of my building."

"Your building? I'll tell them."

As one man pressed the call button, Able and his men entered the open elevators as they arrived. The doors closed.

We loaded back up in our hovervehicles and were allowed to leave the parking bays by Macro security. We flew in the sky traffic but had no place to go. They yelled until their voices were gone. They cried until there were no more tears. I was witnessing the end of a dynasty

I managed to get in the same hoverlimo as D.G. and Echo. I hadn't seen Judo or Pro. It was only the three of us in the rear compartment.

"You asked why we wanted to escape," D.G. said softly. "We will tell you."

The moment was profound as I, the outsider, was about to be told about the inner, private world of their society. But their society was no more.

"Hiero used to be a company of honor. There was business we didn't do. Because it was beneath us and the province of commoners. Violence was to protect. Never for revenge. Never against innocents. But they grew corrupt. They ordered us to kill innocents, to kill children. Hiero became a company of degenerates, no longer interested in honor or business. Vile depravity was what occupied their days. They reveled in the power to do anything they wished without restraint or regard to decency because they could. Our forefathers would have executed us all for the shame we brought to the name of Hiero. We were no better than a street punk stealing coins from elderly women and children coming from school. We got into drugs, prostitution slavery, murder-for-hire. That was the Hiero of today, not the Hiero of yesterday that helped build Metropolis into the supercity, greater than all the world. Our masters had become monsters. We were going to escape it all. But there is nothing left for us."

"Seppuku? Is that what you're telling me you'll do? Ritual suicide. Cut your belly for your blood and guts to spill out on the ground."

"You're an outsider and do not understand."

"It would seem to me that your motives were honorable but your plan was not. You were going to escape when you're the only ones who could stop them."

"We are bound by oaths," Echo said. "We cannot raise a hand against our company or its masters."

"I'm sorry, Mr. Echo, but that sounds like a big excuse to me. The answer is to commit suicide and let them get away with it all to carry on forever. Is Macro the same?"

"The same."

"Digital Samurai, you have unfinished business. Your Hiero forefathers are counting on you to do what they can't."

"Do you believe your words will appeal to my humanity?" she asked.

"You do have humanity left inside of you, or we would never have met. Don't go halfway trying to be a good guy. You started the journey. Go all the way. Finish it. Only you know their true selves. Once you're gone, there'll be no others to act. You need to finish it. Macro-Hiero remains."

"Hiero-Macro!" Echo yelled.

"Hiero is dead. Macro is alive. If Hiero dies, shouldn't Macro follow?"

A small smile came over D.G.'s face. "Is this why you've remained with us, Mr. Cruz? To be a spiritual guide."

"Every step of your plan things have gotten worse. You believe it can't get worse, but we both know it can. Metropolis doesn't need a corporate war spilling into the streets."

"You make intellectual arguments, Mr. Cruz. Emotional arguments are often far more powerful."

"D.G., you already made the emotional arguments. They are the same as the owners of Hiero. Macro is a company of degenerates with no honor. Vile depravity is what occupies their days."

The elevator opened and I stepped out and through the main lobby of Cybercrimes. The routine was the same as I was checked by both human guards and robotic sentries. I showed ID, they took my photo, fingerprints and palm prints, did the retinal scans, and I walked under several scanning arches and a final scanning tunnel. I had no mobile or other devices on me.

Another officer escorted me through the doors of the Cybercrimes Division, where Agent Delphi waited.

"Mr. Cruz, I'm both surprised to see you and not," he said.

"Surprised to see me alive?"

"Not really. You do have a habit of surviving."

"Makes me sound like a cockroach, so I won't take that as a compliment."

"I hear your men visited Hiero."

"My men?" I grinned.

He led me from the waiting area, through the bull pen of dual cubicles, single cubicles, to the offices with glass walls for the higher-ups. As we walked I glanced over to the area of whiteboards on the other side of the room. Agents stood there watching me with arms folded. All the whiteboards were turned away so I couldn't see them. I smiled and waved at them.

"Still have my family, friends, and associates up on the board?" I asked Delphi.

"We've moved on from you, Mr. Cruz. The Hiero case is closed, because there is no Hiero Corporation. And since you don't work for free and they have no money to pay you, you're involvement with them has ended, and so is our interest in you."

I followed Delphi into his office.

"Have a seat, Mr. Cruz."

Through the walls other agents stood up from their chairs, looking at me.

"What do you have for me today, Mr. Cruz?"

"You raided Hiero today."

"We did. Seized everything that could be taken or downloaded. Hiero laid off their entire staff, but we got there just before to take them into custody for a brief chat before they headed to the unemployment line. No one complained since all of Hiero's attorneys were also laid off with them."

"Any useful information?"

"No, but that wasn't the point."

"Kick the man when he's down. I get it. What about Macro?"

"What about them? We have nothing on them. Our focus was Hiero and they no longer exist."

"A great triumph for Cybercrimes. The end of Hiero, which incidentally had nothing to do with your division at all."

"We take what we can get, Mr. Cruz."

"No, you're going to do more than sit back and take what you can get. You're going to take down Macro too."

"Are we?"

"How bad was Hiero?"

"We had this conversation already, Mr. Cruz. Cyber-terrorism, cyber-extortion, cyber-warfare, cyber-harassment, cyber-contracts for murder, kidnapping, and whatever else."

"Drugs and prostitution?" I asked.

"Mr. Cruz, every possible crime you can think of was part of Hiero's illegitimate businesses. They were heinous criminals, including your clients—the enforcers for their business."

"I know that, but my clients were escaping. That's what set all this in motion."

"You can believe you want. I chose not to. I'm law enforcement and they're criminals. Criminals should be dead or in jail."

"Delphi, you don't have to lecture me. Most of my clients are criminals of some sort or doing something they shouldn't be doing. How many cases would you be able to close or how many convictions could Metro PD get if they couldn't rely on slimy informants? We're not in the Sunday school business. When you work in hell you're not going to come across too many angels. I took criminal justice ethics when I interned for the police as a kid in high school. I aced my exams. You draw your ethical lines; I'll draw mine. At least I have lines I won't cross. Most of the detective firms out there don't."

"Your point?"

"Isn't Macro the same?"

"Of course, Macro is the same. They merged because they were exactly the same."

"Then it's your lucky day, Mr. Delphi. Hiero's gone, and Macro will follow."

"How would we do that, Mr. Cruz?"

"We? No. My clients, former clients, will do it for you. But you need to do something for them."

"Are you still working for your clients?"

"I want you to do something, Mr. Delphi. Then I want you to keep Metro PD away from the site. Let nature take its course. You'll never get this opportunity ever again. Your chance to roll up not just Hiero, but Macro too."

The attorney led me into some kind of dimly lit computer terminal command center. Agents wearing visor glasses and headphones were at terminals in row after row. In the center of the room was a pit of larger terminals with code scrolling down. Teams of agents sat at each one. The lawyer led me down the steps into this pit where Delphi had assembled other senior agents.

"He's all set," the lawyer said.

"I'm going to get a copy of that non-disclosure agreement with all that legalese?" I asked.

"It's called an NDA and that's a 'no,'" Delphi told me. "Tell my team what you told me."

"Is this them? Your tech-jacks?"

"Yes."

"Cybercrimes' own cyber-warfare section."

"It's called fighting crime," one said sarcastically.

"Then all you have to do is shut off all power to the Macro Headquarters building and use every trick in the book, all at once, to breach their mainframes."

"Shutting off power is under Metro PD," one said.

"But you can get them to do it."

"Why are we doing this?" another agent asked. "We have no probable cause. No evidence that we can present to any judge."

"So?" I said.

"So, we need that."

"Are you all telling me you've never harassed or jammed up a suspect without probable cause or evidence? Really? Never? Delphi, tell your men to do it. You said criminals should be dead or in jail. For Macro, we're skipping the jail part."

"Sir, what is he talking about?" an agent asked.

"Since you don't want Metro PD going in, am I to assume that your remaining Hiero clients will be going in?" Delphi asked.

"Yes, and they don't care about warrants or evidence. Their only interest is revenge. We're going to let them. This is a once in a lifetime chance, Delphi. If we don't take them down now, how many innocents and law enforcement officers are we condemning to future death, harm, and terror? How many of my descendants, yours, and your agents' will be fighting this evil company? Because they always manage to survive for centuries, not decades or years."

Delphi looked at his men. "Do it."

FINAL SHOWDOWN

O nce I planted the seed, Delphi did the rest. The objections that flew out of the mouths of his men had less to do with whether they thought it was strictly legal, and more to do with the fact I, a civilian, had suggested it. The back and forth among them went on for about ten minutes, but Delphi settled it. They'd do exactly what I suggested.

"Call the power division," Delphi directed. "Most of these megatowers take up an entire grid; if not, take it all down."

"The second we do their lawyers will have us in court," an agent said.

Delphi ignored him. "Synchronize the launch of the intrusion to coincide with the power shutdown. Whatever tasks our tech-jacks are on, put on hold. This is the priority for the day."

"Should we notify the chief?" an agent asked.

Delphi pondered for a moment. "Not yet. Let's see how this all turns out. Find a place for Mr. Cruz to relax."

"I won't be here," I said.

"Where will you be then?"

"Macro headquarters."

"Are you insane? You're going in with them?" Delphi yelled.

"Yes."

"Why would you do that?" Delphi asked.

"I'll be okay. Someone has to be on the inside. How else will we know how it all turns out?"

"If you're dead, we won't know."

"I'll be fine. All I have to do is stay out of the way. Also, someone has to be on the inside to call the police."

"Call the police? Funny, Cruz," Delphi said.

"If you have a better idea how to know what's happening after you shut off all the power with my clients and Macro's forces locked inside, I'll listen."

"It's your funeral, Cruz."

"Not my funeral, Delphi. When I do call the police, just make sure you come with everything."

It wasn't lost on me that Bubble Baha—the good one and the jerky one—were deeply involved in this case. Case? I had no case. The case was over the second we learned Hackasaurus was dead. I was a spectator now along for the ride. B.B., however, knew things from the inside before we found out.

In the message he left for me to call the last time, he left the means to reach him again. And I did. I used a secure room at Metro PD to call him back.

"Cruz, I'm disappointed."

The call was audio only like last time.

"Well, I'm not calling you from Cybercrimes," I said.

"But you are calling me from the police. Police is police, Cruz."

"Where else am I going to go with potentially a lot of unfriendly people out there?"

"No one is looking for you anymore, Cruz. You're free to move about the cabin."

"Hiero's dead and Macro reigns supreme. Is that it?"

"What happens going forward isn't your business. You have nothing to prove. Move on, man. The ship is going down. Get on your personal escape pod and go. Who cares who's left on the ship at this point?"

"I guess you're not going to tell me who killed the Hack."

"Because I don't know. If someone paid me for the info I might find out, but you don't have that kind of money."

"That's not why I called. You said you were a cyber-gremlin."

"Yes I did."

"I don't have any money, but maybe you can use the insider info I could give you to exercise your malicious ways and identify the funds to pay yourself—whatever you think is fair."

"Cruz, what are you and the cops about to do?"

"Do you want a payday or not?"

"You're talking about Macro, aren't you?"

"For Hiero-Macro or Macro-Hiero to go away, Macro needs to go too."

"They're too powerful."

"Don't worry about them. The police will occupy their mainframes, but I think you could do far more damage than they could. Plus you're far more creative. You can even see if they have any money lying around for you."

"You're crazy enough to do it. You talked the cops into it too, didn't you? How do you know I'm not working for Macro or will call them after I disconnect with you?"

"B.B., I'm thinking that getting a piece of all their money is a better incentive than the possibility of a mere fee. Am I wrong?"

"No, you're righter than right. You're going to have me working with cops. Working with the very cops who'd like to put me in a cell without computer access for the rest of my life."

"Yep, put all your other projects to the side for today."

"Already done."

I strolled into the Macro headquarters building minutes before noon. A hovertaxi dropped me off in their parking bay. Security was heavier than the last time—corporate soldiers, same black suits and ties with white shirts, laser machine guns and long guns everywhere. I wanted to make sure that I was seen from the second I arrived. I was directed to the elevator bays.

When I stepped onto the first level of the executive levels, the coffeehouse and an open dance club had remained. The same beanbag lounge chairs in every color were there, equipped with full entertainment audio and screens. But all of them were empty.

Gone from the executive reception were the tall buxom females in inappropriate attire. In their place were several huge cyborg soldiers.

"Mr. Ming," I said. "I was told he was here."

"There is no one by that name," one them answered.

"Then please call Mr. Able. Tell him Mr. Cruz is here to see Mr. Ming. Should I wait here or in your play area?"

"You can wait here."

The cyborg touched his metal ear and began whispering. I didn't have to wait long. Mr. Able appeared, but he wasn't alone. Six armed thugs were with him.

"Why are you here, Mr. Cruz?"

"I'm here to meet with Mr. Ming."

"Mr. Ming is unavailable."

"Mr. Able, I simply have a message for him from Mr. Echo. It's my last task, then I'm done with my Hiero business. If you're scared of one unarmed street detective, maybe Macro is the wrong business for you."

Able smirked.

"Okay, Mr. Cruz, we'll play. Search him again," he directed his men.

They patted me down and when they were satisfied, we all walked to another set of elevators.

"Is Mr. Ming a prisoner?" I asked.

"Why would you think that?" Able asked as we stepped onto the elevator capsule.

"He was the CEO of his own megacorp, and now he has to get permission from you to see anyone."

"Mr. Cruz, do you know you've crossed over from the line of benign amusement to honest annoyance?"

"Mr. Able, I'm delivering my message and I'm gone. I'm just the messenger."

"I hope that's all, for your sake."

The elevator didn't open into a hallway but an executive office. Another megacorp office with lots of open space, taking up most of the floor, with sparse but expensive furniture. Mr. Ming stood alone, waiting. Same as before, wearing all black—suit, tie, and shirt, his white Fu Manchu mustache past his chin.

Able led me and his men to Ming.

"A message from Echo?" Ming said. Not even a courteous hello.

"Yes, sir. Mr. Echo said to tell you that they will rescue you from Macro."

"What!"

Not only was Ming shocked, but so was Able.

"Rescue? What do you mean?" Ming yelled.

"Yes, The Digital Samurai is already in the building," I said.

Sirens blasted. Emergency lights flashed. Able screamed over his wrist communicator as one of his cyborg guards held me by my neck. Ming glared at me with clenched teeth.

"Echo has brought only shame and dishonor to Hiero," he yelled at me.

I had a snappy comeback, but it probably would have led to me getting my neck snapped.

Able returned to us. "You're going to tell us precisely what they said to you."

"Able, I told you everything they told me to say."

"They wanted you to say that and expected you to walk out of here?" he asked.

"Able, I don't know."

He reached into his jacket for a gun. He pointed it at my forehead.

"I don't care how I find out what I want to know. I don't care what I have to do to you, but you will tell me what I want to know."

"Don't point weapons at me," I said.

"Are you going to answer my question?"

"They plan to crash into the parking bay and come up from there."

Able lowered his weapon and yelled to his men in another language. Even though I couldn't speak any other language besides English, I could at least place other languages. Not this time—I had no clue.

I was pushed along as we all entered the elevator. Ming didn't take his cold gaze from me. His behavior seemed strange to me. He seemed right at home as a Macro man, despite the end of his Hiero empire.

When the door opened, we exited into another vast room. Security screens hung from the ceilings, security stations everywhere. I was in Macro's security command post. At the other end I saw the windows going black; the building's blast walls were coming down. Building lockdown was in effect.

The elevators opened again and Mr. Glyph exited with dozens more armed men. They joined us.

"The detective said they're planning to breach our security at the parking bay," Able told him. "The bulk of our soldiers are en-route."

"To rescue Ming?"

"That's what he said."

Glyph stepped closer to me. "Was he armed?"

"No," Able replied.

"You come into my building without guards or weapons. Are you dumb or know something I don't know? When this day is over, we're going to have to have a long talk."

Everyone panicked. The power went off.

The room was pitch black, then emergency reserve power cut on. The ceiling lights were a dim blue but on. Able yelled at the guards in that language and Glyph did the same.

"Did he say she's in the building?" Glyph asked.

"That's what he said."

"Get her. I don't want to take any chances!" Glyph yelled.

Able dashed off with a group of the corporate soldiers following.

"Where is she?" Glyph yelled at me.

"How would I know?" I said. "Ask Ming. He knows more about her than me. I still don't believe the urban myth of her ability to travel via the Net to get to her targets and kill them. But ask Ming."

Glyph went crazy. "Turn off all the terminals! Manually disconnect them from the power source."

"Sir, the connections cannot be disconnected," someone yelled out.

"Pull them apart! Shoot the connections with your guns!"

Glyph left us in a frenzy to personally watch the work of his men. I heard smashing and gunshots everywhere.

The same half-dozen cyborgs and Ming remained with me. His expression, his whole demeanor was different—relaxed.

"Does she plan to kill me?" he asked in a whisper.

"She didn't say that. I'd say her target is Glyph."

"Her target is much more than one man. His death changes nothing. It will be Macro Corp itself."

"Makes sense."

"What role do you play in this plot?"

"Watch the situation unfold as a spectator. What else can I do? I'm unarmed and I'm not tough enough to take on six cyborgs."

"You come naked to the snake pit," he said.

One of the security stations exploded, and all we heard were screams and saw shadows of bodies falling to the ground. The dim blue lights flickered; we were practically in darkness again. When the second and third explosions happened, I quickly knelt to the ground. It was then I noticed that all of the six bodyguards guarding me were lying on the ground dead—their throats slashed. I looked up. Ming was gone.

I wasn't going to wait. I grabbed weapons from one of the cyborg guards and ran to one of the terminal stations in the chaos. A fourth explosion. People were running and yelling all around me. I dove behind an empty partition wall for cover. Took off my fedora and slicker. With my white shirt and black tie, I'd at least blend in and look like a corporate soldier in the dim light.

"Cruz is gone!" a voice yelled out.

"Use full power!" The voice sounded like Glyph.

Then there was light. The lights of the entire room came on. There was nothing but silence. I slowly peeked out from behind my partition.

From across the room, everyone was watching me. The security techs were gathered together on one side. The corporate soldiers on another with Mr. Glyph. Able began walking faster to me with a dozen guards. I saw how they knew exactly where I was when I turned. Closer to me, pointing, was a certain woman in a tight, black full-bodysuit.

"Drop it," she said.

I dropped my gun to the ground.

The look in Able's eyes told me that the second he had his hands on me, he was going to hurt me bad. He had the look of a hyperventilating bull, half-running to me he wanted to hurt me so badly.

"Ming! Make your move now!" I yelled at an imaginary point beyond the corporate soldiers.

It worked. Everyone looked behind. I dropped to the ground for the gun and aimed point-blank at Able's head. Not only did no bullets fire, but Voodoo Child sliced the gun's barrel off with a translucent sword and kicked me in the chest.

"Ming, come out!" Glyph yelled.

"Never!" Ming yelled, but we didn't see him.

Able reached me and grabbed me by the collar.

"You're going to regret ever walking into this building."

"I should tell you then," I said.

"Tell me what?"

"You should turn on your computers."

"No, no, no!" Able immediately dropped me to the ground and ran to Glyph.

Voodoo Child stayed with me. I gave her a sad face, but with her mask on her expression, if any, was invisible.

"Bring him here!" Glyph yelled.

The Voodoo woman picked me up like nothing—another cyborg. She walked to them and dropped me down. Glyph held up a tablet to my face.

"What are you doing?"

The screen had flashing red code behind a flashing security warning message.

"Who's doing it?" Glyph yelled.

"Looks like Metro Cybercrimes but—" one security tech said.

"But?" Glyph asked angrily.

"They're not the problem, sir. There's, maybe, a dozen or more hackers in the system too. The only way to know what they're doing is to get in there."

"Can we stop them?" Glyph yelled.

"We need to get the computers online, but we don't have the power to both maintain the security measures and divert full power to cyber-defense."

"Divert all power to cyber-defense! If I have to choose, I choose that."

"Yes, Mr. Glyph."

The entire floor of security techs ran en masse to the exit stairs at the end of the room.

"They'll be able to get in now, Mr Glyph," Able said.

"Then we'll deal with them."

"Mr. Ming?" Able asked.

"We don't need him anymore. We'll deal with him and his Hiero soldiers all at one time."

"The detective?"

"We're burying everyone in the same grave."

I didn't like being threatened. Corporate soldiers stood guard over me as the Voodoo woman joined Mr. Glyph and his sidekick, Mr. Able. They disappeared from the room, using the stairway. More corporate soldier reinforcements arrived from the same stairwell.

One of them ran directly to the dozen watching me. He had a black bag with him and pulled out handcuffs. "Put these on him," he told them.

Unlucky for them, they didn't know the man was Pro. He dropped the bag and his laser sword came from out of his suit. He thrust, cut, and sliced his way through my twelve minders. I reached into the black bag filled with my weapons.

Gunfire erupted between the different groups of corporate soldiers. Judo led the men to me. I looked around at the security stations in the room.

"Ming was here," I told them. "I didn't see where he went."

"He's not here," Judo said to me.

"How do you know?"

"He's not here. We find Glyph."

"Voodoo Child is with them."

"D.G. knows."

"Are you sure you're staying?" Pro asked me.

"I'm sure."

"Then you will need this."

Pro reached into the black bag and took out packet after packet.

"Corporate soldiers have tools of the trade too. Slap patches are used for any deep cuts or wounds. The patch automatically cleans and sews up the gash. If you need more, this is a personal surgery kit. The robot is the size of a thumb but can do full operations, including anesthesia and aftercare. These are pain patches. We don't use them because pain is a thing of the mind. But you are a civilian. If you do lose a body part, use this cryo-bag to carry and keep the parts fresh until they can be reattached."

To say that I was overwhelmed was a gross understatement. Pro stuffed them all in a carry belt and helped me fasten it around my waist under my clothes.

The important thing was that I had all my personal weapons with me, including my omega-gun. I had no intention of getting shot or losing a body part so that some robot-in-a-bag would need to operate on me.

"This time we save you," he said.

Judo gestured to the men. Corporate soldiers stood shoulder-to-shoulder and raised their mortar guns. They blanketed the floor with rounds, then we casually walked to the stairwell. I, of course, wanted to run as fast as I could, but I stayed with them. We reached the stairwell and I heard a click from one of the men. I didn't see it, but heard the blasts followed by the rush of hot air. The entire level was engulfed in flames.

In the stairwell was an all-out gun battle between ex-Hiero and Macro corporate soldiers. We went down one level and exited. The hallway was filled with soldiers. Not too far away was a giant hole not only down to the floor below, but three floors. Men set up a crane above the hole and dropped a rope.

"Can you rappel?"

"Yes," I answered.

"Then keep up if you can," Judo said.

Judo jumped on the rope and slid down faster than I'd ever seen. Soldier after soldier simply jumped down the hole and grabbed the rope and slid down. I couldn't do all that. I jumped on the rope and down I went. I wondered why they weren't using any hover-tech, but knew there was a good reason.

I heard an explosion below me. I stopped and looked. No one was there. All I could do was continue. Three levels down. I looked up through the holes. I saw a small figure of Pro looking down; he waved. I continued on.

Gunfire, explosions, sounds of metal on metal. When I walked through the only open doors on the level, my eyes didn't know what to focus on first. The room reminded me of the one at Cybercrimes, but theirs was far larger, and this one had a literal corporate war with guns and swords. Fatalities were already high. Fallen bodies and limbs strewn everywhere. Lots of blood, which I made a mental note to avoid, lest it trigger a massive germophobic attack, which I couldn't afford to have happen now.

Glyph was a samurai soldier too. He was trading blows with Echo and was holding his own, which I would never have expected. Then there was The Digital Samurai versus Voodoo Child, both using double swords to fight each other. Two fights I wanted to see, but too much was happening around me. I put my back against the wall. Then I saw Judo against Ming! Three fights I wanted to see. If there was only someplace I could stand and watch without getting hit.

I dropped to the ground. Above me, three throwing stars embedded themselves in the wall. That was on purpose. Who threw those at me? I scanned the battle, but couldn't tell. That's what happened when your guard was lowered for even a second. The gunfire was over. It was all sword play. As I watched, I realized that they were all equally matched. They had the same training, moves, and countermoves. The battle could go on for hours without any significant advance from either side.

I'd found my role. Grand arbiter. One of them would cheat eventually. If it were my side, I'd do nothing. If it were Macro, I'd shoot them. Fair was fair. I also didn't see Blur. I'd keep an eye out for her too.

Down I went to the ground. Three more throwing stars, but they didn't come from any of the fighters. They were too busy with each other. Lying almost flat on the ground, I looked up at the ceiling, then down a bit to the screens hanging from the ceiling. I saw him! A two-foot doll of me, dressed in tan fedora and slicker, holding on to the screen with one hand and raising something in his other hand. The Voodoo woman had made another doll of me! But who was controlling it? Was it a killer robot doll? The answers were irrelevant. The doll had to die!

My omega-gun supposedly had a million attachments, but I didn't need all that. The dozen or so I had were fine. I had no doubt that the second it saw me raise my weapon, it would jump away or hide behind the screen. I aimed and fired. As I suspected the evil doll jumped out of my sight, but threw another throwing star at me. I leaned away just as it hit the wall. But my round did hit what

I was aiming at—the line holding the screen to the ceiling. One side crashed to the ground and started a cascade.

The Cybercrimes agents said The Digital Samurai had jumped into computer screens and disappeared. I'd laughed at them. As another screen fell, D.G. did what I thought was impossible. She dove into a screen, and disappeared. Voodoo Child jumped after her, but violently crashed into the screen.

A man's yell. I looked. Ming had impaled Judo with his sword. Echo saw it, lost his concentration and lost a hand by Glyph's blade. Judo yelled again and rushed Ming. I fired and hit Ming in the neck, but he didn't go down. I fired again. This time Ming blocked my blast with his sword and ran to me. I fired as fast as I could, but he blocked every one. I'd never seen anything like it in my life. Other ex-Hiero soldiers lost focus and were killed. Ming laughed as he got closer.

"You're good, but try now!" I yelled.

I fired at him in machine-gun mode. He didn't block them but didn't flinch a bit as the bullets riddled his chest.

"I kill you!" he said.

Ming was a quivering mass of rage. He fell forward, face-first. His back had dozens of throwing stars embedded in it. He was dead. I looked at Judo, who saluted me and collapsed to the floor where he stood.

Three Macro men killed their ex-Hiero opponents and charged other ex-Hiero corporate soldiers. I shot all three of the Macro men dead. I'd upset the balance and we suffered for it. All because of that doll. But the balance was restored.

Voodoo Child had her eye on me. She rose to her feet with her sword arms to her side. She was going to charge me. Then she dodged it—a sword thrown through the air. The Digital Samurai leaped out of a screen and ran at her nemesis. D.G. didn't have her second sword, but she was better with the one. Voodoo Child blocked the blows but barely. All the screens flickered, then strange symbols appeared.

D.G. was hit by electric blasts from multiple screens at the same time. She screamed out.

"Don't use all the power!" Glyph yelled.

Glyph's final mistake in life. Echo sliced off his head, hands and legs at the knees. He threw his sword at Voodoo Child but she swatted it away.

D.G. collapsed to the floor. Echo pulled another sword from his jacket and marched to Voodoo Child.

With Glyph dead, the Macro men stopped fighting and ran for the door. The remaining ex-Hiero men remained where they were.

"If you can't beat her, how can you beat me?" the Voodoo woman asked him.

"You will join your master," Echo said and moved in a circular motion around her.

"He might not want you to do that," she said.

Another doll hopped out of nowhere. A replica of Echo! Another appeared—one of D.G. Then my doll appeared.

"I say this ends now," she said.

I twisted my body to touch my back and I could feel them.

"Yes, Mr. Cruz. They are there," she said from afar, not even needing to look at me. "Feel free to shoot your mech-clone. Kill it. Kill yourself. All with one shot."

Damn! I was enraged.

Echo knelt to the ground, dropped his sword, and reached into his jacket with his hand. He slapped a patch on the stump that used to be his left hand.

"I'm sorry my master did that to you, Mr. Echo," she said. "But he's dead and soon you will be too."

"Who will be your new master?" Echo asked her.

"My honest annoyance has turned to burning rage." Able stood at the door's entrance with more corporate soldiers, and Blur at his side.

"It's all gone!" Able yelled. "We've been locked out of our own accounts!" Able's gaze turned to me. I could see his mind racing. "This was your doing!"

I shook my head. "I'm the spectator."

"You did this. Half the building is burning. The entire parking bay is destroyed. Locked out of our accounts. All systems down. You!"

"Not me."

"Voodoo," he said.

I looked at her. D.G. still lay on the floor unconscious.

"Mr. Cruz," she said, watching me, but never ignoring Echo, who was still kneeling on the floor.

"Didn't I tell you not to make another one of those creepy dolls of me again?" I said.

"I'm sorry that I chose to disregard you."

"Did you think I'd let you do the same thing twice?"

"Why not."

"I didn't."

"Do it now!"

Ex-Hiero soldiers threw a flurry of throwing stars at Able, but his men jumped in front of him as human shields. The men were hit and fell to the ground. Echo charged Voodoo Child, sword in his right hand. She was ready.

I flicked my wrist but this time no pop-gun. Blur disappeared. We were all engulfed in the EMP blast. Weapons with any kind of electronics shorted. The dolls fell to the ground; circuits exploded on Voodoo Child and some of Able's cyborg soldiers. One of them fell to the ground.

I yelled. A throwing star was embedded in my hand. I shot the corporate soldier who did it in the chest with my omega-gun. But I didn't stop. Corporate soldiers threw their bodies in front of Able as I showered them with laser fire. Able ran out of the room. I turned and fired an explosive round—blowing my mech-clone and the other dolls to bits. The Voodoo woman threw her sword at me, but another sword hit it away from me. It was Echo's. How he did that, I didn't know. He was definitely a master and I, the civilian. But he stood there without a sword. Voodoo Child looked at him, then at me, not knowing who to go after.

She sprinted at me. Someone yelled in Japanese. Voodoo Child stopped and turned. The Digital Samurai was standing again. The pulse had affected some of her implants too but she was a different kind of cyborg, like Voodoo.

"Come back here," D.G. said.

I fired another round at the Macro corporate soldiers and blew one into the wall. It was then that Voodoo Child raced back out the entrance. The main doors slammed shut and we heard a massive lock.

The room was where we were supposed to make our stand. Instead, we were wounded and had to go chasing after people. At least Ming and Glyph wouldn't be among them. But Judo was dead too.

Echo yanked the throwing star out of my hand then slapped a patch on it.

"Ready for more?" he asked.

"I wish we'd gotten at least one of them. Voodoo or Blur," I said.

"Able is a samurai master too," Echo said.

"Him?"

"Yes."

"He doesn't look like one."

"Looks can be deceiving. You know this."

"What are we doing?" I asked. "Can we really win this fight now?"

"You do not understand yet. Centuries ago the society took over the corporation. Corporate soldiers would run the company. Only the best would control. Samurai soldiers on the board. Samurai masters to lead."

"You're telling me, Mr. Echo, that the society killed its civilian masters way back then."

"They were weak and corrupt."

"And today."

"The corruption and evil overcame us again."

"May I suggest that we call the authorities now?"

"No. We finish this," Echo said.

"This is their building. You can't defeat them with only swords. Take some guns, the laser machine guns; instead of smoke bombs use real bombs."

"No," Echo said. "Leaders of the society do not fight that way."

"Don't they?" I said.

"No," D.G. said to me. "You stay here. We finish it. Only us. For society alone. When it's done, we don't care what you do."

PJ, my cyborg secretary, would have punched the door off its hinges. D.G. crisscrossed the door with her sword at blinding speed. The door disintegrated into falling confetti. D.G., Echo, and their Hiero soldiers walked through the opening.

I sat in a massive room of corpses. It was fair to say that I was out of my depth. Why was I even here? I was a street detective, not a samurai soldier. I wasn't getting paid anymore. There was no real case to be solved. What was I doing? I was a roadkill watcher. It was like a big crash in hovertraffic. Drivers stopped to see the carnage on the ground below. Morbid curiosity. That's what I was doing here. I wanted to see how it ended. Morbid curiosity got people killed, whether in hovertraffic or here. I was a civilian and I had no business being here. What was wrong with me?

The little nugget of info that Echo shared was enlightening. Hiero Corp and Macro Corp were run by their corporate soldiers. I'd never heard of that before. If only the best ruled, with samurai soldiers at the top of the food chain, that's why Echo deferred to D.G. She was a more powerful fighter than him. Able didn't defer to Voodoo Child because he was more powerful than her. The only people to lead cyber-assassins would be cyber-assassin killers. Was Blur the true head of Macro-Hiero?

I could ponder all day and never know. I still didn't know who killed Hackasaurus, but did it matter? What would that knowledge get me at this point? Nothing.

The building was on reserve power but security measures were not fully operational. People could slip out. I hoped Cybercrimes wasn't completely stupid and had a cordon around the tower to at least prevent that from happening.

Where could I go to wait things out? I walked the floor, checking each terminal to see if there were any not blown out by my EMP weapon. Everything was off. I examined the walls the farthest from the main entrance. In our preparation for our final mission, I got to see the plans to the building. I found what I was looking for. The secret door opened and I closed it after me. The back way to private meeting rooms, each with their own security station. I picked one, entered, and locked the door. The terminals were on and waved my hand in front of the screen to turn it back on.

To pass the time I'd try to connect to the building surveillance cameras. It could take hours.

"Surveillance feed," I said.

The screen switched to one of the levels that was engulfed in flames.

"Number of floors on fire."

The screen showed twenty different floors.

"Number of floors with human detection."

Macro corporate soldiers advanced on the floor where I'd left Pro and his men. The laser fire was relentless and the ex-Hiero men were retreating.

On another floor Echo was fighting Voodoo Child and Able alone! Black smoke exploded. I couldn't see any of them.

The other camera showed me the lobby where more and more corporate solders were pouring in from the streets.

The final camera was my level. The room outside with all the corpses—Ming, Glyph, Judo, etc. I didn't see anything on the screen, but the camera was detecting something. I stared at the feed. I didn't see anything. Another camera feed appeared on my screen. D.G. came back through the hole. Her eyes were glowing like hovercar high beams. She stopped. Blur materialized in front of her.

Was Blur a cyborg or robot? And could Digital Samurai beat her? If not, I knew Blur was coming to get me.

"All is lost," Blur said to her. "Defeating me is impossible. I was made to exceed all of your abilities. You have modified your eyes to disrupt my disorientation effect. Give my compliments to your tech, if they still live."

"The detective created it for me. He built hovercars in his previous life."

"An outsider?"

"I have learned that sometimes we need the eyes of an outsider to see more clearly."

"Cruz, yes. I believe he saved your life last time." Blur pointed to the wall. "He's in the rooms there. He will not be able to help you this time. When I kill you, I will deal with him."

"Are you so certain of my defeat?"

"I am."

"What will you do when we're all dead?"

"I will run Macro-Hiero for the next fifty years. We have lost much today, but we will find suitable companies to take over."

"None of the megacorps will allow that, nor will the Council."

"We have many assassins. We are not concerned with the Council."

"You would go to war with the Council too."

"We would go to war with any to protect the society, which you have betrayed."

"You have killed many cyber-assassins like me. My mother too."

"You were told? Echo gave his word that he wouldn't. Shame upon shame is all that you have brought to Hiero."

"You took away my only chance for true life. We would have gone away peacefully. Disappeared."

"No one leaves the society. I sent Voodoo to kill that man to stop you. We didn't have to track him because we knew where he was at all times, as we do with all our employees."

"You should have let us go. We would have had our freedom. You would have had the company forever. Was it worth it to you?"

"I would ask you the same."

"I know it's over. But I'm not sorry I tried."

"The fact that you are not is further proof of your dishonor to the society."

"Honor? The society ceased to be honorable a long time ago. We became as corrupt as the civilian masters we overthrew. Look what we became. We began as an honored company that helped found this city."

"An honored company that will control this city one day."

"No. It ends for me, my brethren, but it ends for you as well."

"Brethren? They are certainly all dead."

"No. Echo is superior to Able and Voodoo."

"Are you willing to wager your life on it?"

"What is the wager?"

"He wins, I let you go. He loses and you perform the ritual of atonement as you should have done from the beginning of your betrayal."

D.G. nodded. "I accept."

"You accept so quickly. When he's dead now."

"If he's dead, then have Able and Voodoo join us."

"I will. In fact, Voodoo arrives. Look what she brings."

Voodoo Child came through the hole in the main entrance dragging Echo's lifeless body, facedown. D.G. looked on without emotion, quiet, as Voodoo came along Blur's side.

"Your former teacher was no match—" Blur began.

Blur thrust her sword through Echo's back. He yelled out but swung and sliced her legs at the knees, but not before she whipped out a second sword and decapitated the Voodoo Child impostor.

D.G. lunged at her. Blur threw a flurry of mini darts at her. D.G. swatted them away. An explosion. D.G. was blasted back but contorted to land on her feet. She threw her own star. Blur caught it and threw it back at her. D.G. swatted it away.

Blur had no legs but it didn't seem to bother her. She jumped away from Echo's body. Echo managed to stand up. Blur clapped her fists together and a laser blast blew through his chest. His sword dropped from his hand. D.G. yelled out. Blur had used a weapon illegal to the rules of combat within the society. I told them as much, but then they told me not to come to the building for this final showdown. Neither of us listened.

As Echo collapsed he threw something else. Blur tried to jump away. The explosion was unlike anything I'd seen before—a combination of flame, electricity, and smoke. It also blew out the surveillance cameras. The rumbling effects of the device passed through the thick walls, shaking me, my chair, the table, the terminal.

For all their rules of combat, ways of honor, customs going back centuries, they were humans trying to kill each other. Junior men used guns, higher level used guns and swords, leaders and masters faced each other with swords, using misdirection devices. Mass destruction devices weren't supposed to be used by anyone. But D.G. and Echo had said it: the society wasn't supposed to kill innocent people or engage in all manner of lowly activities. But they did.

I came out from my office and out the secret door. I waited as the smoke cleared. Something came crawling out of the smoke cloud—Blur. Her body had been incinerated, her mask and clothing were gone, the flesh of her face and body charred. The Digital Samurai also came out of the smoke, walked up behind the mangled body of Blur and stomped what remained of Blur's body to a pulp. D.G. stopped and collapsed to the ground.

I'd been ready to blast Blur again with my pulsator, but D.G. had ended it. I already knew what happened to the others. Pro and his men defeated all the Macro forces, and sent three men away to help Echo. Pro and his men never knew what hit them. The new forces flew up the stairs via jetpack and slaughtered Pro and all his men, except for the three sent away.

Echo had defeated both Able and Voodoo Child, even with one hand. He killed her in the smoke and with her gone, concentrated all his effort on Able. Knowing he was losing the sword fight, Able tried to run and Echo killed with a shower of throwing stars.

One of the three men impersonated Voodoo Child, changing into her costume. The last two entered the room with their weapons. They surveyed the area, saw me, then ran to D.G. We heard the commotion. New forces were on our floor. We had to move fast. I opened the secret door and the two ex-Hiero men carried D.G. through for us to escape.

What a mess. The fire burned on thirty floors now. We were in a real towering inferno, so no need to call any authorities. All of Metropolis was watching the Macro megatower on the news. Police had arrived too, streaming in from the ground and air on multiple levels.

I looked at the three of them. Two shell-shocked kids. D.G. collapsed and barely awake, a blank stare at the ceiling. They were what remained of the "great" Hiero and Macro Corporations. All else was gone.

What a horrible mess. A corporate war no different than any other. I regretted my decision to stay. I shouldn't have been there. The case was over. Morbid curiosity could have gotten me killed and did nothing but leave me disturbed for who knew how long. I wanted to witness the end of Hiero-Macro. I did. Happy? Hell no. All I wanted was to go home.

GARAGE SALE

"**I**'m sorry it didn't work out as you planned," I said. The two kids were dead. I'd only left the room for a bit to walk around and clear my head. I came back to see the two of them slumped over in pools of blood. I wasn't surprised. Their faces had an emptiness of crushing despair. Their company was dead, their brethren, the society, their whole world and way of life was over. They lived for the life and without it, there was nothing. Western culture said even an old dog can learn new tricks. Eastern preached the reverse.

That's what I said to a lone Digital Samurai, lying on the ground, tears still dripping from her eyes. "I'm sorry it didn't work out as you planned."

"The plan was doomed to fail," she whispered.

"What happens now?" I asked.

"I don't know."

She said it with desperation. She truly didn't know. She was alone and afraid. There was no advice I could give her. Who could? The fact that she said she didn't know meant that ritual suicide was not an option for her. Maybe because she was at the highest level of their society or maybe because of all her body-modification and bionics, suicide wasn't as easy as for the rest of us.

"I wish I really could slip into the Net and live out my life in the virtual world. To live in my dreams."

"But you're The Digital Samurai."

"All deception. Built-in holo-projectors, cloaking suit, computer interface by touch. Many people to assist from near and from afar to aid in my illusion."

She was telling me all her secrets. Not a good sign. She wanted to die.

"Maybe we should ask someone who might have answer," I said.

"What answer?"

"What to do now? I'm not qualified to answer it, but I know people who might be. Asking questions never hurt."

"Questions mean hope. There is no hope."

"They should have let you go."

"They should have. All would have lived. None of us do, now."

"If the plan had worked, where would you all have gone?"

"We hadn't decided on a final place. A simple life in another country. Off-world was not a possibility because it would be where they'd expect us to go. We were going to stay here on Earth."

"It's a big planet. Lots of places filled with people to get lost in."

D.G. closed her eyes. The emotion welled up inside of her again. I glanced at the bodies of the two corporate soldiers near her. Kids. So young, but gone. She was the last of her society. What a mess.

The building blast walls lifted to once again expose the bay windows. I saw a police cruiser hovering in the air outside my window. A standard five-seater hovercraft with two officers, but circling the building were much larger hovercruisers that could carry dozens of police soldiers.

But there were many more red hovercraft in the sky. Part of the air was black with smoke. The building was still burning. While police personnel wore silver-and-black uniforms, fire officers were in red-and-black gear with the word "FIRE" on the chest and back of their uniforms. Their mechanical uniform enhancements were much more pronounced than those of the police. They appeared to be eight-foot tall, muscle-bound giants when you saw them. In these days, using drone robots would have made more sense. But the Fireman's Union wouldn't allow one single, solitary fireman— or firewoman—to be replaced by a robot, so they did the next logical—and more expensive—thing: they merged the two.

Fire cruisers fired high-pressure water from cannons, while others launched fire suppression bombs at the engulfed floors. They would explode in expanding foam to saturate and suffocate the fire.

I heard commotion outside our wall. When I stepped over to the terminal, I saw on the security feed dozens of police swarming through the hallways, pointing laser rifles. They were outside the wall and with their enhanced infrared could see as if the wall wasn't there.

"It's Cruz," I said, knowing their audio pickups would hear me clearly. "Notify Agent Delphi in Cybercrimes." I raised up my hands just to be on the safe side.

"Come out from behind the wall!" a voice boomed.

"D.G."

She sat on the floor looking at me.

"I know you think this is the end, but let me try. I'll ask the question for you. You don't have to do anything. See what I come up with. That's why you hired me. I came through before."

"You did."

"Nothing will change what has happened. Nothing will bring back your brothers. But maybe there's more story for you to live after today. Let's find out."

She slowly stood up, then raised her hands.

I sighed a relief. At least I wouldn't be in the middle of another all-out gun battle.

"We're coming out, Officers!"

The police handcuffed D.G. immediately. They knew exactly who and what she was. Dozens and dozens of troops rushed in, guns pointed, while a police hovercruiser with cannons hovered outside the window. Yes, they knew who she was all right. But she looked unconcerned. Her head lowered and her eyes cast down.

The police took me to the elevators. I don't know why they put me in handcuffs too. If they knew who she was, they knew me—most Metro PD knew me by sight. On the ground level, they had me sit on the lobby floor as police and fire personnel streamed back and forth. The security was tight; I counted no less than eighty officers on guard throughout the lobby.

Finally, Delphi arrived, with a group of his men following.

"Officers," he said.

Two policemen lifted me from the floor and unhandcuffed me.

"Mr. Cruz, you made it," Delphi said.

"Are you satisfied?"

"I might have been if we didn't find out that all of Macro's corporate bank assets were siphoned off during this whole operation. We're tracking it all, but the hackers seemed to know of our operation beforehand and were ready. Do you have any thoughts as to how they might know that?"

"None at all," I said.

"I thought you'd say that. However, they did leave behind all the records for us. Cyber forensics will be able to use those records to paint a full picture of the megacorp's inner workings, both legal and criminal."

"Delphi, you won't have to worry much about arresting anyone, since they're all dead."

"Yes, I was told. A burning building filled with bodies. With you in the center of it."

"I told you. Roll up both Hiero and Macro."

"Yes, you said it and that's what happened. Would have preferred not to have a burning megatower in the city sending smoke that can be seen from hundreds of miles away and space, and so many bodies that the coroner says it could take weeks to process the scene."

"Would you have preferred the bodies to have included your men or the police?"

"No."

"Then you should be satisfied."

"We are."

"What happens to Digital Samurai?"

"Cruz, the case is over for you—completely. You've done more than enough."

"If it wasn't for her and her people, we wouldn't be here to mop up. They brought down Hiero and Macro."

"That will all be taken into consideration, but again, she's an assassin. Surely, you don't think that can be ignored."

"Nor should it. Aren't there other assassins out there? Other criminal societies?"

"There are."

"Sounds like a plan is coming together, Delphi. Maybe a new Special Ops Cybercrimes unit."

Delphi held back a laugh. "Cruz. I'm glad we got to work together. I'll see to it that you find out what happens to your former client, for your own peace of mind."

"Thanks, Delphi."

"But before you go home, the chief wants to see you too. And the Council."

"Delphi, I want to go home."

A giant corporate hovercraft descended above the main entrance lobby. Police had everything cordoned off; even the media was kept far back. The side door opened and there was Chief Hub. The six-foot, muscle-bound, veteran officer, who ran the largest police division in the world of five hundred thousand personnel—the Metropolis Police Department. Why was he exiting a Council hovercraft? Then a Caucasian woman in a kimono-style slicker followed with two corporate soldiers, a male and female. The last time I'd seen Hub and her together they were on opposite sides with their own armies behind them, about to blow each other to bits.

"Chief," I said.

Hub squinted at me. "Cruz. What is about you in being in buildings in some state of mass destruction?"

"It's not my fault," I said.

"How many times have I heard that?"

The woman and her guards reached us.

"Madam President," I said. "So the president of the Council of Corporations is outside of her tower headquarters again, and providing shuttle service for the chief of police. The last time I saw you two together you wanted to kill each other."

Two of the most powerful forces of nature in Metropolis—the government, and megacorporations—Metro PD and the Council of Corporations.

"As much as I'd like to chat, I do want to go home," I said.

"Mr. Caveat has kept me abreast of your activities, Mr. Cruz," she said. "You've been very helpful to the Council. The chief and I were discussing that assistance on the flight here. The Hiero and Macro Corporations had become threats to both of our interests. No one will be sad to see them dissolved."

"What happens now?"

"A 'garage sale,' Mr. Cruz. With the leadership of both companies gone—"

"You mean dead."

"We prefer to use softer language."

I laughed.

"I'm glad you find me amusing, Mr. Cruz," she said.

"After the day I've had and you see inside for yourself, you'll know why I need any chance to find a reason to laugh."

"I understand, of course. The Council will acquire ownership of the building, it will be sold, and all their civilian employees will easily find other employment. Any financial assets left will be donated to the police department."

"Oh, that's why you and the chief are buddies now."

"Yes, we are," Hub said.

"What else? You didn't have me wait to tell me that."

"We have to stress upon you, Mr. Cruz, to keep all this confidential. No media interviews, no sharing with friends, associates, and family. Keep it all to yourself until at least the sale of the buildings."

"Also, remember that you signed NDAs with Cybercrimes," Hub said.

"Chief, please. I know how to keep secrets. You know this already."

"It had to be said," Hub said.

"Take no offense, Mr. Cruz. There are other Hiero and Macro Corporations out there. You can understand our desire to manage this situation properly," Madam President said.

"Don't worry about me. I want to forget it all as fast as I can. However, my only ask is to do right by The Digital Samurai."

"You mean the assassin," Madam President said.

"A bio-engineered and illegal killer cyborg," Hub added.

"Yes."

"You wouldn't be so quick to defend her if you knew all that she'd done," Madam said.

"I have no doubt. But I don't know. I can only judge her by my interaction with her on this case. Limited, I admit. Naive even, but her people are lying dead in there, but none of your people or yours, Chief Hub. They did the suicide mission for you. Remember that. That's all I'm saying."

"Everything will be taken care of," Hub said.

"You said what you had to say. I said my part. Chief, can you have officers take me home? I'm so exhausted that I'll sleep for days, assuming Cruz Jr. lets me."

Hub smiled. He summoned two officers. "Take this man home."

I sat in the passenger compartment of the police cruiser making one last call before I got home.

"Not much fun and games in this case," PJ said from the vid-screen.

"No, not much at all. We forgot the rules of the game. My posthumous mentor, Wilford G. said: 'Never forget the detective business is not a game. You can die at any time.'"

My posthumous mentor, Mr. Wilford G., the ninety-two-year-old private eye, who worked the streets of Metropolis until the day he died. His sixty-page book titled *How to Be a Great Detective with 100 Rules* remained my bible to the biz. There was deep substance behind each rule from the endless cases he solved, said in his witty, dispassionate, direct way.

"We were stupid on this one," PJ said.

"We saw throwing stars and smoke and forgot why we're here."

"Do you wish you didn't take the case?" PJ asked.

"Taking the case wasn't the problem. On this one I didn't walk away when I should have. This one could have ended real badly."

"*C'est la vie*," PJ said.

"That is the life. I won't forget ever again."

"I'll take care of everything at the office while you see your family. Take a vacation. You deserve it."

"Thanks, PJ."

The "garage sale" happened as Madam President said in the days and weeks ahead. Each building was purchased by the Council and leased to many more than only two megacorps—hundreds. Part of their new billion-dollar profit megacorp promotional blitz. People would soon forget about Hiero, Macro, and the burning megatower in the middle of the supercity. Every day would be another puff piece in the media on another one these new companies to pass the threshold of a billion dollars of profit. The Council of Corporations could maintain control of hundreds of new smaller megacorps. Hiero and Macro, both of which existed even before the Council, had grown too big and dangerous to be controlled. The Council wouldn't allow that to happen again. They could do nothing about Up-Top megacorps, which were not part of the Council and never were. The Council would not allow such megacorps to exist on Earth, if they had anything to do with it. I hoped that D.G. would not find herself with a new vile master to answer to, but I didn't worry. If so, she'd rebel against them too.

LA FAMILIA

I was never so happy to see that beautiful, ugly granite block of a building called the Concrete Mama—home! My no-frills monolith tower of legacy housing, which could withstand a planetary shockwave from a nuclear blast or an asteroid crash, was home to the Cruz family. I thanked my police drivers and couldn't get inside fast enough. The building doorman, Mr. Post, yelled "hello" from his station. He'd done such a great job getting rid of the lobby johnnies that used to hang out in the lobby before. My feet kept me moving to the elevators.

Out I came on the 150th floor and straight to room number 9732. The door was open and there she was. China Doll, called China by women, men called her Doll, but my family and I called her by her real name—Dot. I hugged my wife and gave her a long kiss.

My wife, always the consummate fashionista, was in a sparkling pink body hugging dress, though she told me that it was called a *cheongsam*. Her hair tied back, with the ponytail carefully resting on one shoulder, her colored neck scarf of the day was a matching pink. Every finger had a colored ring, and each wrist had multiple bracelets. Yep, my wife looked like a movie star. I'm not going to lie.

"Look who's here," I said and picked him up in my arms. "What have you been up to all these days, Cruzie?" I gave him a kiss on the cheek and he laughed.

I was home and wasn't leaving the apartment for days. I wasn't even going to leave to check my Ford Pony in the parking bay. That would wait. We had brunch and we talked and played catch with Cruz Jr. I'd forgotten that I was exhausted and wanted to sleep. I'd sleep and when I did it would probably be for twenty-four hours.

Besides learning about the Macro-Hiero "garage sale" from Mr. Mick, I got word about the fate of Digital Samurai. "Her name is *Hú dié*. It means butterfly," Delphi told me.

"I'm glad you know how to pronounce it, because I can't. What's going to happen to her?"

"The chief made a few calls. The Council wanted her, which meant us having her would cause all kinds of political friction. She's going to work for Interpol."

"The Interspace Police."

"But you didn't hear it from me. We'll never see her again."

"I'd say a Digital Samurai would be able to do a lot more Up-Top in their world of digital tech than here on Earth."

"True. Hope it works out for all involved. Take care, Cruz."

"You too, Delphi."

He was right that I would never see her again. But six months ago, I received an email message from an unknown sender. It simply said: "I am free. DG." I knew nothing more and would never know anything more. But I smiled. That message was all I needed to mentally close the case of The Digital Samurai in my mind.

REVIEW REQUEST

Dear Reader,

I hope you enjoyed *Digital Samurai*.

Can You Write Me a Review?

I'd greatly appreciate an honest review on one or more of the following sites:

Reviews are the best way for readers to discover good books. My writer's motto is simple: "Readers Rule!" Thanks so much.

Always writing,

Austin Dragon

CONTINUE THE ADVENTURE

Also by Austin Dragon

See all my books in science fiction, horror, and fantasy at:
http://www.austindragon.com/books

ABOUT THE AUTHOR

Austin Dragon is the author of the *After Eden* Series, including the *After Eden: Tek-Fall* mini-series, the classic *Sleepy Hollow Horrors*, the new epic fantasy adventure *Fabled Quest Chronicles*, and cyberpunk detective series, *Liquid Cool*. He is a native New Yorker, but has called Los Angeles, California home for the last twenty years. Words to describe him, in no particular order: U.S. Army, English teacher, one-time resident of Paris, political junkie, movie buff, Fortune 500 corporate recruiter, renaissance man, dreamer.

He is currently working on new books and series in science fiction, fantasy, and classic horror!

Connect with Austin on social media at:

Website and blog: http://www.austindragon.com

Pinterest: http://www.pinterest.com/austindragon

Goodreads: https://www.goodreads.com/ADragon

Other books by Austin Dragon

See all my books at: http://www.austindragon.com/books